I0651852

William E. Chandler, Hiram Tuttle

The Statue of John P. Hale

erected in front of the Capitol and presented to the state of New Hampshire by

William E. Chandler of Concord. An account of the unveiling ceremonies on August

3, 1892

William E. Chandler, Hiram Tuttle

The Statue of John P. Hale
*erected in front of the Capitol and presented to the state of New Hampshire by William E.
Chandler of Concord. An account of the unveiling ceremonies on August 3, 1892*

ISBN/EAN: 9783337398644

Printed in Europe, USA, Canada, Australia, Japan

Cover: Foto ©Andreas Hilbeck / pixelio.de

More available books at **www.hansebooks.com**

THE STATUE

OF

JOHN P. HALE

ERECTED IN FRONT OF THE CAPITOL
AND PRESENTED TO THE

STATE OF NEW HAMPSHIRE

BY

WILLIAM E. CHANDLER

OF CONCORD.

AN ACCOUNT OF THE UNVEILING CEREMONIES ON

AUGUST 3, 1892,

WITH A REPORT OF THE ADDRESSES DELIVERED BY THE DONOR AND

HIS EXCELLENCY GOVERNOR HIRAM A. TUTTLE,

COUNCILLOR GEORGE A. RAMSDELL, CHAIRMAN, AND MESSRS.
DANIEL HALL, GALUSHA A. GROW, GEORGE S. BOUTWELL,
FREDERICK DOUGLASS, AUGUSTUS WOODBURY,
AMOS HADLEY, AND ALONZO H. QUINT.

Published by Direction of the Governor and Council.

CONCORD, N. H.:
REPUBLICAN PRESS ASSOCIATION, RAILROAD SQUARE.
1892.

THE HALE STATUE.

The statue of JOHN PARKER HALE, of Dover, New Hampshire, now standing in front of the capitol at Concord, was tendered to the state by a letter, as follows :

UNITED STATES SENATE.
WASHINGTON, D. C., April 14, 1890.

To the Governor and Council of the State of New Hampshire :

GENTLEMEN : — I have the honor to state that I have made a contract for the erection of a statue of John P. Hale in the state house yard at Concord, which I hereby donate to the state of New Hampshire, and ask the acceptance thereof.

The statue will be of the same size as that of Daniel Webster, now in the state house yard, and will be cast at the same bronze foundry in Munich after designs of Mr. F. Von Miller, artist and director of the bronze foundry. It is expected that the statue will be ready and in place for unveiling in the month of September, 1891.

I have requested Col. Daniel Hall to present this communication.

Respectfully,

WM. E. CHANDLER.

On April 22 the offer was considered at a meeting, in Concord, of the governor and council ; pres-

ent : Hon. David A. Taggart, president of the senate, acting as governor, and Councillors Charles H.
Horton, Edward C. Shirley, William S. Pillsbury,
and Frank C. Churchill.

On motion of Councillor Horton,—

Voted, That the governor and council, in behalf
of the state of New Hampshire, cordially and gratefully accept the statue of John P. Hale, donated to
the state by the Honorable William E. Chandler,
and will reserve for it an eligible site in the state
house yard, to be determined hereafter in confer-
ence with Mr. Chandler or his representative.

On November 6, 1890, a vote was adopted by the
governor and council exactly fixing the site, as follows :

On motion of Councillor Pillsbury, it was voted
to grant to Hon. William E. Chandler a plot of
ground in the state house yard as a site for the
statue of John P. Hale ; the plot to be in the front
of the yard, next to Park street, north of the central walk, and occupying a position corresponding
to that granted for the erection of the Stark statue.

There was delay in the completion of the statue
until the summer of 1892. On the 28th day of
June, at the suggestion of Senator Chandler, Councillors George A. Ramsdell and Henry B. Quinby,
with Secretary of State Ezra S. Stearns, were designated by His Excellency Governor Hiram A. Tuttle as a committee of arrangements to prepare for
the unveiling and the acceptance of the statue ; and
Col. Daniel Hall was designated and invited as
orator of the occasion.

The ceremonies took place on the third day of

August, 1892. The final instrument of conveyance of the statue to the state is as follows :

CONCORD, NEW HAMPSHIRE, August third, 1892.
The bronze statue of John P. Hale, this day unveiled in the state house yard at Concord, and the granite pedestal and the bronze tablets thereon, are hereby given and conveyed by me to the state of New Hampshire unconditionally and forever.

WILLIAM E. CHANDLER.

The statue is of heroic size, standing eight feet and four inches above the die. It represents Senator Hale as an orator, wearing an open frock coat, with a small roll in his pendant left hand, while the right arm and open hand and fingers are extended in an expressive gesture. The form and face make an excellent likeness, and the statue as a work of art has been commended by all observers.

The pedestal is of Concord granite, cut by the New England Granite Works, of Concord. This rises nine feet and eight inches, making the whole monument eighteen feet high. The die is three feet and nine inches square, and rests on three bases : the first, eight feet square and fifteen inches thick ; the second, five and one half feet square and fourteen inches thick ; and the third, five feet square and twenty inches thick.

The statue faces east. On the front of the pedestal, in heavy raised letters cut in the granite, is the name,—

JOHN P. HALE.

On the three other sides are bronze tablets ; that on the north inscribed,—

JOHN P. HALE.
FIRST ANTI-SLAVERY U. S. SENATOR.
HE SECURED THE ABOLITION OF FLOGGING
AND THE SPIRIT RATION IN THE NAVY.
BORN AT ROCHESTER 1806.
DIED AT DOVER 1873.

The south tablet contains, from Mr. Hale's North Church address of June 5, 1845, the sentence,—

THE MEASURE OF MY AMBITION WILL BE
FULL IF WHEN MY WIFE AND CHILDREN
SHALL REPAIR TO MY GRAVE TO DROP
THE TEAR OF AFFECTION TO MY MEMORY
THEY MAY READ ON MY TOMBSTONE,
HE WHO LIES BENEATH SURRENDERED
OFFICE, PLACE AND POWER RATHER
THAN BOW DOWN AND WORSHIP SLAVERY.

On the rear are the words,—

PRESENTED TO THE
STATE OF NEW HAMPSHIRE
BY WILLIAM E. CHANDLER
OF CONCORD.
1892.

The artist who designed and made the statue is Ferdinand Von Miller, Junior, manager of the Royal Art Foundry at Munich in Bavaria, a sketch of whose life and works is given in this memorial volume.

August third, 1892, the day of the unveiling ceremonies, was fair, and the attendance was unexpectedly large, although no special invitations had been given. At half-past eleven o'clock a procession left the Eagle Hotel, conducted by City Marshal G. Scott Locke, and headed by Governor Tuttle and Councillor Ramsdell, who acted as chairman of the proceedings. Besides those who took part in the exercises, there were present Mrs. John

P. Hale, Mrs. William E. Chandler and John Parker Hale Chandler, Mr. and Mrs. William H.
Jaques, Mr. and Mrs. William D. Chandler and
their son Clark, and also ex-Governors Nathaniel
S. Berry, of Bristol, James A. Weston, of Manchester, Benjamin F. Prescott, of Epping, and
David H. Goodell, of Antrim, and many state offi-
cials and prominent citizens.

From Rochester, Mr. Hale's birthplace, were
present the following :

Mayor Charles S. Whitehouse ; Councilmen Joseph Warren, William Flagg, George A. Bickford, Charles W. Allen, and George A. Bickford,
Jr.; City Solicitor George E. Cochrane, Chief-
Engineer Fire Department William C. Sanborn,
and City Clerk Charles W. Brown.

From Dover, Mr. Hale's home, came the following delegation :

Henry R. Parker, Mayor; Eli V. Brewster,
Charles H. Horton, and Richard N. Ross, ex-
Mayors; Charles W. Smith, President of the Com-
mon Council ; Herman W. Stevens, City Clerk;
George H. Demeritt, Messenger ; William E.
Whiteley, Clerk of Common Council; Joseph T.
Woodbury, George W. Nute, Willard T. Sanborn,
Daniel A. Nute, Charles E. Burnham, Charles
Porter, Charles H. Foss, Albert G. Neal, John J.
McCann, and John Killoren, Aldermen; John W.
Merrow, Fred E. Quimby, John F. Stevens, Alfred
R. Sayer, John A. Goodwin, Erastus A. Crawford,
Charles L. Ricker, John W. Felch, Andrew P.
Folsom, Charles F. Sawyer, Charles H. Morang,
Peter Murphy, Patrick E. Mallon, and James

Cassidy, Councilmen; William F. Nason, City Solicitor; also Prof. Sylvester Waterhouse, Messrs. John Scales, Joshua L. Foster, Elisha R. Brown, Joseph S. Abbott, Oliver A. Gibbs, Joseph A. Peirce, Daniel H. Wendell, Charles H. Trickey, Eben C. Berry, William D. Taylor, Fred H. Foss, Theodore Woodman, Joseph Hayes, Samuel C. Fisher, William Sterns, Charles A. Faxon, George F. Morrill, John C. Tasker, Everett O. Foss, Charles Wood, and Mrs. Daniel Hall, Mrs. E. R. Brown, Mrs. A. H. Young, Mrs. Frank Hobbs, Mrs. James H. Wheeler, Miss Mary A. Hoitt, Miss Mary Woodman, Miss Susan Woodman, Miss Kate Adams, Miss C. Wood, and Mrs. Durgin.

The exercises were conducted at the right of the statue upon a raised platform, which was in charge of Col. J. W. Robinson. During the hour preceding, a concert was given by the band of the Third Regiment, New Hampshire National Guard, under the direction of Mr. Arthur F. Nevers. At the conclusion of the addresses, a collation was served by the state authorities at the Eagle Hotel, accompanied by music from Blaisdell's orchestra.

UNVEILING CEREMONIES.

At half-past eleven the assemblage was called to
order by Councillor Ramsdell, the chairman, who,
after music, said :

It is our custom, upon the threshold of important
occasions, to pause and recognize the Divine presence. It is highly appropriate that we do so at this
time. Let silence be observed while Rev. Dr.
Quint invokes the blessing of Almighty God.

Rev. Dr. Alonzo H. Quint then offered prayer ;
after which followed the

ADDRESS OF COUNCILLOR GEORGE A. RAMSDELL.

Fellow Citizens : — On the 22d day of April,
1890, Senator William E. Chandler communicated
to the executive department his purpose to present
to the state a statue of the late John Parker Hale.
Governor David H. Goodell and his council made
it a matter of record that the state would gladly
accept the gift, and soon after set apart a portion
of the state house yard for its reception.

A month ago the senator made a second communication announcing the arrival of the statue
from Europe, and his desire to present it to the
state upon the third day of August, 1892.

His Excellency Governor Tuttle at once appointed a committee of the council with the secretary of state, to make arrangements for a proper
ceremonial at the unveiling. In consultation with
the governor and the donor, such arrangements
have been made as seemed to befit the occasion,
and we are assembled to uncover and take to the
care of the state a statue of this noble son of New
Hampshire ——

[The speaker at this point recognized ex-Gov.
Nathaniel S. Berry, who had been escorted to the
platform leaning upon the arm of ex-Senator James
W. Patterson, and given a seat near the presiding
officer.]

It is an agreeable duty, easily performed, to welcome this gathering of my fellow-citizens from all
parts of the state. Nor is it less agreeable, or an
office more difficult of execution, to extend a greeting to these distinguished men about me, representing our own and other states, not a few of
whom have received high honors at the hands of
their fellow-men. But what shall I say to this aged
man, for two years our war governor, who, bending beneath the weight of fourscore and fifteen
years, prompted by a great love, has come from his
retirement to take part in the exercises of this day?
How shall I address this favorite of heaven ? No
words of mine can express the thought which I see
pictured in the faces of all within sound of my
voice. But, as my eyes [turning to the statue of
Webster] rest upon those lips of bronze, I am
moved to say,—"Venerable man : you have come
down to us from a former generation. Providence

hath bountifully lengthened out your life, that you might behold this glorious occasion."

Resuming my theme: We have come together to uncover and take to the care of the state a statue of this noble son of New Hampshire, whose commanding presence, liberal culture, stirring eloquence, and, more than all, whose dauntless moral courage made him such a mighty factor in the formation of that public sentiment which made it possible for this nation in God's own time to throw off the institution of slavery which had come down to us, an almost fatal legacy, from an earlier generation and a ruder civilization.

The number of memorials of this character belonging to the state is small. They can be enumerated in a few moments, and upon the fingers of one hand.

Forty years ago, in recognition of his great service in the early history of our national existence, there was erected by the state, in the town of Hampton Falls, upon our limited sea coast, a marble shaft to the memory of Mesheck Weare, who, during the stormy years from 1776 to 1785, was at the head of civil affairs in New Hampshire.

One third of a century after this work was done and when it seemed that no more names, illustrious in our history before the Civil War, were to be perpetuated in bronze and stone, a distinguished citizen of Massachusetts, always loyal to the place of his birth, presented to the state that statue of Daniel Webster, whose peerless intellect and patriotic statesmanship have given our small commonwealth a name throughout the world.

Yonder statue of Stark has been but recently placed upon its foundation by the state, in obedience to a popular demand that our most prominent figure in the War of the Revolution,—the man who, in that great contest, with no authority but the commission of the state of New Hampshire in his pocket, and (may I not say it) with few men behind him save the citizen soldiers of our state, fought a decisive battle,—should have, in addition to his great fame already secured, all the immortality that bronze and granite can give.

There is, at Thornton's Ferry, upon a lot and foundation furnished by the town of Merrimack, a substantial granite monument awaiting dedication, placed there by the state in memory of the distinguished services of Matthew Thornton, illustrious not only as one of the signers of the Declaration of Independence, but also as a co-worker with Weare and others—a galaxy of noble men—in laying the foundations of our state government.

The last legislature made an appropriation to assist the towns of Peterborough and Temple in building a highway and establishing a public park upon a mountain rising majestically upon their borders and overlooking, like some giant sentinel, upon one hand, the place of the birth of General James Miller, and on the other, the place of his decease, to the end that the memory of this rugged old soldier, so creditable to our state, perish not from the minds of men so long as these evidences of man's work upon that granite mountain shall endure.

The list is not long : Weare, Webster, Stark,

Thornton, Miller ; but, God willing, another name shall be added before the sun goes down.

The statue will now be unveiled by John Parker Hale Chandler, a son of the donor and grandson of the senator to whose memory it is erected.

At twelve o'clock Master John Parker Hale Chandler, a boy of seven years, pulled the cord which lowered the United States flag which had covered the statue, and the unveiling was accomplished amid cheers from the assembly and music from the band.

The chairman then said :

Senator Chandler, have you at this time any communication to make to the state, represented by His Excellency Governor Tuttle ?

SENATOR WILLIAM E. CHANDLER'S ADDRESS OF PRESENTATION.

MR. CHAIRMAN:—John P. Hale was three times elected United States senator from New Hampshire by legislatures sitting in the capitol edifice within the precincts where we to-day assemble. The statue here erected and now exhibited to view I have thought might not inappropriately be presented by me to the state of New Hampshire and the city of Concord, for I was born in yonder house, the nearest to the capitol ; have been twice here chosen senator, succeeding to the term forty years after Mr. Hale's first election ; and, moreover, am able to rejoice in my relation to that child of promise, who, as the only male descendant of Mr. Hale

and bearing his name, has this day fittingly unveiled the statue of his grandfather.

Governor Tuttle, to the state of New Hampshire,
through your excellency, I now tender, by a proper
writing of conveyance, this statue of one of New
Hampshire's foremost sons.

As a work of art, it cannot, I think, be justly
criticised ; and, as a likeness in face and form,
it must be received as being as good as could
be expected in a design made from photographs
never fully satisfactory to the family or friends.

It is a high pleasure to me to give the statue to
my native state and city as an evidence of the
strong affection which I bear to my home and of
my appreciation of the kindnesses and honors
which its citizens have so lavishly bestowed upon
me.

Statues of the illustrious dead and memorial
arches and monuments are principally valuable for
the lessons which they teach to new generations.

No inculcation has sprung from any life more
noble than the one inspired by Mr. Hale's career :
That there can be no higher aim in life than to
espouse a humane and holy cause in the hour of its
gloom and despondency, and to devote one's self
constantly and fearlessly to its service.

Gifted with pleasing form, feature, and voice,
receiving an excellent collegiate and professional
education, and achieving success as a lawyer, at
an early age he became the favorite orator of his
political party, an associate and friend of Franklin
Pierce, its greatest leader in the state, and was
elected a representative in congress. But when he

was called upon to support the forcible annexation
of Texas and an unjust war with Mexico, in order
to extend the domain of human chattel slavery, and
to bring more slave states into the Union, he rebelled and wrote his famous Texas letter, for which
he was expelled from his party and debarred from
congress ; and his now historic proclamation of
resistance was the beginning of the political anti-
slavery movement in New Hampshire.

The conflict upon which he then entered aroused
the best elements of his noble nature, and enlisted
every energy of his soul from 1845, when the
struggle began, down to 1865, when every slave
was free and liberty was universal in America.

The idolized poet of our Merrimack valley (who,
in thought and word and sympathy, is with us
here to-day) greeted the beginning with his earnest benediction and thrilling exhortation :

> God bless New Hampshire; from her Granite peaks
> Once more the voice of Stark and Langdon speaks.
>
> *   *   *   *   *   *   *   *   *
>
> Courage, then, Northern hearts. Be firm ; be true.
> What one brave state hath done, can ye not also do ?

And, when the full fruition came, how gratefully
he praised God in a joyous song of freedom :

> It is done.
> Clang of bell and roar of gun
> Send the tidings up and down.
>
> *   *   *   *   *   *
>
> Fling the joy from town to' town.
>
> *   *   *   *   *   *

On morning's wing
Send the song of praise abroad.
With a sound of broken chains,
Tell the nations that *He* reigns,
Who alone is Lord and God.

Once engaged in Freedom's battle, Mr. Hale's hostility to every form of human debasement became intense, and his reverence for humanity, his respect for man made in the image of his Creator, became the absorbing and controlling principle of his existence.

It was alike abhorrent to him that black men, women, and children should be sold as chattels upon the auction-block, under national laws, and that the sailors of the republic should, by national direction, become besotted by alcoholic drams, and be flogged with brutal whips. To contend against the enslavement or degradation of either the bodies or the souls of human beings of any race, color, or condition, was the deliberate mission of his life.

When he began he laid down office, place, and power to fight in a doubtful and almost hopeless struggle. Before he finished he saw his great works brought to complete success, the paramount desires of his heart fully gratified, and himself crowned as well with honors as with length of days.

No more inspiriting example can be studied by the ingenuous youth of New Hampshire than the life of him whose statue rises before us.

Indeed, the spot whereon we stand abounds in inspiring suggestions.

John Stark was New Hampshire's most renowned soldier in the Revolution. Most fortunate as well as most valiant of warriors, he saved the rear at Bunker Hill, routed the British army at Bennington, and led the van in Washington's critical movement upon Trenton.

Daniel Webster, with his massive intellect, his profound comprehension of the principles of the constitution and the Union, and his intense patriotism, New Hampshire gave to the nation as her greatest statesman and orator.

The New Hampshire soldiers in the War of the Rebellion, to whom yonder beautiful arch is dedicated, gave their best service and, many of them, their lives in battle, to preserve the union of these states.

The memory of these heroes and patriots is gratefully perpetuated by all these permanent monuments.

To these tributes to the distinguished dead to-day is added the statue of another son of New Hampshire—

A citizen of public spirit and high character; an orator of surpassing pathos and power; a fervid champion of the oppressed and the enslaved; an inspired apostle of human liberty; and a conscientious statesman of purity and patriotism.

He was well worthy of commemoration in this enduring form; and his character and life should be comprehended and imitated by the present and every future generation in the state he loved and served.

2

ADDRESS OF ACCEPTANCE BY HIS EXCELLENCY
GOVERNOR HIRAM A. TUTTLE.

MR. CHAIRMAN AND FELLOW-CITIZENS:—In the
mighty struggle that preceded the destruction of
the accursed system of American slavery, New
Hampshire played an important and influential
part. When the able Southern leader attacked
the federal constitution, it was New Hampshire's
greatest son who made answer, declaring doctrines
and principles that have never since been successfully assailed. In that great contest other sons of
New Hampshire occupied an honorable and conspicuous position. Chase, Greeley, Fessenden,
Pillsbury, and others that might be named, man-
fully contended for the principles of liberty and
equality, and dealt mighty blows against the institution of slavery ; but, among them all, one man
stood out preëminent as the leader of the anti-slavery host. That man was John Parker Hale ; a
statue to whose memory, through the liberality of
one of New Hampshire's leading citizens and public men,—Senator William E. Chandler,—is this
day unveiled and dedicated.

In behalf of the state of New Hampshire, I
accept this statue, which will stand here to remind
the people of our state of the great and good. man
whose fame and achievements it is designed to
commemorate. Beautiful and enduring, it may
·inspire to more vigorous and virtuous actions, in
his mature time, the graceful child, in whom are
united the names, Hale and Chandler, and in
whose veins courses the blood of both.

It is well thus to signalize our appreciation of the virtues and accomplishments of men who, like John P. Hale, have brought credit and renown to the state of their birth; and, as the immortal Webster and the heroic Stark are already here in bronze, it is fitting that the eloquent and fearless Hale should also be thus immortalized.

New Hampshire has produced many great men, —a galaxy of brilliant jurists, able soldiers, and consummate statesmen,—but among them all John P. Hale stands out a conspicuous and grand figure. Born in the early days of the nineteenth century, Mr. Hale reached the maturity of his powers at the time when the great question of anti-slavery was agitating the people of the North, and into that contest he threw the mighty force of his intellect and the magnificent powers of his convictions and his purpose. Loving freedom, hating oppression, a true patriot, he entered into the thick of the fight, and never flinched, however hot the battle became. No matter what the odds were against him, he fought as man can only fight when animated by moral convictions and strengthened and upheld by moral forces.

At every step in his career he opposed slavery and the extension of slave territory, including the annexation of Texas. He made no compromises with wrong,—no pledges nor promises that he could not honorably keep. The associate and friend of Franklin Pierce in early life, he broke away from the great Democratic leader when Freedom called him to do battle against oppression. The associate of Chase and Sumner in the senate

of the United States, he was the peer of these great
men, and together they held aloft, in the days that
tried men's souls, the flag of equality and human
rights.

He lived to see the triumph of the cause for
which he battled so long; the abolition of slavery,
the very name of which he hated; the defeat of the
slaveholders' rebellion, and the reconstruction of
the Union upon the firm and abiding foundations
of liberty and justice.   His career was one of
unflinching integrity, of honorable ambitions, and
magnificent achievements.

It is fitting that such a man should be commemorated in granite and bronze.   It is fitting that
such a man, whose life-work shed so much lustre
upon New Hampshire, should be thus honored.
His virtues and deeds are already enshrined in the
hearts and affections of the people of the state, but
it is well that this beautiful statue should be erected
here as an object lesson to the youth of New Hampshire, pointing them, not only to the grandeur of
this man's life, but also reminding them of the pos-
sibilities that lie in the path of those who value
integrity; who love the truth, and whose steps are
guided by the unfailing light of a mighty principle
and an indomitable purpose.

MR. CHAIRMAN : In the name of, and as the
servant of, the great state of New Hampshire, I
accept this statue; and, as the chief executive, I
fervently invoke the renewed devotion of our people to the great doctrines and principles that John
P. Hale advocated and defended with such marvel-
ous ability and matchless eloquence.

His tongue has long been mute, but the words he spoke in life and the heroic grandeur of his character should ever be an incentive and inspiration to noble aims and lofty deeds on the part of all who appreciate and honor the highest type of American manhood.

THE CHAIRMAN : — We are fortunate in having, as the principal speaker of the occasion, one who, from his own boyhood to the day of the decease of Mr. Hale, knew him, admired him, and loved him ; one who can speak out of a full heart. I present our fellow-citizen, Hon. Daniel Hall, of Dover, as the orator of the day.

COL. HALL'S ORATION.

MR. PRESIDENT AND FELLOW CITIZENS : When the illusions of military glory, and the delirious dream of a universal supremacy, had given way to the sober reflections of the philosopher and statesman, the august exile of St. Helena said : "I wanted no statues, for I knew that there was no safety in receiving them at any other hands than those of posterity." In a like spirit, Burke also deprecated a statue in his life-time, saying that such honors belong exclusively to the tomb, and that, frequently, such is human inconstancy, the same hands which erect pull them down. Thus these great men, both with characteristic penetration and discernment, touched upon the profound truth that every man's work is to be tested by time. That is the crucible through which all service is to be passed before it receives its final stamp and authentication. But time is a factor whose relations to history are readjusted. What required an age in an earlier day is now accomplished in a generation, by the diffusion of knowledge, the rapid circulation of intelligence, the electric rapidity of all the interchanges of thought and sentiment. Men do not wait for ages to be appreciated. By these modern instruments of precision, in the quickening of human sympathies, and the broadening of intellectual horizons, we measure the mental and moral altitude of our great actors, and determine their places in the firmament with unerring accuracy, after only that brief lapse of time which suffices for the subsidence of the passions and perturbations of contemporary judgment. And so, before a generation has passed since a great man was gathered to his rest, the people of his state meet, in unbroken accord, to do him honor by raising here a statue to his memory in the public grounds of the commonwealth, under the shadow of its capitol, whose arches have so often resounded with the echoes of his eloquence.

On the 31st day of March, 1806, New Hampshire was enriched with one of those rare gifts, which, bestowed upon her in unusual plenitude, have given her a distinction beyond most other states, as the mother of great men. On that day JOHN PARKER HALE was born in Rochester, of a father bearing the same name, a lawyer of brilliant promise, and a mother who was the daughter of William O'Brien, an Irish exile, who distinguished himself by the daring feat of capturing the first

armed British vessel in the War of the Revolution and died a prisoner of war at the early age of
twenty-three. He was of the heroic stock which
gave birth to William Smith O'Brien. It is hardly
more than idle speculation to fancy that we always
find in race or pedigree the source of special traits
in a great character; but those who are curious to
trace the characteristics of genius back to ances-
tral blood, have readily found Mr. Hale's practical
turn of mind, sound sense, coolness and phlegm in
his sturdy Anglo-Saxon father, and the wit and
humor, warmth and rhetorical fervor which marked
his speech and temperament, in his mother's Celtic
ancestors. Mr. Hale's father died in 1819 at the
early age of forty-four, leaving an honorable name,
but to his mother little of this world's goods where-
with to care for a numerous family of children, of
whom Mr. Hale was the second, and but thirteen
years of age. But she was equal to the duty
imposed upon her. She nurtured her brood with
singular care and industry, and had the satisfaction
of living to see her son enter upon a career of
assured professional success, and also into the
political life which was afterwards so distinguished.
She died in 1832 at the age of fifty-two years.
Through all his life Mr Hale loved and honored
this noble mother with a rare devotion, serving her
with a knightly loyalty in his youth, and in his days
of renown, when he was an illustrious United States
senator and the peer of any living American, he
made a most touching allusion to her in the debate
upon Gen. Cass's resolution of sympathy with the
exiled Irish patriots. Said he, "Sir, my mother,

many years dead, was the only child of an Irish
exile. His name was O'Brien, and I should feel,
if in this place, or in any place, whenever or wherever a word of sympathy is to be expressed for an
Irish exile and an O'Brien, that I should be false
to every pulsation of my heart, to every drop of
blood that flows in these veins, and to that which
no man can be false to, a deceased mother, if I did
not express it. No, sir, let whatever consequences,
personal or political, stand in the way, so long as
the blood of my mother flows in my veins, and so
long as I remember who I am, and what I am,
whatever words of sympathy, of counsel, or of
encouragement an Irish exile can have, that he shall
have from me."

But few of the contemporaries of Mr. Hale's
youth survive, and it is difficult to present any
but an imperfect record of the circumstances amid
which he reached maturity, the processes by which
he was prepared for his destined work, and the
forces which determined the course and complex-
ion of his career. But it is certain that he was a
bright, active, quick, witty, kind, generous, courageous, and helpful boy. His mother's exertions
kept him at school, and he was enabled at an early
age to get a term or two of preparatory study at
Exeter under Principal Abbot, who boasted some
years after that he had five of his boys in the
United States senate, "and pretty good boys,
too,"—Webster, Cass, Hale, Dix, and Felch. He
entered Bowdoin college in 1823, and was there a
contemporary and friend of Franklin Pierce,
Nathaniel Hawthorne, and other distinguished

men. He was graduated there in 1827, with a high reputation for general ability and off-hand oratorical power. He read law at Rochester and at Dover, where he finished his legal studies under the tuition of the late Daniel M. Christie, for many years the honored head of the New Hampshire bar. As a law student he displayed all his characteristic traits of quickness, aptitude, ease of acquisition, and tenacity of memory; so that both his instructors, Mr. Woodman and Mr. Christie, formed the highest hopes of him, and confidently predicted his future eminence. To all who knew him it was evident that he was fitted to play a great part in the world, and was the possessor of powers of which his country had a right to demand an account. From his earliest youth he manifested the activity of his intellect, and read with interest the classics of our literature, and especially the great orators of ancient and modern times. Admitted to the bar and opening an office at Dover in 1830, he at once took high rank in the profession. His entrance into practice realized the highest hopes of his friends; he soon gained a large clientage, and within a few years became known as one of the most astute lawyers and eloquent advocates at the New Hampshire bar. He had consummate skill and tact in handling witnesses, rare keenness in discerning the points at issue and adroitness in meeting them, and extraordinary power before juries in both criminal and civil cases. In the earlier years of his practice he was often the leading counsel against Mr. Christie and others not less distinguished, and his appeals to the jury gave full

scope to his unrivalled wit and humor, his indignation against wrong, and pathos in defence of the
rights of humanity.

As a lawyer, Mr. Hale from the outset manifested the democratic tendencies of his mind and
character. He believed in the people, and was
jealous of every encroachment upon popular rights.
Before his entrance upon the national arena he
made a stand in the supreme court of New Hampshire for the right of the jury to be judges of the
law as well as the facts in criminal cases, and had a
warm controversy on the subject with the late
Chief-Justice Joel Parker. He published a pam-
phlet on the question which was a remarkable pro-
duction, showing great research and polemical
skill, and it is scarcely extravagant to style it a
monument to his acquirements as a lawyer. It
contains well-nigh all the learning on a question of
the deepest importance in its day, which has been
substantially settled at last by the ameliorations of
the criminal law, the progress of society, and the
growth of the institutions of liberty. Although
Mr. Hale was not distinguished for recondite learning, this publication exhibited too complete a
mastery of authorities to be dashed off at a sitting,
too profound an argument to have been prepared
in a day. This debate is chiefly interesting today
as proof that Mr. Hale had unquestionably devoted
time in his early years to the study of the great
books of the common law, to the history and
development of English liberty, and was deeply
grounded in its leading principles. Judge Parker
replied through the New Hampshire Reports in

Peirce et al. v. State, 13 N. H. 536. An examination of these reports from Vol. 6 to 17, inclusive, will show the extent and importance of Mr. Hale's law practice, and that he had every prospect of a great legal career.

Mr. Hale exhibited an early bias towards politics and the consideration of public affairs. With his ardent nature, popular sympathies, and devotion to free principles, it is not strange that he had embraced the doctrines of that democracy which was then in the ascendant in the young republic. In 1832 he was elected to the legislature on a workingman's ticket, an incident thus early indicative of his sympathetic relation with humanity, and a presage of his future career as a champion of popular rights. He soon after became fully identified with the Democratic party, and in 1834, when only twenty-eight years of age, he was appointed by President Jackson United States district attorney, which position he held with distinction till he was removed for political reasons by the Whig administration in 1841. During this time Mr. Hale had developed very rapidly as a lawyer and orator, and in 1843 he was nominated for congress by the Democratic party, and elected on a general ticket with Edmund Burke, John R. Reding, and Moses Norris.

It was the fortune of Mr. Hale to come upon the stage of action at a time of intellectual and moral ferment in New England,—a time of daring speculations, when enthusiasms were aroused, and society, though not recreated by transcendentalism and other more or less Utopian schemes, yet re-

ceived a mighty uplifting, which gave free scope
to the most adventurous thought and philanthropy.
His youth and early manhood were coincident with
this period of moral and intellectual upheaval and
awakening on all subjects ; and if such a man, by
virtue of his environment and the indifference of
the public sentiment in which he was reared, was
as yet callous to the wrong and the danger of
American slavery, it was clear he could not so
remain. It is impossible to conceive that a mind
so comprehensive, a nature so fine and humane, a
temper so bold, a courage so superb and complete,
should not be arrested by a portent so terrible then
rising into domination of the republic, and against
which every generous aspiration of New England
was rising in insurrection. Since, by his own confession, he had encouraged a rude interruption of
an anti-slavery meeting in Dover in 1835, a persecution of abolitionists in which he said he thought
he was doing God service, as Paul did before his
conversion in persecuting the Christians, Mr. Hale
had been a watchful observer of the course of
events and ideas, and when he was elected to congress in 1843, it was known that he would vote for
the abrogation of the twenty-first rule, whereby
congress, at the dictation of the slave power, con-
temptuously refused to receive anti-slavery petitions. He had avowed this purpose, and was
elected with that understanding ; and when the
question came forward in that congress, he, with
Hannibal Hamlin of Maine, came to the support of
Mr. Adams, and valiantly fought to abrogate the
rule. The attempt was not then successful, but at

the next session the "old man eloquent" burst
through the gag rule in triumph.

The slavery of the negro race in the United
States is one of the cruelest and bloodiest passages
in human history. In the same year that the *May-
flower* crossed the ocean, bearing to the western
continent the Pilgrim fathers, another ship buffeted
the same sea, brought with her a cargo of nineteen
slaves, and landed them at Jamestown in Virginia.
That was the fatal seed of American slavery, the
upas tree which struck deep its poisonous root, and
threatened so long to overshadow the whole land.
Mr. Sumner well said that in the hold of these two
ships were concealed the germs of the War of the
Rebellion. As time passed on, negroes were forced
into the country by British greed, and the system
made its way into all the colonies. But the conscience of Puritanism never gave up its antagonism
to the idea that "man could hold property in man,"
and in time the New England colonies one by one
sloughed it off.

During the War of Independence, however,
nearly all the colonies held slaves, though the system was far stronger in the South than in the
North. But the Revolutionary struggle itself
gave rise to certain phrases since called " glittering
generalities of natural right," which in themselves
were held to bar a continuance of the institution.
Before the adoption of the constitution a majority
of the states had inhibited the further introduction
of slaves, and almost everywhere, notably in Virginia under the influence of Jefferson and Madison,
the current of opinion and of political action was

against slavery. That it was considered a mere temporary condition by our fathers, to be very soon eliminated and cast off, is beyond question. It was the fortune of Mr. Hale to demonstrate that on repeated occasions in his political life. The views of the makers of the constitution are clearly shown by the great ordinance of 1787, passed by the congress of the confederation, which dedicated the Northwest to freedom forever by these immortal words: "There shall be neither slavery nor involuntary servitude in the said territory, otherwise than in the punishment of crimes whereof the party shall have been duly convicted."

Then came the constitution itself, in which the founders would acknowledge the existence of slavery in the Union by an euphemism only, by the prohibition of the slave trade after 1808, and by guaranties looking to the ultimate extinction of the system itself. One of the first acts of congress under the constitution was to reënact the ordinance of Jefferson and Dane by extending its provisions to new territory ceded to the Union. But now, soon after the constitution was formed, these strong tendencies towards emancipation and the restriction of slavery began to be reversed. In the Union as first formed, only a small portion, a little strip on the southern Atlantic slope, was adapted to the tropical productions of rice and cotton. But now the Anglo-Saxon "hunger for the horizon" began to operate. The retrocession of Louisiana to France in 1800, and its purchase by the United States from Napoleon in 1803, and the purchase of Florida from Spain in 1819, threw open a vast acreage of new lands, with a deep and fertile soil, under a burning sun, fitted superbly for the growth of cotton and the sugar cane under conditions to which the Caucasian constitution was not adapted. But the most potent factor was the simple invention of the cotton gin by Eli Whitney in 1793, which, concurring with other mechanical inventions of this time, changed the whole aspect of the slavery question in the cotton growing states.

Previous to 1790 no cotton had been exported from America. These events stimulated the cultivation of cotton, opened for it a foreign market, enhanced the commercial value of the slave, and tightened his chains. It is noteworthy how the excess of land in the extreme South fitted into the excess of labor in the border states, and gave to both a common and reciprocal interest in " the peculiar institution." The Louisiana purchase added more land to the Union than we already had. This acquisition of territory thus developed the inter-state slave trade, and Virginia became the breeding ground of a race of chattel laborers, whose wrongs were depicted in such lurid colors and with such lightning strokes of genius in Uncle Tom's Cabin. Thus the institution became an iniquitous and guilty traffic, so far out-heroding any former system of helotism in human history as to call down upon itself the execration of man and the vengeance of heaven. The South became more and more enamored of a system so diabolically profitable, and, elated by holding the fancied monopoly of the world's greatest staple, boldly proclaimed that cotton was king,—that cotton could only be produced by slave labor, and that therefore slavery should be a permanent institution, to be nursed, protected, preserved, extended, and made the corner stone and vital principle of their civilization. From that time the North and South grew wider and wider apart, and the rival systems of freedom and slavery contended fiercely for the mastery in the great masses of territory that had been successively added to the Union. Happily, the great ordinance of 1787, a state paper deserving to take rank with the declaration of independence, which Lord Brougham said should always hang in the cabinet of kings, had predestined to freedom a vast region, a virgin soil where no prior rights had taken root and no tares been sown, and to its efficacy we are indebted for the great free commonwealths of Ohio, Indiana, Illinois, Michigan, Wisconsin, and Minnesota, stretching from the Ohio to the sources of the Mississippi,—though slavery did not give *them* up even without a further struggle. The South, with a bad faith which became characteristic, demanded the abrogation of the ordinance, and an agitation began to be manifested whose dull and distant rumblings, forerunners of volcanic outbreaks, could be heard ever and anon during the next thirty years. But, over the Louisiana purchase of 1803, that vast region extending from the Gulf of Mexico to the headwaters of the Missouri, the old empires of Spain and France had legalized slavery, and consequently the institution was already planted there beyond dispute. Louisiana and Arkansas were taken into the Union as slave states, but at a little later day, when Missouri

applied for admission in 1818, the friends of freedom, then in control of the house of representatives, demanded the exclusion of slavery. There-
upon ensued a memorable struggle lasting two
years, but finally settled by the Missouri compromise passed in 1820, whereby Missouri was admitted with the slavery that has cursed and hampered
her ever since, and the North in lieu of it got the
solemn agreement of the South for the reversion of
freedom in the part of the territory not yet organized, in the following words : *"And be it further
enacted*, that in all that territory ceded by France
to the United States under the name of Louisiana,
which lies north of 36° 30′ north latitude, excepting
only such part thereof as is included within the
limits of the state contemplated by this act, slavery
and involuntary servitude, otherwise than in punishment of crime whereof the party shall have been
duly convicted, shall be and is forever prohibited."
Florida was then admitted in 1821, and once more
the country breathed freely, and peace for the
future was supposed to be secure. But the tiger
craving of the South for conquest and power had
been whetted, and its aggressive and Philistine
character appeared ever and anon, in the discussions upon the tariff, the public lands, the right of
petition, the right of interference with the mails in
search of " incendiary publications," the Creek and
Seminole War, and otherwise, that came up in the
following twenty years. That at the end slavery
had made a distinct advance upon freedom, enlarging its pretensions, aggrandizing itself anew at
every step, and more and more completely subju-

3

gating the public opinion of the North to its uses, is a truth abundantly evidenced by the history of the time. In 1832 Mr. Calhoun had organized the slave power, and brought it forward upon the scene with a distinct purpose and programme of its own; and, less than twenty-five years after the Missouri compromise, that power, now become a propaganda of the most ruthless character, and, holding entire control of the federal government, had adroitly and criminally plotted and brought about the severance of Texas from Mexico, overrun and revolutionized it, and now proposed to annex it to the slave interest in the Union, and make its preponderance final and decisive. This had been notoriously done in the interest of slave extension. These encroachments of the South upon freedom were well calculated to arouse the latent and slowly-growing anti-slavery sentiments of the North, and, in fact, brought a crisis which enlisted the energies of many noble souls.

At this juncture John P. Hale took his seat in the national house of representatives—into this seething caldron of slavery agitation his political life was cast. He had inherited no anti-slavery principles—such as he had were the fruit of a steady growth of heart and brain. He had been awakened by the trend of events and ideas between the Storrs meeting in the Dover church and 1843, and he found his conscience and his whole better nature insurgent against the slave system. Perhaps no man ever entered congress with more flattering prospects. His reputation had preceded him, and his gifts as an orator gave him an imme-

diate hearing in the house. In the opening days
of the session he entered freely into the debates,
taking a very prominent stand as an advocate of
Democratic principles, and attracting wide and
admiring attention by his oratorical power. There
was the fire of a passionate sincerity in his eloquent
improvisations; and I well remember the contemporary characterizations of him as the "Democratic
Boanerges," the "Granite State cataract," and
other like expressions. He proposed measures of
retrenchment in regard to West Point, the army,
and the navy, and advocated a reduction in postage
rates, and the abolition of corporal punishment in
the army. On the 3d of June, 1844, he set in
motion a great movement for humanity by moving
an amendment to the naval appropriation bill, abolishing flogging in the navy, and his eloquence
carried it in the house, but it was lost in the senate.

Then came the act of Mr. Hale which may fairly
be regarded as the initial point of his great career
upon those lines which he afterwards followed with
such devoted singleness of heart and purpose. The
annexation of Texas was the pet scheme of President Tyler, but was supported zealously by the
extreme pro-slavery party at the South with Mr.
Calhoun at their head. He was their leading intellect, and it was soon seen to be a scheme in the
direct and exclusive interest of slavery extension.
Accordingly, as its character unfolded, the spontaneous feeling and expression of the North were
opposed to it. The project of slavery extension
was opposed by all the accredited organs of Democratic party opinion in New Hampshire, alike by

the leaders, the press, and the masses of the party
itself. It was denounced by the press in unmeas-
ured terms as a design "black as ink and bitter as
hell." This was the undoubted attitude of the
Democratic party of New Hampshire in 1843 and
1844. But the South had obtained complete control of the national councils and patronage, and the
word had gone forth that Texas was to be annexed
to the Union for the aggrandizement of slavery,
and such was the power of the South over the
national convention that Mr. Van Buren, for whom
the Democracy of New Hampshire had unanimously
instructed their delegates, was defrauded of the
presidential nomination on account of his opposition to the annexation of Texas, and Mr. Polk
nominated because he favored the scheme. Therefore, to keep in line with, or rather to obey the
behests of, the Southern Democracy, the Democratic
newspapers and public men of New Hampshire
had to change front, and to eat their own brave
words of resistance to that domination. In fact,
the annexation of Texas had been first hinted at,
then timidly suggested, and at length boldly
avowed as the Democratic policy in the teeth of all
the anti-slavery feeling of the Northern states;
and not only this, but as a treaty of annexation,
which the whole North believed to be the only constitutional way of acquiring foreign territory, could
not be carried through the senate, it was resolved
by an unscrupulous and domineering slave party to
defy all constitutional restraints, and annex Texas
by joint resolution. So complete was the domination of Southern men and interests over the Demo-

cratic party of the North that at their dictation the
New Hampshire Democracy reversed its course,
and the legislature in December, 1844, passed resolutions instructing the senators and representatives
in congress to vote for the annexation of Texas.
It was true that Mr. Hale had powerfully and effectively advocated the election of Mr. Polk, who was
known to be in favor of annexation, but he had done
so, undoubtedly, with the understanding that
annexation was to be effected, if at all, by constitutional methods, by the treaty-making power which
all the great organs of constitutional interpretation
had insisted upon, and also that as many or more
free than slave states were to be added to the
Union, and thus the area of freedom was to be
extended at least equally with that of slavery.
This was the language of Northern speakers, and
the Democratic press, headed by the *Democratic
Review*, all through the campaign. This was Mr.
Clay's opinion, and some Southern men opposed
the annexation upon the very ground " that Texas
as an undivided slave country, though a foreign
one, was preferable to Texas carved up into an
equal number of slaveholding and non-slave-
holding states." The New Hampshire legislature
in these very resolutions of instruction expressed
the belief that the annexation of Texas would add
more free than slave states to the Union. But
Mr. Polk had been elected, and the South proceeded at once to pluck the spoils of victory.
Before the inauguration so eager were they for the
consummation of the scheme that at the session
commencing in December, 1844, the Texas project

was brought forward. All the pent-up fires of Northern opposition to slavery extension and aggrandizement were fanned into a flame, and a fierce contention arose. Mr. Hale, evidently with no idea of breaking with his party, instead of bending to the dictation of the Southern leaders, proceeded simply to carry out the opinions he was known to entertain, which he had avowed in New Hampshire, which he had expressed by his action in vindication of the right of petition, and in which he had every reason to suppose he would be sustained by his Democratic constituents at home. He accordingly moved a suspension of the rules in order to move to divide Texas into two parts, in one of which slavery should be forever prohibited; but though his motion was carried by a majority, it failed for want of a two-thirds vote. This, and the scornful defeat of every movement looking to a division of Texas between freedom and slavery, showed only too clearly the animus of the whole scheme. In fact, if Texas, or any part of it, had been let in with a constitution prohibiting slavery, subsequent proceedings would have interested its advocates no more.

Mr. Hale then addressed to his constituents, "the Democratic Republican electors of New Hampshire," the famous letter dated July 7, 1845, in which he took ground against the Texas scheme, exposing its character in no measured terms, as purely in the interest of slave extension. He declared his unalterable opposition to the annexation by congress of a foreign nation for the avowed purpose of extending and perpetuating slavery.

He stigmatized the reasons given by its advocates
in its behalf as "eminently calculated to provoke
the scorn of earth and the judgment of heaven,"
and thus appealed to the patriotic traditions of one
of the most patriotic of the "old thirteen":—"When
our forefathers bade a last farewell to the homes of
their childhood, the graves of their fathers, and the
temples of their God, and ventured upon all the
desperate contingencies of wintry seas and a savage coast, that they might in strong faith and
ardent hope lay deep the foundations of the temple
of liberty, their faith would have become scepticism,
and their hope despair, could they have foreseen
that the day would ever arrive when their degenerate sons should be found seeking to extend their
boundaries and their government, not for the purpose of promoting freedom, but sustaining slavery."
This letter for a moment gave pause to political
movements in New Hampshire, but was very soon
met by a storm of denunciation from the party
leaders. The decree went forth that Mr. Hale was
to be thrown overboard for his contumacy, and at
a convention of the party called for the purpose
February 12, 1845, his nomination was rescinded,
his name struck from the ticket, and another substituted. But there was a public conscience that
only needed to be aroused, and the letter had struck
a chord that was only waiting to be touched by the
hand of a master. Immediately there were signs
of a revolt in the Democratic party against this
despotic sway at the dictation of the slave power,
and under the lead of Amos Tuck and John L.
Hayes a small party styling themselves Independ-

ent Democrats rallied about the standard of Mr.
Hale. This was the first meeting in a state where
the party rule was absolute—which had been under
Democratic control since 1829, and had given Mr.
Polk 6,000 majority. Meanwhile, although faithful
sentinels on the watch towers of freedom fore-
warned the North of the direful consequences of
annexation, it was carried in the house by 134 to
77, showing the gains slavery had made, John P.
Hale and Hannibal Hamlin alone among the Northern Democracy refusing to bow the knee at the
party behest. Thus the administration of Mr.
Tyler, not otherwise illustrious, was distinguished
at last by the admission of Texas. The election
came off March 11, 1845. Mr. Hale received about
8,000 votes, and the regular Democratic candidate
lacked about 1,000 votes of an election. Mr. Hale
had taken no very active part in it. He had not
been hopeful of a successful resistance to the party
despotism, and had made arrangements to retire
from political life, and take up the practice of his
profession in the city of New York. Many years
afterward he said in the senate,—"When I went
home from Washington at the close of the session
in 1845, I had no more idea of being returned to
congress than I had of succeeding to the vacant
throne of China." Moreover, in his letter to his
constituents, he had rather incautiously said : " If
you think differently from me on this subject, and
should therefore deem it expedient to select another
person to effectuate your purpose in congress, no
person in the state will bow more submissively to
your will than myself." With a perhaps over-

scrupulous sense of honor, he regarded this as a sort of pledge to leave the result with them without interference. But the result of the first trial convinced him that New Hampshire was not yet irrevocably mortgaged to the slave propaganda, nor wholly prepared to execute the edicts of party tyranny. His friends gathered around him, and demanded that he take the field in person. Their summons to him was the appeal of the Andalusian king to the ancient Douglas :

> "Take thou the leading of the van,
> And charge the Moors amain ;
> There is not such a lance as thine
> In all the hosts of Spain."

Mr. Hale yielded to these importunities rather than to any ambitious views or hopes of his own. He assumed the leadership ; he canvassed the state ; he delivered speeches wherever he could get a hearing, to audiences large and small, in halls, in churches, in vestries, in school-rooms, in the open air, everywhere stirring and thrilling the people with his warm and glowing eloquence, and his impassioned appeals to duty and manliness. He was then in his full prime. His figure was noble and commanding—

> "A combination and a form indeed,
> Where every god did seem to set his seal,
> To give the world assurance of a man."

His voice was resonant and flexible ; his countenance was one of striking manly beauty ; he had perfect command of words, and perfect command of his temper ; his self-control, his chivalrous courtesy, were superb ; his sincerity and loyalty to his convictions were manifest, and it required a crisis like this, the liberties of man hanging in the balance, to give full sweep to his unrivalled powers, his wit, his humor, his brilliant repartee, and bring into play all the resources of his large mind, his humane spirit, his liberty-loving heart. The circumstances had never had a parallel. Here was a man who was voluntarily putting to hazard the highest hopes and brightest prospects—renouncing all by a sublime act of political abnegation and self-effacement—making way for liberty like Arnold Von Winkelreid charging the Austrian army ; giving up a party whose ascendency in his own state was so pronounced as to be beyond question, whose particular pride and pet he was, and by whose generous suffrages he had been set forward in a career of political advancement whose goal he might without unwarranted pretension easily see in the highest honor of the world. As far as human forecast could reach, this course opened to him no road to favor or patronage. As no man could be so visionary as to indulge a hope of breaking the spell of Democratic victory in New Hampshire, adherence to his party connection and obedience to party direction were unquestionably the readiest and only path to influence and promotion. Concurring with this was Mr. Hale's natural fondness for popular applause and for political life, his alleged ambition, and his growing popularity as an orator and statesman. But all were renounced. He hazarded wealth, power, political preferment,

and held out no lure to his followers but the cold
and hunger which Garibaldi promised to those who
should strike with him for the deliverance of Italy.
In his own words, he sat on no stool of repentance.
He maintained the defiant attitude he had taken
up, and defended his position before the people
with imperturbable wit, with infinite good humor,
and incomparable eloquence. In this extraordinary
crusade of Mr. Hale there was a certain romantic
knight-errantry, which, with the charm of his personality, his gallant and chivalrous bearing, his
noble heart, his freedom from all vindictiveness as
from every selfish ambition, captivated the imagination of the people, and made him an ideal popular
hero. Brave men flocked to his standard, and
gladly bared their own bosoms to the shafts of the
pro-slavery hatred aimed at him. He was a popular idol, and made of political coadjutors devoted
personal friends. They lived in his "mild and
magnificent eye," and loved to follow wherever his
white plume danced in the eddies of the fight.
They were his disciples, and asked nothing better
than the title of "Hale men," thus identifying
themselves with this eloquent champion of liberty
sans peur et sans reproche. I shall never forget
how a noble old man once told me that in those
days no night ever passed when he and his wife
did not together send up their prayers that God
would bless, and protect, and keep John P. Hale.
And not alone were their aspirations wafted heavenward for his welfare ; but thousands in New Hampshire, and everywhere in America where human
hearts were beginning to stir with new thoughts of

freedom, sent up daily their petitions to the Most
High to cover his head in battle, and shelter him
under the shadow of His wing. The "Hale storm"
of 1845 is the heroic and romantic episode of our
political history, and veterans who lived in and
have survived that time turn back to the period
fondly as one when it was worth while to live.
Thus the conflict went on through the summer
days, and

> "His was the voice that rang
> In the fight like a bugle-call."

Perhaps its most striking incident was the celebrated meeting of Mr. Hale and Franklin Pierce at
the Old North church in Concord on the 9th of
June, 1845. The circumstances were suited to
exhibit Mr. Hale's extraordinary powers, and they
were displayed to the greatest advantage. During
that week, the legislature commenced its session. A
meeting of Independent Democrats, to be addressed
by Mr. Hale, had been called, and there was an
unusual assemblage of people in town in attendance
upon various religious and benevolent anniversaries.
The Democrats, apprehensive of the effect of such
a speech upon an audience so intelligent and conscientious, resolved that he must be answered on the
spot, and Franklin Pierce was selected as the only
man at all fitted for such an encounter. The old
church was crowded beyond its capacity. Mr. Hale
spoke for two hours, making a calm, dignified, and
effective vindication of his principles and conduct.
Occasionally rudely interrupted, he never lost his
temper, nor that splendid equanimity which availed

him on so many occasions in debate. He rose to a
surprising eloquence in denunciation of slavery, and
at the end it was manifest that, whether they agreed
with his conclusions or not, all were convinced that
he had been actuated by pure motives and a high
sense of public duty.

Mr. Pierce was himself a nervous, energetic, and
brilliant orator; but, for the task set before him, he
was handicapped by the inconsistencies of the Democratic record, and by Mr. Hale's glowing appeal to
the nobler sentiments of humanity, lifting the plane
of discussion entirely above its ordinary dead level.
He replied to Mr. Hale in a passionate and imperious, not to say insolent, manner, accusing him of
ambitious motives, and defending, as he only could,
the party in power for its efforts to extend the area
of the republic by bringing the vast territory of
Texas under its sway. The advantage in temper
was very manifest, and when Mr. Hale had rejoined
with a triumphant vindication of his own motives
and purposes, he closed with this magnificent appeal:
" I expected to be called ambitious; to have my
name cast out as evil. I have not been disappointed. But, if things have come to this condition, that
conscience and a sacred regard for truth and duty
are to be publicly held up to ridicule, and scouted at
without rebuke, as has just been done here, it matters little whether we are annexed to Texas or
Texas is annexed to us. I may be permitted to
say that the measure of my ambition will be full, if,
when my earthly career shall be finished and my
bones be laid beneath the soil of New Hampshire,
when my wife and children shall repair to my grave

to drop the tear of affection to my memory, they may read on my tombstone, 'He who lies beneath surrendered office, place, and power, rather than bow down and worship slavery.'" In the opinion of Mr. Hale's friends, his victory was indisputable. No debate in New Hampshire ever had such interest, and none results at all comparable with it in importance. Beyond doubt Mr. Pierce's effort that day made him president of the United States, and Mr. Hale's led to the triumph of his party, whereby he became the first anti-slavery senator and the recognized pioneer champion of the Free-Soil movement. On the 23d of September, 1845, the third trial was held for representative in congress, resulting in a Democratic defeat by about the same vote as before, the Hale men holding the balance of power between them and the Whigs. November 29, 1845, a fourth trial left the Democrats in a still more decisive minority; and then the final struggle for mastery in the state was postponed to the annual election, March 10, 1846. During the winter, Mr. Hale canvassed the state again, everywhere the admired champion of a cause now manifestly advancing to certain triumph. The result was a complete overthrow of the party in power in New Hampshire, the Whigs and Independent Democrats together having both branches of the legislature, and a considerable majority of the popular vote, though there was no election of governor or congressman by the people. Mr. Hale was chosen a representative from Dover, and, by a coalition of Hale men and Whigs, was made speaker of the house. Mr. Colby, the Whig candidate, was elected governor, and, on the

9th of June, 1846, Mr. Hale was chosen United
States senator for the full term of six years commencing March 4, 1847. Thus, upon an issue distinctly joined, the Democracy had been signally
defeated, and the Gibraltar of the North had passed
into the hands of the combined opposition. The
first and strongest outwork had been carried in a
square contest against the extension of a system
which met the moral reprobation of the world, and
the victory proclaimed that never again was New
Hampshire to sit supinely by, to take the orders
and register the edicts of slavery. The note of defiance and of resistance to further slavery aggression
rang out clear and strong from these New Hampshire hills, and was heard throughout America.
No ear so dull that did not hear it; no brain so
sluggish that did not comprehend it. As armies
in mythologic story paused in mid-contest to watch
the issue of a single combat, so in some sense the
people of America turned to observe the outcome
of this struggle; and Mr. Hale's success in New
Hampshire in resistance to slavery, and to party
subserviency and tyranny, was the first lightning
gleam of victory lighting up the dark clouds that
hung over the country. It was an encouragement
and a challenge to other states and the friends of
liberty elsewhere. An inspired singer and prophet
of anti-slavery had watched the struggle with
breathless interest from his home just across our
border, and it called out from him that immortal
tribute to New Hampshire, which will live with her
fame and the name of John G. Whittier forever:

"God bless New Hampshire—from her granite peaks
Once more the voice of Stark and Langdon speaks.
The long bound vassal of the exulting South
For very shame her self-forged chain has broken,—
Torn the black seal of slavery from her mouth.
And in the clear tones of her old time spoken!
Oh, all undreamed of, all unhoped for changes!
The tyrant's ally proves his sternest foe;
To all his biddings, from her mountain ranges,
New Hampshire thunders an indignant No!
Who is it now despairs? Oh! faint of heart,
Look upward to those Northern mountains cold.
Flouted by Freedom's victor-flag unrolled,
And gather strength to bear a manlier part!
All is not lost. The Angel of God's blessing
Encamps with Freedom on the field of fight;
Still to her banner, day by day, are pressing
Unlooked for allies, striking for the right!
Courage, then, Northern hearts!—Be firm, be true:
What one brave state hath done, can ye not also do?"

Here were the first fruits of John P. Hale's manly resistance to slavery in America. At first but a
feeble protest, scarcely heard amid the hosannas of
Northern servility to the slave power, it had swelled
into a volume of indignant opposition, which had
swept away the strongest muniments of oppression
in the North. It gave courage everywhere for the
great struggle just opening before this people. In
the words of Cardinal Newman, "We did but light
a beacon fire on the summit of a lonely hill; and
anon we were amazed to find the firmament on
every side red with the light of a responsive flame."

And now, is there occasion for either hesitation
or apology in making claim in behalf of John P.
Hale for pioneership in the great Free-soil movement which finally overthrew slavery in the United

States? New Hampshire was the first battle-field of the new crusade, and John P. Hale commanded the vanguard. Aye, more, in his Texas letter he had formulated the issues upon which the fight was to be made and won, the identical postulates which were afterwards to be the principles of a great political party not yet born, under whose lead the war was to be fought and emancipation come to the country and the slave. The Hon. Amos Tuck, one of the earliest, ablest, and most faithful of the followers of Mr. Hale, at Downer Landing in 1878, met the claim of Massachusetts that the Republican party was founded there in 1848, by showing that that party was anticipated in every one of its ideas by the Hale party in New Hampshire in 1845, and that John P. Hale won his election as the first anti-slavery senator, and sat in that body, alone, as such, for two years before a friendly senator came to join him, and two years before the date which Massachusetts claims for her patent. This claim for New Hampshire and for Mr. Hale is impregnable. Therefore I say that no man can precede Mr. Hale as the founder of the Republican party, and all that is implied thereby: and that whatever of merit may attach to such a sponsorship—and I know full well that many still regard it as a cause for condemnation rather than praise—that whatever of glory or shame there be in it, belongs to him more than to any other man. I must ask indulgence for the use of political terminology, which I employ because I find our resources of expression inadequate to convey any clear ideas without using the terms Democrat and Republican.

4

Mr. Hale took his seat in the senate, December 6, 1847, and for the first time American slavery was confronted in his person by the aroused moral sense of the American people. From his first dramatic appearance in that body this solitary representative of freedom was the object of the bitter hatred and disdain of the slave oligarchy. He entered a senate composed of thirty-two Democrats, twenty-one Whigs, and himself. Declining to be classified with either, he unfalteringly took up and held the position of an anti-slavery independent. He declined the obscurity to which both sides would have relegated him, and for two years before he was joined by Chase in 1849, the anti-slavery movement centred around his striking personality, and he stood there alone, resisting at every step the aggressive measures of slavery, maintaining his ground with unsurpassed resources of wit and logic, eloquence and good humor. He entered resolutely into the public business and had to stand in the breach and contend single-handed with the entire senate, containing then not only the great triumvirate of oratory and statesmanship, but also many others of the highest distinction and ability. He met them face to face, and dealt sturdy blows for freedom in every emergency. His weapons were of that firm edge and fine temper that might be broken, but would not turn, in their impact upon the brazen front of oppression. Every means of silencing him was resorted to, threats, insults, sneers, ridicule, derision. He was treated with studied contempt by the South, and with cold neglect by the North. He was denied the common courtesy of a place on senatorial committees, being told publicly by a senator who was afterward expelled from the body for disloyalty, that he was considered outside of any healthy political organization in the country. But this discipline was lost on him. He had the moral courage which shrinks from no duty—that calm, firm, cool, inflexible, resolution which clinched its determination to go straightforward with Luther's exclamation, " I will repair thither though I should find there as many devils as there are tiles on the house tops. I cannot do otherwise, God helping me." It is not practicable to refer minutely to the debates in which Mr. Hale mingled in the senate. In 1848, in the discussion upon the admission of Oregon, he proposed as an amendment the ordinance of 1787 excluding slavery, which gave rise to a fierce debate, in the course of which he was the subject of most personal and inflammatory denunciations. He defended himself with consummate ability, declaring his determination to press the prohibition of slavery according to his own judgment. Said he, " I am willing to place myself upon the great principle of human right, to stand where the word of God and my own conscience concur in placing me, and then bid defiance to all consequences." Early in April, 1848, upon resolutions of sympathy with the up-risings of the down-trodden nationalities of Europe, Mr. Hale spoke in the senate in a strain of sadness mingled with enthusiasm and a lofty hope for the disenthrallment of all men, in America and Europe alike.

In a debate occasioned by certain mob demonstrations against the office of the *National Era* in

Washington, Mr. Hale introduced a resolution copied from the laws of Maryland, providing for the reimbursement of persons whose property should be destroyed by riotous assemblages. This led to a controversy with Mr. Calhoun, in which the great Southerner forgot his usual urbanity and became violently personal, and ended his speech by saying, that he "would as soon argue with a maniac from Bedlam as with the senator from New Hampshire on this subject." Mr. Hale retorted by telling Mr. Calhoun that it was a novel mode of terminating a controversy by charitably throwing the mantle of a maniac's irresponsibility upon one's antagonist. In this debate, Mr. Foote of Mississippi, after many insulting expressions, and denouncing Mr. Hale's bill as "obviously intended to cover and protect negro stealing," turned to Mr. Hale and said: "I invite him to visit the good state of Mississippi, in which I have the honor to reside, and will tell him beforehand in all honesty, that he could not go ten miles into the interior before he would grace one of the tallest trees of the forest with a rope around his neck, with the approbation of every virtuous and patriotic citizen; and that, if necessary, I should myself assist in the operation." Mr. Hale replied: "The senator invites me to visit the state of Mississippi, and kindly informs me that he would be one of those who would act the assassin, and put an end to my career * * * Well, in return for his hospitable invitation, I can only express the desire that he should penetrate into one of the 'dark corners' of New Hampshire, and, if he do, I am much mistaken if he would not find that the people in that 'benighted region' would be very happy to listen to his arguments, and engage in an intellectual conflict with him, in which the truth might be elicited." The ruffianism of the assault, and the nobleness of the reply, have consigned Senator Foote, though a brilliant and by no means a bad man, to the pillory of history, with a soubriquet given him by the public instinct which will last forever.

He opposed the whole system of measures pursued in prosecuting the war with Mexico, because, in the language of Mr. Webster himself, it was "an iniquitous war made in order to obtain, by conquest, slave territory." In December, 1849, Mr. Hale again proposed to incorporate the ordinance of 1787 into Mr. Foote's resolution, declaring it to be the duty of congress to provide territorial governments for California, Deseret, and New Mexico.

At a later day the compromise measures of 1850, including the fugitive slave law, which he loathed and defied, were fought by him with all the weapons of his logic, wit, ridicule, and sarcasm, and with all his parliamentary resources. He occupied two days in an elaborate argument, vindicating the principles, measures, and acts of anti-slavery men.

This was, perhaps, the most powerful of his senatorial efforts. In it he grappled resolutely with the morality, the statesmanship, and the policy, of Mr. Webster's 7th of March speech, quoting his former declarations against himself, agreeing with Mr. Webster in 1848, but dissenting from him in 1850, and saying: "Yet the senator says he would not reënact the laws of God. Well, sir, I would. When he tells me that the law of God is

against slavery, it is a most potent argument for
our incorporating it with any territorial bill " He
closed with an eloquent presentation of the principles and aims of the Free-Soil party, of which he
was the foremost champion.

The abolition of flogging in the navy was a con-
genial field for the exertion of his humane spirit.
In the senate he promptly renewed the efforts he
had commenced in the house. In July, 1848, he moved to insert in the naval appropriation bill a clause
abolishing the spirit ration and prohibiting corporal
punishment in the navy. He addressed the senate
in its favor, but only four senators rose with him.
In February, 1849, he again presented petitions,
and made a strong speech, in which he depicted in
glowing colors the brutality, degradation, and outrage of punishment with the cat-o'-nine-tails, but
was voted down by 32 to 17. In September, 1850,
he made a final impassioned appeal to the senate to
stand no longer in the way of the abolition of flogging in the navy, and on the same day it was carried as a part of the appropriation bill by a vote of
26 to 24, and was concurred in by the house. Thus
at last his efforts were crowned with success. It
was a joyful day for the American navy and for
humanity. It was one of the most gratifying incidents of his life when, two years after, he was received by Commodore Nicholson and crew on board
the man-of-war *Germantown* in Boston harbor, who
thanked him for his noble efforts in abolishing flogging in the United States navy, presented him
with a medal, and manned the yards in his honor.
It was not till twelve years after, however, that he

secured the abolition of the spirit ration. His agency in these beneficent reforms is one of his chiefest titles to honor, and is most fittingly commemorated on the pedestal of this statue.

Thus upon every question that arose he sustained his part with a manliness, a courage, and a nobility of soul which extorted the admiration of foes as well as friends. To adapt the language of Junius, " The rays of Southern indignation collected upon him served only to illumine, they could not consume." The estimate placed upon his services and character was manifested by his unanimous nomination for the presidency by the Liberty party at Buffalo in 1847. He magnanimously relinquished this candidacy, and submitted himself to the will of the later Free-Soil convention at Buffalo in 1848, thus making way for Mr. Van Buren, who was there nominated over him by a majority of 40 votes. Mr. Hale afterwards said that if he had had any idea that the Barnburners had in mind only to revenge Mr. Van Buren's wrongs upon Gen. Cass in 1848, he would have lost his right hand before he would have been a party to such a fraud. In August, 1852, the Free-Soil party at Pittsburg nominated Mr. Hale as its candidate for president, and under the banner of Free Soil, Free Speech, Free Labor, Free Men, No More Slave States, and *no* Slave Territories, he received at the election 155,850 votes.

His first term in the senate is the period of focal interest in Mr. Hale's career. He was the gallant leader of a forlorn hope. He was the *avant courier* of a new *régime*. In him were concentrated in germ all the forces of the new era. Every attempt to

suppress him proved unavailing. He stubbornly
contested every inch of ground. He stood up and
battled unfalteringly for his principles against all
threats, all intimidations, all allurements. And yet
he steered clear of all the breakers and shoals in
such a dangerous course. His tact and disposition
alike kept him always within the proprieties of debate. The enemies who hated him watched in vain
for some word, some purpose disloyal to the Union
which they affected to champion, but were foiled by
the absence of all vindictive feeling or speech, and
by a marvellous moderation and self-restraint in
the face of provocation. Ignored, socially tabooed,
insulted, he showed no resentment. Assailed ran-
corously on all sides, he replied with good-natured
vehemence, but a never-failing courtesy. Occasionally, however, he carried the war into Africa, and
transfixed the slave power with the keen arrows of
satire and invective. He gave the giant wrong no
rest and no quarter. He charged its defenders
in front and flank and rear, and, returning again
and again to the combat, while his assaults were
redoubled, he at length secured a comparative immunity from personal attack. Thus his position
lifted him into a grand and superb isolation; and
now that we stand on the vantage ground which
he won for us, we are able in some degree to enter
into that high companionship, and into the elevation
of spirit that sustained him in his self-appointed
role of austere political solitude. As has been said
of General Gordon " we know to-day that he alone
was awake in a world of dreamers."

Thus for two years one great heroic figure was

prominently before the eyes of America. Solitary
and alone, he represented in the senate the dawn-
ing hope of freedom. But may we not be sure
that he already heard behind him, in imagination,
the on-coming hosts' of the new era, closing their
ranks and advancing to the last onset against slavery, which should sweep away the embattled pha-
lanxes of oppression? Did he not have something
of the fine instinct of that Scottish girl, who, laying
her ear to the ground, exclaimed, with streaming
eyes and transfigured face, "Dinna ye hear the slo-
gan? It's the Campbells a comin'!" So, again, on
a larger battlefield than Lucknow, where greater
issues hung in the balance, "the Campbells were
a-comin'," and it was given to this inspired prophet
of anti-slavery to cheer up the beleaguered garrison of freedom, to make one more struggle and hold
out for the victory. The Campbells came—Chase
and Seward and Sumner were their vanguard—a
glorious reënforcement, and from that moment the
forces of liberty were to grow and grow, till the
exasperated enemy should compass its own destruction by raising its hand against that very Union
whose sacredness had been for seventy years invoked in its defence.

One can but wish for a more elaborate treatment
than is here permitted of Mr. Hale's senatorial labors, and to reproduce some of the many thrilling
appeals and noble sentiments which broke from his
lips in the great discussions of his first term. But
the student of the history of that exciting period,
and the lover of eloquence, will be repaid by the
perusal of those great debates, and will rise from

them with an enhanced appreciation of the splendid powers, no less than the grand earnestness and
the priceless services to liberty, of John P. Hale.

At the expiration of his first term his opponents
were in control of New Hampshire, and chose his
successor. Mr. Hale then proceeded to carry out
a long cherished design to practise his profession
in the city of New York, but was recalled in 1855
to fill the senatorial vacancy occasioned by the
death of Mr. Atherton. He served out that term,
and was then reëlected for a full term commencing
in 1859. During these ten years of senatorial service his course was as straight as gravity. He
stood undismayed and with unshaken constancy
amid the surges of a fierce contention, and nothing
deflected him for one moment from that line of
conduct which he had marked out as the path of
conscience and duty. In the long struggles of
that momentous period Mr. Hale was found in the
forefront of every debate where liberty was drawn
in peril. His speeches on the various phases of
the Kansas controversy, the Oregon question, the
Dred Scott decision, on the constitutional status of
slavery, on the province of the supreme court in
the settlement of questions of law and political
policy, on the homestead bill, on the nefarious
attempt to seize Cuba—all questions antedating
the war, are among the historical headlands of the
epoch; and he was ever the same bold and fearless
advocate of that policy which was at an early day
to take control of the destinies of the United
States.

Meantime, although Mr. Hale had gained a hear-

ing for freedom in the United States senate, and
the subject of slavery was now open for discussion
everywhere, yet it is beyond denial that the institution had made a distinct advance in its aggressions upon the North, so far as public measures
and its apparent hold upon public opinion were
concerned. The decade from 1850 to 1860 was
the aggressive decade of slavery. Up to that time
a geographical barrier had stood against its advance beyond certain definite limits. But that was
broken down by their success in securing the passage of the fugitive slave law by the aid of Northern votes, and in enforcing it in the streets of
Boston, where the master *did* " with his slaves sit
down at the foot of Bunker Hill monument," as
Mr. Toombs had insolently boasted to Mr. Hale,
although in defiance of the ominous ground-swell
of liberty that shook the walls of Faneuil Hall,—
by their victory in overthrowing the Missouri compromise, by the border-ruffian outrages in Kansas
whereby a soil predestined to freedom was drenched
with the blood of freemen, and by the Dred Scott
decision. At the opening of that decade the Democratic party had already fallen into the deepest
degradation and servility to slavery. The rabble
of the cities, poisoned with race antipathies and
the vanity and pride of power, had been played
upon by the pliant demagogues of the North till
they exhibited a sort of rabies at the mention of
the subject of slavery. The Whig party, whose
public utterances had been till this time full of
sounding phrases protesting its fidelity to liberty,
was rapidly and surely passing under the yoke.

Cotton and trade, greed and conservatism, had done their work, had honeycombed that great organization, and left it only a thin and superficial veneering of anti-slavery sentiment. So determined was the North to stand by all the legal pretensions of slavery, that all hope of its removal in the Southern states, which idealists and ultra abolitionists were dreaming of, was now foreclosed. The only problem left was to prevent its extension. It could not be hoped to recede—how far should it advance? Indeed, the friends of freedom had confined their labors to the exclusion of slavery from the territories, not venturing to assert their power over it even in the District of Columbia, where the clanking of the bondman's chains was to be heard till the nation should be shaken by the throes of the Civil War. The Free-Soilers never claimed any right to legislate against slavery in the Southern states. Within those limits it was safe; was entrenched behind the constitution, and might have remained undisturbed to this day, had they abided by that line. But the South was judicially blind, and made every advance a pretence for a new aggression, until every congress was the theatre of a conflict on the subject ever growing more and more intense.

Look at a partial catalogue of its excesses in this decade. In 1850 by the compromise measures congress renounced all authority over the internal slave trade, exempted California, New Mexico, and Utah from all restriction as to slavery, and enacted the fugitive slave law, throwing to the North the poor sop of abolishing the slave trade

in the District of Columbia. The Missouri compromise was overthrown in 1854, and the territory
north of 36 deg. 30 min., supposed to have been
shielded from the possibility of contamination,
thrown open to slavery. The climax of outrage
upon the North was reached in the Dred Scott decision, whereby the highest judicial tribunal of the
land delivered a judgment which overturned the
law of the world that slavery was a merely local
and municipal institution, and announced the doctrine that the constitution protected the slave-holder
in his "property" wherever he might go. By this
decision, making slavery national and freedom
sectional, slavery became the public law of the republic; and its unparalleled infamy justifies Mr.
Hale's indignation when he said in 1864, "In my
humble judgment if there was one single, palpable,
obvious, duty that we owed to ourselves, owed to
the country, owed to honesty, owed to God, when
we came into power, it was to drive a plowshare
from turret to foundation stone of the supreme
court of the United States."

Slavery felt itself secure only so long as it could
push itself into new fields; and therefore not only
was the door to every territory thrown open, but
a raid was organized upon Cuba, and a piratical
jingoism held out a most tempting lure, even to
cool Northern statesmen, who could but warm to
the idea of a universal sway over the world's destinies. Sixty years before, the founders of the
constitution were ashamed of slavery, and tried to
hide it away under obscure phrases from history
and the public opinion of the world. Now, minis-

ters of the gospel unblushingly defended it. The presence of slavery had of course subjugated the Southern churches—and the North had largely followed suit under the stimulus of the commercial greed that occupied the pews. Mrs. Stowe's satire upon the clergy was warranted by the "South-side Views" so plentifully served up to us, and by the overworking of the texts in which Canaan was cursed, and Onesimus sent back by Paul to his master Philemon. Even Dr. Channing's society deserted him in the later years of his life on account of his anti-slavery views.

During this awful time, while the republic was writhing under its Nessus's shirt of slavery, goading and irritating it at every step of its painful progress, cowards and time-servers were lapping themselves in the comfortable assurance that slavery, being wrong, was a doomed institution—and in the conservative belief or the dastardly pretence that change was to come about solely by supernatural means, by slow spiritual influences proceeding from personal religion. And so we saw everywhere around us that spirit of concession, the lack of moral firmness, the recreancy to principle, the abject submission to Southern usurpations, which invited constant aggression. During this period freedom was indeed under a ban at Washington. Adulation of the slave oligarchy was the fashion. To be a Free-Soiler was to be excluded from the common courtesies and privileges of the capital. All cabinet positions, all public offices, all committees in the senate and house were held by pro-slavery men. An infamous code of morality, both

national and international, prevailed. Mr. Buchanan boldly proclaimed in the Ostend manifesto that
if Spain should refuse to sell Cuba to the United
States, "then by every law, human and divine, we
should be justified in wresting it from Spain, if we
have the power." In the raids upon Cuba and Central America, the ill-concealed designs against
Mexico,—then disorganized, disintegrating, and
liable at any moment to fall into our hands under
one pretence or another,—and the scarcely veiled
purpose to establish a great continental slave
empire,—in all these the perfidy and rapacity of
the system, and its thirst for rapine and subjuga-
tion were fully displayed; and in these acts how
vividly we now see, as if on a canvas painted by
lightning, all the black features of the moral mon-
ster, which, in the war that followed, displayed the
wild and frenzied ferocity, the desperate abandon
of cruelty, which was seen in the reign of terror
of the French regicides.

Never in our history, however, were all appearances so deceptive as in this terrible decade
when slavery was holding high carnival in the
great republic, when it dominated society, and had
seized upon every attribute of power in the government. There are those here who knew Washington between 1850 and 1860. The star of slavery
was at its zenith, and as it began to descend to its
setting, it lit up the western horizon with unwont-
ed brilliancy. One saw its characteristic pride, its
patrician charm of manners, its stately elegance of
forms and ceremonies. But these were only a
meretricious gilt of hospitality and courtesy,

shrouding the darkest designs that ever lurked in
the heart of a dominant class. As the Count de
Ségur said of France in the day of her approach-
ing doom, "the old social edifice was undermined,
although there _ was no slightest sign of its ap-
proaching fall."

There lay latent there the revolution, to be precipitated by its own madness indeed, but a revolution surcharged with the dormant energies of liberty,—revolution, which the Duc de Broglie calls
"that delicate and dreadful right which slumbers
at the feet of all human institutions, as their sad
and final safeguard." The slave oligarchy, like a
man smitten with mortal disease but thinking himself in perfect health, was never fuller of arrogance,
of fire, of the pride that goeth before a fall. Washington was full of such characters as only appear
in a society on the brink of perishing,—its Masons
and Slidells, its Davises and Footes, its Soules and
Brookses, and Wigfalls. But let us thank God
for the irrepressible instincts of every institution at
war with the social order. Slavery was a Philistine that could not keep the peace. , Conscious
that it could only live by extending itself, it was
ever aiming at new conquests. It overreached itself. Encroachment after encroachment, outrage
upon outrage followed, till at length, under the
faithful resistance of a few men, of whom John P.
Hale was the pioneer, the question of slavery became flagrant and omnipresent. It met men at
every turn in debate, in some form or other it mingled in every discussion of fact or principle, and
finally became the sole issue to be tried on the

battle-field of American politics. The delicate silence, the bated breath with which "the peculiar institution" had been regarded, gave way to the open discussions of congress, of the pulpit awakened to its high office, of the press, and of the hustings all over the land. Its supposed sacredness and immunity from criticism were things of the past. No longer was this gangrened sore, this leprous stain, shielded from public gaze by the denial of the right of petition, of liberty of debate, or by a profound unconsciousness, or indifference, or the trembling fears of those who profited by a political or commercial alliance with slave-holders —that mercantile class which Burke described as "snuffing with delight the cadaverous scent of lucre."

Nor was the time without other hopeful signs. The wheat was getting sifted from the chaff. The Whig party became defunct in 1852, and the Democratic party, under its heavy load, was tottering to its fall. The Conscience Whigs were being differentiated from the Cotton Whigs, and Seward, Adams, and Palfrey, Sumner and Wilson, Allen and Dana, appeared, while Chase and Banks, Wilmot and Grow, Rantoul and Boutwell, answered back from the Democratic ranks, and took their places in the line that was being formed against slavery. And so, as the end of this decade approached, over which slavery was to plunge into a yawning abyss, the clouds that had been gathering on the horizon began to overspread and blacken the political sky. The air was overcharged with electricity. The day of retribution

5

was at hand, and we stood in the vestibule of the
rebellion. But when the sky darkened and the
storm came on, such had been the charity, the for-
bearance, and the love for his whole country of
the first anti-slavery senator, that he could with a
perfect conscience say with the parliamentary General Waller, " The great God who is the searcher
of my heart knows with what reluctance I go upon
this service, and with what perfect hatred I look
upon a war without an enemy." He had stood,
proclaiming the solemn warnings of history, for
thirteen years in the United States senate. By
masterly argument, again and again had he dem-
onstrated the departure of the country from the
principles of the constitution and of the men who
made it, and in burning eloquence shown that slavery was a barbarism and an anachronism. In vain
were his appeals; but he, at least, had stood

" Among innumerable false unmoved,
Unshaken, unseduced, unterrified,
His loyalty he kept, his love, his zeal ;
Nor number, nor example with him wrought
To swerve from truth, or change his constant mind
Though single. From amidst them forth he passed
Long way through hostile scorn, which he sustained
Superior, nor of violence feared aught ;
And with retorted scorn his back he turned
On those proud towers to swift destruction doomed."

I would not willingly offend even the shred of
what was once conceived to be a party sentiment,
by any word of indictment of American slavery,
much less of the men, some of them honest and
honored, who tried to save it in its fall. But if I

rightly apprehend the present conditions of public opinion, the horror of it and the hostility to its extension and aggrandizement which guided the political course of Mr. Hale, are now become the sovereign and universal principle of men and nations. We have cast slavery aside into the outer limbo of things we would fain forget. We have flung it into the dark dungeon of loathsome things; the foul heap of discarded relics of barbarism and cruelty; the stakes, the racks, and thumbscrews; the Towers and Bastiles of the bloody past of humanity, and there are none to-day so poor as to do it reverence.

Political liberty is a development, and in reading history we mark the various stages of its evolution. The controversy of one generation becomes the settled doctrine of another, and the stone rejected of the builders becomes the head of the corner. I protest that I thresh over the old straw of controversy only because it is impossible to realize the stress of Mr. Hale's heroic warfare, and the significance of this memorial, without trying to understand, as the present generation can only faintly do, the nature of that institution which it was the business of his life to destroy. Ah! dear friends, how many fearless young men, then in the flower of their strength, are now sleeping beneath the sods of the battle-field! How many maimed and wounded! How many families still in mourning! How many mothers, wives, lovers, in tears that will not cease to flow! How many homes desolated never to be rebuilt! What a sad conflict between two sections of one great people! And what

a price did the country pay for the peace it could
have had for the asking by listening to the voice
of warning and of conscience uttered for the first
time in the senate by JOHN P. HALE!

During the war Mr. Hale stood unflinchingly by
all those principles with which his name and fame
were associated, and about which the battle raged
for four long years. He bore a conspicuous part
in all the debates of the senate during the great
struggle,—in vindication of the principles and conduct of New England and New Hampshire, in
denunciation of the fugitive slave law and efforts
for its repeal, in defence of himself as counsel in
the fugitive slave cases in Boston, and in December, 1860, he made an eloquent appeal for the
Union, which he loved with a devotion far deeper
and warmer than that of those who had invoked
its sacred authority in behalf of slavery for
thirty years. As the contest progressed, and the
black flag of slavery went down upon one after another of the bulwarks that had been erected for its
defence in those sad years of its Quixotic blind-
ness, he had the satisfaction of helping to wipe out
the black code of the District of Columbia, and
abolishing slavery itself there in 1862. Towards
the close of his senatorial career he took a joyous
part in the last mighty blows against the slave
system, which blotted it out forever from our
escutcheon—the emancipation of the slaves of rebels, the repeal of the fugitive slave law, and, finally, the adoption of the 13th amendment to the constitution, which prohibited slavery forever thereafter by the organic law of the land, amid the

jubilations and fervent thanksgivings to God of the slave, and of every lover of liberty the world over.

We are apt perhaps to lose sight of Mr. Hale's great merits as a general legislator in the splendor of his services for liberty. But a study of the public records will disclose his vigorous attention to the general business which came before congress, in which he labored with a tireless activity, an omnipresent vigilance, and an inflexible persistency of purpose on every great question of administration as well as innumerable matters of detail. He participated in nearly every debate that took place in the senate, and was ever found the consistent advocate of a well defined administrative policy. He was an old-fashioned economist. Like Fox, he might perhaps have boasted his ignorance of the " dismal science " of political economy; but of the economies and frugalities of the truly republican house-keeping of our early days he was an unswerving devotee. He was invariably for reform, for the reduction of expenses, the correction of abuses, the curtailment of extravagance, the lopping-off of superfluities and sinecures, of perquisites and excesses in official emoluments. He was against constructive charges and salaries, jobbery, and profligacy of every kind. He was against aggression and against spoliation; he was the implacable foe of monopolies, of unjust claims, of extortionate raids upon the treasury, of frauds and corruptions of every kind. He was the friend and champion of the laborer on the public works, the private soldier, and the common sailor. The *Congressional Globe* for twenty years is replete with his untiring efforts

for the masses against the classes. He returned
daily to the ever recurring struggle on these lines
with a vigilance, a courage, a boldness, and fertility
of resource admirable in the last degree, and in un-
changing fidelity to these principles was never
found wanting for sixteen years in the United
States senate. Not the least of his titles to praise
is found in the brave stand he took against the
corruptions of the navy department, and his fearless
independence in exposing maladministration in his
own party, at a time when by so doing he subjected
himself to the criticism of some friends, though he
supported every step of Mr. Lincoln's administration
in putting down the Rebellion. His activity as a
senator diffused itself over all the questions of his
day:—the homestead law, internal improvements,
foreign and domestic commerce, the tariff, the army
and navy, education, the judiciary, patents, banks,
appropriations, the civil lists, pensions, public lands,
sub-treasury, printing, the census, the franking
privilege,—these all felt his touch. The topics he
discussed embraced the whole range of our foreign
and domestic relations, our trade and administration
in every variety of form. His views were always
clear, practical, comprehensive. His logic, wit,
and humor, his tenacious memory of legislative precedents, his old-fashioned frugalities, his apt illustrations, his parliamentary skill, which justified
General Cass in calling him " a most adroit parliamentary tactician,"—all these were brought into full
requisition in the general business of the sessions.
He was not a man of one idea. He was an idealist
indeed, but no idealist ever had a more stalwart

common sense, or less of the visionary about him; and, though he was not always right, no public man ever took so decided a part on a great variety of subjects and made fewer mistakes. Despite his anomalous position as a senator, he accomplished many things in general legislation which entitle him to public gratitude, and was frustrated by the extravagant tendencies of his time in others which would have been still more beneficial to the country, had it been wise enough to follow his lead. He was the most typical Jeffersonian Democrat of his time. Mr. Hale was not much of a party man. He was not one of those,—

"Who, born for the universe, narrowed his mind
And to party gave up what was meant for mankind."

He was

"For a patriot too cool, for a drudge disobedient,
And too proud of the right to pursue the expedient."

Political ties always sat loosely upon him. He used party connections to subserve purposes, and when he thought his duty lay in another direction he burst asunder the partisan leading-strings without compunction. He was neither a party leader nor a party follower. He was not pliant; his mind was simple and direct; he wanted policy, and was no more tolerant of wrong in his own party than in any other. Hated by the enemies of liberty on the one hand, he was assailed by zealots of freedom on the other for his conciliatory temper, his freedom from political acerbity, and his refusal to endorse projects of disunion or any other extravagances.

A sound discretion, and even a wise conservatism governed him. He loved to travel *super antiquas vias*, and the precedents of Anglo-Saxon freedom were the guiding stars of his political life. Unwilling to go all length, and too independent to submit to dictation, he represented no party, no group even,—he was no exponent of others; he was a type of himself. Without affecting airs of independence, he was the most truly independent man in America. Those of us who loved him and would stand guard over his fame, are not pained to hear, as we sometimes do, that he knew how to behave in the minority much better than in the majority.

Mr. Hale's general political views were broad and well defined and coördinated, and gave unity of purpose to his political life. His creed at bottom was embodied by Burke in his definition of the principles of true politics as " those of morality enlarged," or, in other words, that in politics " nothing is right that is not *right*, just that is not *just*." He had none of that revolutionary spirit which rudely breaks with all the traditions of the past. If there were contradictions in our institutions, he was content to tolerate them till the general conscience and intelligence should be awakened to such anomalies, and make those institutions homogeneous. He was no innovator or fanatic. He stood by the fabric of the constitution, and the Union he reverenced with a fervor not surpassed even by Webster himself. In this respect, in his willingness, often expressed, even to abide by and carry out fairly, honestly, and in good faith what were termed the compromises of the constitution, he differed *toto coelo* from Garrison,

Phillips, and others of the abolitionists. Let us do justice to those from whom Mr. Hale differed in this respect. Such was their view of the pro-slavery clauses of the constitution that they indignantly spurned them, and fled for refuge to that "higher law" which Mr. Webster in derision said "soared an eagle's flight above the tops of the Alleghanies." They dealt only with the abstract question of right, claimed a discharge of conscience from all complicity with slavery, and demanded an immediate and unconditional manumission.

It is still an unsettled question whether the efforts of statesmen like Mr. Hale were hampered by impracticable theories of doctrinaires who renounced political action as implying allegiance to a constitution which recognized and sanctioned slavery. Many regarded these scruples as puerile, and a hindrance to the progress of the cause within constitutional and legal lines. There was, however, but little danger to liberty from those who refused to obey the fugitive slave law. History is full of proofs that a disobedience of the statutes of men may imply a higher and deeper reverence for the laws of God. Admitting the danger of leaving citizens, each for himself, to judge of the law and their obligation to obey it, yet those who are so tremblingly afraid of stranding the ship of state on this Scylla, should remember the awful dangers of the Charybdis on the other side, and that no government worthy to live was ever wrecked by those who obeyed the behests of conscience.

We are not here to-day to cast a doubt upon those men who formed the American Anti-Slavery soci-

ety, which Mr. Frederick Douglass calls "the most
efficient generator of anti-slavery sentiment in the
country," and whose heroism has given them an
enduring place in history. But, whether it be to
his credit or discredit, it is certainly true that Mr.
Hale had little or no sympathy with extremists;
made no assaults upon church or state; stood aloof
from all schemes of disunion, and discountenanced
every thought of disloyalty. This was not his line
of thinking or of action; he proposed to act politically *in* the Union, by circumscribing slavery and
pressing it to death by a cordon of free states. Mr.
Hale took the ground that the constitution was
essentially an anti-slavery document. The Buffalo
convention of 1848 admitted that slavery in the
states was protected by the constitution, and the
Free-Soil party had no intention to attack it where
it existed under the sanction of law. The Free-Soil
convention at Pittsburg in 1852 neither raised nor
lowered the standard; and its lineal successor, the
Republican party, did not at all grapple with emancipation in the states,—not even in the District of
Columbia,—its whole policy looked simply to its
circumscription. But the event shows how urgent
and how indispensable was the need of a Free-Soil
party. That want Mr. Hale and others supplied,
no doubt holding, in solution at least, the faith
which Mr. Lincoln afterwards so tersely formulated
in the memorable words: "If a house be divided
against itself it cannot stand. I believe this government cannot permanently endure half slave and
half free." They had found the heel of Achilles;
they had divined the weakness of slavery, and the

essential conditions of its progress and immunity.
Then only the great problem approached its solution when "no more slavery extension" became the
watchword of a distinct political organization, drawing to itself more and more the humane sympathies
and the generous ardor of the world.

I have said that Mr. Hale stood by the constitution. So thoroughly loyal, indeed, was he to that
instrument, that amid the thunder and agony of
the Rebellion, he parted company with his political
friends on the confiscation bill, which he opposed
because it was not in accordance with the constitution. Said he: "I want constitutional liberty left
to us when the war is over. Constitutional liberty
is the great boon for which we are striving, and we
must see to it that, in our zeal to put down the Rebellion, we do not trample on that; and, that when
the war is over, and our streamers float in the air,
in that breeze also may still float the old flag, and
over this regenerated country may still sway a
sacred and unviolated constitution, in the faithful
maintenance of which in the hour of our peril and
our trial we have not faltered."

But he was no priest of the constitution. His
divinations were at another shrine, even that of
liberty. We have had such a priest. He stands
there, [pointing to Mr. Webster's statue] overlooking us with his awful solemnity, his brow of Jove,
and all the majesty of his god-like presence to-day.

But with Mr. Hale the constitution was no fetich.
He loved it for what it was, and as he understood
it. He could reverence it only for what it meant;
and, if shown that it meant the perpetual domina-

tion of one race or class and the bondage of another,
he would have looked upon it as the *Liberator*
proclaimed it in 1844, as "a covenant with death,
and an agreement with hell." If it meant that, John
P. Hale could no more have obeyed and endured it
than could Pym or Hampden the star chamber, the
collection of ship money, or the exactions of arbitrary prerogative, or Samuel Adams the enforce-
ment of the stamp act, Luther the sale of indul-
gences, or Mirabeau the perpetual dominance of the
Bourbons. His was a higher and nobler interpretation of the organic law of our fathers; and, claim-
ing shelter under its broad ægis, he stood forth in
defiance of the delusion of his time to assert the
essential brotherhood of man, and his right to the
liberties formulated in the Declaration of Independence. In other days, a century or two before, this
intrepid stand in the face of power would have subjected him to a glorious imprisonment or to the
block. But truth was already emancipated from
the grosser forms of tyranny. Who can doubt
that even if the old means of extirpating freedom of
thought had still existed, John P. Hale would have
taken his life in his hand, and proclaimed unfalteringly the faith that was in him, like John Pym,
who, in the crisis of English liberty, cried that he
"would much rather suffer for speaking the truth
than that the truth should suffer for want of his
speaking."

Those are rightly accounted great who blaze out
new pathways for the race. Says Froude, "Those
whom the world agrees to call great, are those who
have done or produced something of permanent

value to humanity." Do any of our American statesmen better answer this requirement? In a great crisis his was the initiative. He grappled single-handed and alone with the greatest problem and the highest duty of his time. Slavery lay like a night-mare upon the republic, weakening, poisoning, degrading it, arresting its development, stifling its liberty. And who, we may well ask, aroused it from its torpor, from the body of its death? Who so emphatically as he gave the word for the resurrection of the true national spirit? It was he, indeed, who impressed the heart and brain of his generation, who pronounced the right word at the right moment, and uttered it in accents that burned it into the imaginations and feelings of millions. When other men called great were dallying and compromising, and striking hands with an evil with which there should have been no truce and no terms, he assailed it in its stronghold, and carried its strongest outwork. He first attuned the voice of a state to the rhythm of liberty, and from his lips first sounded the high note of freedom in the United States senate. And in that great body, where mediocrity cannot for any length of time seize the palm of excellence, where no pretence can escape detection or weakness pass for strength, he maintained his position triumphantly against all assailants for sixteen years. He mingled in all the contentions of the most tempestuous period of our history; one after another he broke lances with all the great actors on the national scene and was never discomfited. He has left in the public records a body of utterances worthy of the study of after-times, made un-

der every variety of circumstances, under insult and
contumely, under taunt and provocation; yet no-
where, on his part, is there any recrimination, any
appeal to passion, to unworthy prejudice, to unman-
ly feeling; but everywhere and throughout a genuine sincerity, a noble philanthropy, a sublime enthusiasm for humanity, and an unswerving faith in its
ultimate destiny.　You shall find in all his impassioned appeals not one doubt cast upon the reality of
human progress, or the eventual triumph of those
principles which had asserted their control of his
political life.

From a recent review of this whole series of
speeches and votes in and out of the national arena,
I am impressed with the conviction that there is no
more honorable and conspicuous record in American
public life.　It is a record marked by a high ethical
tone, by conscientious conviction, by fidelity to truth,
by a standard of public duty modelled upon the
best traditions of Anglo-Saxon freedom, and by
maxims drawn from a wide study and clear reading
of the history of human liberty and progress in all
ages.　I go further.　He was the man for his time
and mission.　He had a message for his generation,
and, as much as any man ever was in political an-
nals, was providentially sent and equipped for the
great tournament in which he played his part.　And
I add the further belief that no intelligent, reflective,
and unprejudiced mind, conversant personally with
the events of that time, can rise from the study of
his public efforts and the story of his life, without the
conviction that no other public man in America was
equal to what he did,—that none had the peculiar

qualities in so high a degree to fill the great post to which he was called as the first anti-slavery senator.

Engaged in the work of statesmanship, which largely diverted him from the studies and practice of his profession, Mr. Hale was still a most distinguished lawyer. He occasionally appeared in the courts of New Hampshire throughout his career; and there was no time after 1840 when his services were not sought in cases of the highest importance, and when he was not esteemed to hold a place as an advocate in the front rank of the profession. In 1851 he was engaged as senior counsel, with such lawyers as Dana and Ellis, in the argument of the slave rescue cases in Boston. In his recent book Mr. Dana speaks of him as having argued the case of Lewis Hayden nobly and with passages of great eloquence. It was in this case, in the defence of the rescuers of Shadrach, that occurred that wonderful burst of eloquence:

"John Debree claims that he owns Shadrach. Owns what? Owns a man! Suppose, gentlemen, John Debree should claim an exclusive right to the sunshine, the moon, or the stars! Would you sanction the claim by your verdict? And yet, gentlemen, the stars shall fall from heaven, the moon shall grow old and decay, the sun shall fail to give its light, the heavens shall be rolled together as a scroll, but the soul of the despised and hunted Shadrach shall live on with the life of God himself! I wonder if John Debree will claim that he owns him then!"

In one of his letters Mr. Sumner said that Mr. Hale had said many things better than any of the rest had been able to say them, and referred to this speech particularly as one that had been reported to him as worthy of Curran or Erskine.

Still later he was leading counsel in the defence of Theodore Parker, who stood indicted for obstructing thê fugitive slave law process in the case of Anthony Burns. The trial came on in April, 1855, and attracted universal interest. The indictment was quashed by the court upon the argument of Mr. Hale's associates, and so odious was the prosecution that the representatives of the government were only too eager to hide themselves from public scorn by entering a *nolle prosequi* in all other cases.

But Mr. Parker afterward published a noble defence, which he dedicated "to John Parker Hale and Charles Mayo Ellis, Magnanimous Lawyers, for their labors in a noble profession," and speaks of them as "generous advocates of humanity, equalling the glories of Holt and Erskine, of Mackintosh and Romilly, in their eloquent and fearless defence of truth, right, and love."

In this "Defence" Mr. Parker also refers to Mr. Hale as "the noble advocate of justice and defender of humanity," and as "renewing the virtuous glories of his illustrious namesake, Sir Matthew Hale,"—and, again, of "the masterly eloquence which broke out from the great human heart of my friend, Mr. Hale, and rolled like the Mississippi in its width, its depth, its beauty, and its continuous and unconquerable strength."

To those who knew Mr. Parker, himself an orator, philanthropist, and one of the grandest characters of his age, such tributes to Mr. Hale's genius

are an offering of no small value, and not without
a deep significance.

The earliest efforts of Mr. Hale announced him
an orator of unusual force and power. Even before
practice had given him a national reputation, he
was endowed highly with the gift of persuasion and
a captivating charm of manner. He possessed in
an uncommon degree many of the external advan-
tages of a popular speaker,—an imposing person,
a countenance of extraordinary manly beauty and
nobleness, a well modulated and resonant voice, a
prompt command of words, a perfect command of
his temper. His language was fluent; his manner,
easy, confident, unaffected; his delivery, impressive;
his self-possession, perfect. His eloquence was
spontaneous, rather than the fruit of patient labor.
It yielded to no rules of art; it was clogged and en-
cumbered by no useless impedimenta of learning or
philosophy; but it came like a fountain bursting
from the earth; it was the warm effluence of a sympathetic heart, a fervid soul, a deep humanity, finding utterance on the tongue, inspiring every accent,
and informing every feature.

In the presentation of a cause to a popular audience he was wellnigh irresistible. His clear and
copious diction, his imperturbable good nature, his
fairness and generosity, his apt stories, his manifest
sincerity and disinterestedness cleared all obstacles
from his path and gave him a power before great
popular assemblies in which he had but few rivals.
Traditions still live of his triumphs as a popular
orator before great masses of people under the open
sky, which alone seemed to give room for the full

6

play of his faculties, as it did to O'Connell, as well as those forensic contests where verdicts were charmed away from the leaders of the bar by the sorceries of his eloquent tongue.

He was the most natural of orators. His best efforts were short, impassioned improvisations, apparently without study or forethought. He did not torment invention for words. He affected no theatrical attitudes, and was little solicitous for either diction or manner, but was content to grasp strongly, and present forcibly and earnestly, the substance of his argument, and always with a definite purpose in view.

His speeches underwent no revision. He never cared to give them the last polish of his pen. They were dashed off with a careless and negligent ease, and were extemporary in the sense of having never been composed in set phrase, or laboriously fashioned into periods. He scattered these gems of speech like a king whose resources were as capricious as inexhaustible. He was thoughtless of their fate, and now they have to be laboriously hunted out from the columns of the *Congressional Globe*, or of fugitive newspapers. But they will repay the search. If they are not marked by literary finish, they are instinct with fervent earnestness and impetuosity. Everything was done by him without apparent exertion. His efforts seemed to flow from an exuberant fountain, and bore no marks of labor or tension of mind.

Without any pretensions to profound learning, Mr. Hale had those immediate intellectual resources that give readiness in debate. To the very marked combination of parliamentary talents already named, he added a prodigious memory, holding his facts firmly in hand, and drawn up ready for instant mobilization. It would be a mistake to suppose him lacking in mental power; he was never wanting, when occasion demanded, to the logical support of his positions. Although he was never very patient of laborious research, nor inclined to

"Scorn delights and live laborious days,"

yet his constitutional learning, especially in all those departments requisite to the defence of personal liberty, was ample; but what is better, the learning he had was aglow with vitality, always at the command of a tenacious memory, and warmed by his eager blood and intellectual vehemence. If any doubt his great ability, even when stripped of the glamour of oratory, let him carefully read his speeches on the constitutional status of slavery, the Dred Scott decision, the supreme court, and the repeal of the fugitive slave law. He sustained himself with ease in the senate in competition with the giants of debate, and did all with such good nature as to provoke no hatred or personal violence. He went in and out unarmed amid the murderous assassins of slavery, holding aloft the banner of freedom, "still full high advanced," till Chase and Sumner, Seward and Wade came and interlocked their shields with his, and the invincible phalanx of Liberty was never broken.

I am at a loss to compare John P. Hale with any

other orator. In the spontaneous and easy play of
extraordinary natural powers he was not unlike
Fox, the great English orator and statesman. Nor
was he unlike that greatest debater that ever lived
in the vehement rush and torrent of his declama-
tion; and hearing him sometimes, when he rose
almost above competition in bursts of indescribable
power, we seemed to realize Porson's meaning
when he said,—"Mr. Pitt conceives his sentences
before he utters them. Mr. Fox throws himself into
the middle of his and leaves it to God Almighty
to get him out again." So it was with Mr. Hale.
He soared to the most-adventurous heights of eloquence; but, when you were trembling for his fall,
he always came safely to earth again from the most
daring flight, and alighted on his feet, the orator of
common sense, of shrewd mother-wit, of homely
and commonplace illustration, as well as the emo-
tional, kindling orator of enthusiasm, his heart on
fire, and his lips touched with a divine flame.

But, after all, there is in every great orator a
something indescribable, a something peculiar to
himself, which differentiates him from all others.
Mr. Hale imitated no one, and was himself inimitable, though he had studied the great orators of
antiquity, and had kindled his torch at the altar
of Chatham and Burke, Fox and Erskine. His
spontaneous style, not formed by extensive reading,
and able to dispense with a critical literary knowledge, was not like that of Burke or Gladstone, but
resembled more the splendid oratory of John Bright,
an instrument capable of sounding all the depths of
passionate emotion, of touching the deepest chords

of human feeling, and of lighting up the sentiments of freedom with unspeakable pathos and splendor.

But if, as all its true devotees do, we ascribe to eloquence a heavenly origin, and give it that office which so wins our hearts, if we say that no man is ever a true orator without being the spokesman of some great cause, that God touches no man's lips with that celestial fire without intending thereby to burn up some giant wrong, how nobly does Mr. Hale fill the character! Who, in this sense, among all our historic Americans, was truer to his divine appointment than he?

Mr. Hale was unique in this, that much of his effectiveness as a speaker was due to his overflowing wit and humor. His quick perceptions, genial temperament, and acute sense of the ludicrous made him a natural humorist. In repartee he was incomparable, and his apt and homely illustrative stories enlivened the United States senate for sixteen years. An ardent admirer of Mr. Hale most happily says,—"The jests which lightened his public addresses were not, however, without their disadvantages. They sometimes gave an impression of levity which formed no part of his character. As there is in art an ignoble and a noble grotesque, and in poetry a sardonic and a just yet not malignant satire, so there is in oratory a humor which degrades and another which attracts to uplift the hearer. This was the humor of our orator; like the wit of Lincoln, it was always serious in its application, an instrument for noble appeal or impressive illustration, a foil for grave discourse or earnest invocation."

It would be pleasant to recall some of those sayings of his which so illustrated his good nature and broad catholicity of spirit, while they drove home some truth as no other means could. For instance, he compared statesmen who were afraid to oppose the Mexican War to the Western man who said he "got caught by opposing the last war, and he did n't mean to get caught again; he intended now to go for war, pestilence, and famine."

Speaking of President Polk's back-down in the Oregon treaty, he said, "The president exhibited a Christian meekness in the full scriptural degree; but he did n't inherit the *blessing* of the meek—he did n't get the land."

He said,—"As to whether the Missouri compromise had, as claimed, given peace to the country, he did n't know how that might be, but he knew that it gave peace to the politicians who voted for it. It sent them down to their political graves, where they have rested in peace ever since. It settled them, if it did n't settle the country."

Senator Westcott called him to order, but informed him that he meant nothing personal. Mr. Hale said, "I am exceedingly obliged to the senator for his explanation. The question of order has been raised but twice since I have had the honor of a seat in the senate, and each time it was raised by the senator from Florida upon the senator from New Hampshire. That satisfies me that there is nothing personal about the matter."

Mr. Clemens, in a violent speech, asserted that

the Union was already dissolved. Mr. Hale good-humoredly replied that it would be very comforting to many timid people to find that the dissolution of the Union had taken place and they did n't know it. " Once in my life," said he, " in the capacity of a justice of the peace, I was called on to officiate in uniting a couple in the bonds of matrimony. I asked the man if he would take the woman to be his wedded wife. He replied, ' To be sure; I came here to do that very thing.' I then put the question to the woman,—whether she would have the man for her husband, and, when she answered in the affirmative, I told them that they were husband and wife. She looked up with apparent astonishment, and inquired, ' Is that all?' ' Yes,' said I, ' that is all.' ' Well,' said she, ' it is n't such a mighty affair as I expected it to be, after all.' If this Union is already dissolved, it has produced less commotion in the act than I expected."

In reply to Mr. Calhoun's complaint that the Missouri compromise had disturbed the equilibrium of the country, he said that it had disturbed no equilibrium but that of the Northern representatives who voted for it; that it threw them entirely off their equilibrium, which they had n't regained yet, and never would.

General Cass, in December, 1856, hoped God, in His mercy, would interpose in this slavery question before it was too late. Mr. Hale interjected, " He came pretty near it in the last election," whereupon General Cass was greatly shocked at the levity of so referring to the Supreme Being.

Garrett Davis introduced a resolution that " No

negro, or person whose mother or grandmother was
a negro, should be a citizen of the United States."
Mr. Hale said, if in order, he would like to amend
by putting in his great-grandmother also. Of
course Mr. Davis was highly indignant at such
buffoonery on a sacred subject.

The records are full of such pleasantries as
these, which had a cutting edge of truth, but
contributed not a little to allay the irritation and
soften the asperities of debate. But Mr. Hale
never indulged in personalities. He was a gentleman from the heart out. There was no bitterness in his jests. He threw no poisoned arrows.
He struck without hatred or malignity, and his
blows left no ranklings and no immedicable wounds
behind.

> " His wit in the combat, as gentle as bright,
> Ne'er carried a heart stain away on its blade."

Consequently, when he retired from the senate, he
had as warm friends south as north of the line, and
among them was one who had learned to hold him
in a high personal esteem, the learned and eloquent
Henry S. Foote, of Mississippi.

But little remains to be added to the record of
Mr. Hale's public life. In March, 1865, he was appointed, by Mr. Lincoln, minister to Spain. This
was a service suited neither to his temper, his taste,
nor his capacity. He had cultivated no drawing-
room arts; he knew nothing of the assiduities of
ante-chambers; he was incapable of intrigue or
flattery; he was as free from servility as from
arrogance; he had not merely a speculative lik-

ing for, but he was a practical exemplification of, democratic principles. The oratorical temperament, which he possessed in so high a degree, harmonizes not with the cunning or even the unsleeping and tireless discretion of diplomacy, whose methods were foreign to the guileless frankness of that noble nature.

In the heat of the hour, when Mr. Hale broke from allegiance to his party, and espoused the cause of the slave, he was the object of ungenerous imputations and even rancorous abuse. But party feelings seldom survive the generation they control, and the little hatred that had been mingled with these accusations had been outlived. But,

> "Be thou as chaste as ice, and pure as snow,
> Thou shalt not escape calumny."

In his new position abroad, his ignorance of the language of the country, and the amiability of his character, involved him temporarily in the toils of an adventurer. He had what some one has called "a want of clear sharp-sightedness as to others," and was exposed constantly to the arts of schemers and self-seekers. The mistakes of his life, which subjected him to unfounded aspersions, all arose out of his ingenuous and generous trust in others who were unworthy of his confidence. He became for a brief moment the victim of the calumnies of an unworthy subordinate, who had compromised him, as he had attempted the ruin of his predecessors in the same way,—one of those Jesuitical reptiles that infest the diplomatic purlieus of Europe, and wriggle in and out of the ante-chambers of royalty.

For a time, as Burke said, "the hunt of obloquy pursued him with full cry." The shafts fell really harmless at his feet, but the injustice done him temporarily by some venomous newspapers embittered his own last days, and clouds the memory of his friends.

I disdain to enter upon the vindication of the integrity of a man who was careless, generous, of simple habits, who neglected his own interests, was indifferent to money, and who with abundant opportunities to enrich himself, had he been base enough to use them, neither made nor spent, nor left a fortune,—the man who was content to tread a thorny road; whose life was one of plain living and high thinking for himself and his family; whose face, one of the noblest I have ever looked upon, was itself a refutation of calumny; whose heart was as open as the day; and whose integrity, shining like a star in the dark night of our country's trial, was "the immediate jewel of his soul."

But I rest his exoneration not there—not upon such moral certainties as triumphantly satisfy his friends: but his defence, if defence were needed, may be rested upon legal proofs that will convince any court or jury of his absolute innocence. I have examined the whole case, and others of more authority than I, and I aver that the evidence against John P. Hale of any conscious dereliction of duty, anywhere, or at any time, is lighter and more unsubstantial than the summer zephyrs that float among these tree-tops over our heads; and that, according to all the canons of evidence in such inquiries, in that blameless life, public and private, there was nothing in the face of which he might not hold his head erect before the bar of God!

His career was drawing to a close. He remained abroad five years, the last being spent with his family in travel on the continent, and in the vain hope of recruiting his shattered energies. His health, never good since the National Hotel sickness in 1857, of which he was a victim, had now become seriously impaired, and he came home in 1870 with a broken constitution. He was welcomed on his return with formal receptions by his neighbors at home and by the legislature, of which a conqueror might have been proud. He lingered with us for three years afterwards, but with strength gone past recovery, and one ill following another made his last days painful ones. As one of his eulogists grandly said, " He was like a war-frigate which lies in port in peaceful times, its mighty armament and its scarred bulwarks only suggestive of stormy days when its ports were up, and its great guns dealt havoc upon the foe."

At length, on the 19th of November, 1873, the worn-out gladiator of freedom " fell on sleep," and joined the great company of his co-workers in all ages—the servant of God passed to " where beyond these voices there is peace."

I have spoken mainly of the public life of Mr. Hale. But to his friends there seems something lacking in the sketch of a man so much loved and admired, without analyzing his character a little more closely, and drawing a portrait of somewhat warmer coloring, as befits his noble nature. Sometimes a nearer view of public men diminishes the

admiration and reverence we feel at a distance.
Not so with Mr. Hale. His dearest place was in
the hearts of his friends. Those who knew him in
his domestic privacy, or where the statesman was
sunk in the social intercourse of friendship, most
unreservedly loved him, and speak in fullest admiration of his virtues and his genius. His morals
were pure without austerity, and his life exem-
plary by its observance of every detail of duty,
whether it involved the active exertion of influence for good, or abstinence from everything evil
and not of good report. He was exempt from
social and personal vices. In 1852 he said in the
senate, "I have not tasted a drop of spirits for
twenty years," and he never afterwards departed
from that principle.

In religion he was a liberal. He was averse to
external ceremonies, and his love of personal independence made him jealous of every kind of eccle-
siasticism. His religion was a matter between himself and his God. As Burnet said of Sydney, " He
was a Christian, but a Christian in his own way."
Let none doubt for a moment, however, the essential reverence of spirit of this free-thinking soul. If
ever man had the Unseen but Indwelling Presence,
if ever man was governed by those great invisible
moral sanctions that we are wont to call the laws of
God, if ever man had the faith which connected
him with powers above him, but which he felt working through him, it was John P. Hale. Sweetness,
and light, and love, were indeed his creed and his
practice. He went forth to the duties of life " as
ever in his great Taskmaster's eye,"—

" He went in the strength of dependence
To tread where his Master trod,
To gather and knit together
The family of God ;
With a conscience freed from burdens,
And a heart set free from care,
To minister to every one,
Always and everywhere."

Endowed with noble gifts, Mr. Hale had what
was greater, an aggressively noble character. He
never cringed to power. He never sold himself for
a vulgar or temporary applause. He was never
false to his convictions; and he always *had* convictions. He did n't crawl and sneak through the
world—he never lapped himself in that comfortable
indifference to the moral law which is the devil's
easy chair in which he hypnotizes the human conscience for a base acquiescence in wrong and
iniquity.

His principles were rooted in his character,
and had an organic growth,—and he lived as if he
had taken holy orders in their service. He was
essentially a reformer, and had the courage to
stand alone, which is the first requisite of leadership in a great cause. The blandishments of power
had no attractions, and no terrors for him. He
might have sat at the right hand of the throne, but
disdainfully rejected the temptation, and held fast
to his principles and his integrity. He perilled his
political career to resist the further advance of
slavery. His courage was superb; he never
quailed before the face of man. He would have
been equal to martyrdom, and would have gone to
the block saying with Sydney, " Grant that I may

die glorifying Thee that at the last Thou hast permitted me to be singled out as a witness of Thy
truth, and, even by the confession of my opposers,
for that old cause in which I was from my youth
engaged."

To him the service of liberty was neither prosaic
nor perfunctory. It gave zest to his life. A strain
of high devotion runs like a nerve of fire through
all his public efforts. He had deeply pondered
upon Sir Henry Vane, Algernon Sydney, Pym and
Hampden, Bradshaw and Henry Martin, and the
great judges who had stood for the liberty of the
subject against kingly prerogative; and no man
was more deeply imbued with free principles—not
the loose and unsandalled vagaries of the French
Revolution, not the wild passions of communism
or *sans cullottism*, but the fundamental maxims
which had found expression in Magna Charta, the
petition of right, the execution of Charles Stuart,
the deposition of James, and the bringing over of
the Prince of Orange, the writ of habeas corpus,
and the trial by jury, the great landmarks and
muniments of English liberty, guarded and regu-
lated by law. These were his ideals, the stern
leaders of political thought and action in the days
of the Commonwealth and of antiquity.

He surpassed all the men I have known in love
of Nature in all her varying scenes and moods.
His soul was open to every divine influence. He
was the friend and familiar of birds and flowers,
mountains, trees, and streams. Never was there a
more enraptured lover of natural scenery; none
who from the hilltops more lovingly drank in the

clouds and the landscapes, the song of the stream-
let, the kindling star, the full glory of the noontide
sun. What a reverent observer and worshipper of
nature he was! His eye kindled and his bosom
swelled as he beheld the pillars of the forest, the
arches of the sky, the gray cliffs and shadowy
cones of the mountains, and listened to the roll of
the unresting and unsearchable sea. Every spot
about his home was familiar ground to him, and
his friends, one by one, under his lead, had to climb
to the top of every mountain and hill within its
horizon. He loved New Hampshire, and every
hour he was absent from it in the public service his
heart was still "in the highlands." His familiarity
with natural, local, and family history gave an
uncommon charm to his easy conversational powers, and made his companionship delightful.

How can those who lived on terms of intimacy
with Mr. Hale convey to others any adequate impression of the attractive human traits that shone
out in his daily intercourse? Those who knew him
in his prime, and before· sickness had rusted the
Damascus blade, dearly remember his easy acces-
sibility, his hospitable mind, his apposite stories,
and his rich fund of wit and anecdote. He was not
simply loftily interested in mankind, but his heart
went out to every man, woman, and child in the
concrete. How well his townsmen knew this, and
how heartily they loved and admired him for his
·unaffected interest in their personal welfare, their
health, their children, their business, their pleasures,
their plans, and hopes, and fears. In early life his
mind had been promoted, but his heart never rose

above the ranks. He had a warm sympathy with
humanity in all its phases—

> " No fetter but galled his wrist,
> No wrong that was not his own."

He was a faithful friend, and assisted those he
thought deserving, or who managed to ingratiate
themselves into his confidence or his sympathies.
Not infrequently he was the dupe of the designing,
but such mistakes never chilled his philanthropy,
nor closed his purse or his heart against the appeal
of distress, whether genuine or counterfeit.

At home, as at Washington, he was the un-
bought counsel and defender of innocence, and no
calculating spirit was ever the mainspring of his
action. Milton had a forecast of his character
when he wrote of Bradshaw,—" If the cause of
the oppressed was to be defended, if the favor or
the violence of the great was to be withstood, it
was impossible in that case to find an advocate
more intrepid or more eloquent, whom no threats,
no terrors, and no rewards could seduce from the
plain path of rectitude."

Such a man could gain but little of this world's
possessions. He cared less for what he should
leave than for what he should take with him; and
he held unaltered to the end this noble conception
of the use and duty of life, its consecration to
helpful service for mankind, and for the poor, and
weak, and oppressed, above all others.

In the still more intimate privacies of his own
home he was the endeared centre of a family circle
to which he was devotedly attached throughout a

stormy and exciting political career, whose stead-
fast love supported, and whose tenderness soothed
him to the last. In him the sentiment of home and
family was strong and beautiful. How pleasant he
was in that circle! All admitted there felt the
sweetness of his temper, the easy gentleness of his
manners, and the charm of his society. He told a
story with a grace snatched beyond the reach of
art, and never one anywhere that would sully the
tongue or the imagination of a maiden. Who that
knew him there can ever forget his perfect natural-
ness, his frankness and sociability, his womanly
tenderness, his delicacy of speech and conduct, his
playfulness, his absent-mindedness, his childlike
simplicities and whimsical oddities, coming out in
his liking for old ways and old places, and for this
or that bizarre article of food, or drink, or raiment?
Beautifully does the admirer already quoted say,
" These are some of the traits which made us often
forget in the man and the friend even that public
record of patriotism and services for humanity
which places him first in the proud roll of the distinguished sons of New Hampshire."

Such was the man who so bore his great commission in his look, and so nobly filled the ideal of
a knight-errant of liberty that Marshall P. Wilder
most appropriately introduced him at the New
Hampshire festival in Boston in 1854 as " the
very embodiment and incarnation of human freedom,"—the man in whom the microscopic power
of slander could find no spot of impurity, and who,
God be thanked for such a statesman in the nineteenth century,—

7

"Through all the tract of years
Wore the white flower of a blameless life."

There is no exaggeration in this description of
Mr. Hale. I know it is the voice of affection, and
of a domestic grief not yet entirely assuaged.—

" Ars utinam mores animumque effingere potest,
Pulchrior in terris nulla tabella foret."

It would be unworthy the occasion, the theme,
the audience, to sketch the character of Mr. Hale
in any other spirit or colors than those of truth and
discrimination; and yet, in delineating him, something must be yielded to the partiality of private
friendship. God forbid that we should ever fail
to dwell on the virtues of our friends, and throw
the mantle of charity over their frailties. Although
none could know him truly without a warm admiration for his noble character, I know how valueless is
mere indiscriminate panegyric. No character is
flawless, and like other men Mr. Hale had his limi-
tations. Nor do I mean to deny the proper meed
of praise to the other great actors of his time,—

" Vixere fortes ante Agamemnona
Multi."

Most of these are now passed away, and there is
no reason for restraint, but we may speak with
posthumous frankness. Undeniably the historians
of the period have not ascribed to John P. Hale
that part in the things accomplished in his time to
which he is really entitled. "On Kansas soil,"
says ex-Gov. Robinson in his recent book, " was
gained the first decisive victory against the Slave

Power of this nation." Not so. More than ten years before the Kansas conflict, the first strong outwork of slavery was carried in no insignificant battle, and John P. Hale, its leader, became the first anti-slavery senator,—not by accident, but by the might of his own invincible arm and indomitable heart, in a hand-to-hand struggle in a state that up to that gallant fight had been the very citadel of Southern slavery. Yet this fact has been persistently ignored, his name and fame have been treated with a studied neglect, and those who came in at a later day, some even at the eleventh hour, have succeeded in reaping the glory and the reward of the movement to which he gave the first impulse and impetus. I distinctly insist that he it was who won the first political success, and who has a valid historical claim to pioneership in the great uprising which terminated slavery. Doubtless its doom was written in the book of fate; doubtless others would have come and set the ball in motion; but certainly he *did* come, and it is as unreasonable and unjust to deny to him the credit as to deny to Luther that of the Reformation, or to Sam Adams and Franklin that of the Revolution.

The state, among whose lofty mountains freedom loves to rear her mighty children, rescues him to-day from this neglect, and demands for him the recognition of history to which he is entitled, as one who early announced and clearly formulated the principles upon which the victory was finally won. If elsewhere this injustice to a great man is continued, it shall not be without protest in New Hampshire, for we announce by a solemn public act that

John P. Hale should stand on the pages of history foremost among the champions of liberty, to whom America owes her emancipation from slavery. Neither John P. Hale nor New Hampshire shall be shut out hereafter from primacy in the successful effort to rescue the republic from the talons of this bird of prey.

And so, with all the ceremony and demonstration of respect which the presence of the official dignitaries of the state, its culture and its worth, can lend to so imposing an occasion—in the presence also of official representatives of the two cities where Mr. Hale drew his first and his latest breath, where he was born and where he had his home till the last, and in whose soil he was finally laid to his rest, whose representatives are most appropriately here and commissioned to assist in this tribute of honor and of justice to their most eminent son and most beloved citizen; in this presence and in that of some of the veteran coadjutors of Mr. Hale who, at his call, buckled on their armor and fought with him the good fight for liberty; in the honored presence, also, of some of the renowned champions of freedom in the United States, who are here to give the dignity and authority of their names to this observance—and in the presence of that still unbroken family circle that loved him most on earth,—we place this great man here in the goodly company of Webster and Stark, all men of distinct types, differing as the stars differ in glory,—the expounder of the constitution, the tribune of liberty, and the hero of the Revolution on the field of battle. We set up their effigies here in token of our reverence for their separate and conjoined excellencies of character and achievement.

"It is at the tombs of great men that succeeding generations kindle the lamp of patriotism." A nation is known by its ideals, and by such memorials as this we realize the continuity as well as the immortality of human excellence in the universe. The stream of humanity is unbroken. There is no real line between the living and the dead.

> "There is
> One great society alone on earth,
> The noble Living and the noble Dead."

The waves of human life come and go; they dash against and sweep away what have been esteemed the proudest monuments of human exertion, but they will not wash away the works that have been built up and founded upon the rock of human love and fidelity. These will remain when not one stone shall be left upon another of the temples erected to merely intellectual or military renown; and in the expansion of the moral horizon that comes to successive generations, posterity shall preserve and cherish the memory of every true man who has connected his name with some step in the progress of the race.

When the passions and prejudices aroused by the contest against slavery shall have died away; when we are farther away from the calculating spirit of family, and local, and coterie partiality and selfishness; when the final story of the anti-slavery struggle in this country shall be written, among

those statesmen who wrought for liberty and progress in our age of civic and military valor, and
who transmuted their own God-given energies into
current coin for the daily use of humanity, no name
will shine with a purer lustre on the historic page
than that of John P. Hale.

I have supposed, and do suppose, that this is the
true glory and significance of his career,—that this
is the emphasis of his life and the distinctive mark
he made upon his time,—that in which the affections of posterity are to hold and garner him.
Without this, without his connection with the great
movement for emancipation which has glorified our
age, and given it an unapproachable exaltation in
history, he would be entitled to public honor as a
good case lawyer, an eloquent advocate, a useful
senator, a faithful son, husband, father, and a
genial and fascinating friend,—but would scarcely
be entitled to be commemorated by a statue in the
public grounds of his state. We give such only
to great services to humanity, and that political
freedom to which all nations, though by indirect
and devious routes, are tending: and such we give
also, only when time has tested, and set its seal
upon such services. Such men as John P. Hale
have an imperishable hold upon the moral world,—

> " Ever their phantoms arise before us,
>   Our loftier brothers, but one in blood ;
> At bed and table they lord it o'er us,
>   With looks of beauty, and words of good."

He bore the test of service for liberty at a time
when such service was the supreme, the inexorable

demand of the hour. Tried in a time which tested men's integrity, men's courage, men's souls,—tried as by fire and not found wanting,—he fitly stands here as the New Hampshire representative *par excellence* of the spirit of the new era under whose scorching breath slavery withered up like a scroll, and went down to its dishonored grave. The moral courage and intrepidity of this man in the face of that public opinion whereby the slave power dominated and subjected the North was the forerunner, the flaming evangel, of the great uprising of conscience in the North, and the harbinger of that martial courage which, twenty years later, on a thousand fields of battle, was to eclipse the highest achievements of chivalry and cast romance into the shade. This spirit, this dauntless courage and persistency, this contempt of martyrdom, ranks him with the apostles of liberty in other ages who occupy the highest niches in the Pantheon of freedom.

Mr. Depew says we shall never have a Westminster Abbey. Perhaps we never shall, but America will write on her heart the names of her champions of liberty, her heroes in council, and on the field of battle.

You shall find in what I say of this great man no political hints or innuendoes. What Mr. Hale did was for men of all parties. His work contributed to the common stock of freedom which all parties enjoy and recognize. I am not so unworthy of the duty laid on me this day as to throw into the scale of our current politics even the weight of an obscure suggestion in any phrase I may employ to

express my admiration for Mr. Hale's truth to
human freedom; and it is the highest tribute our
generation can pay to his genius and labors, to
admit that in political philosophy, in recognition of
universal human brotherhood, all of us begin where
he left off, and stand on the vantage ground he
gained for us.

Mr. Hale's political life was cast in a grand and
fruitful time. He lived when his country was in
full health, and occupied with momentous subjects.
Others there have been whose spirits, like his, were
in tune with the Divine purpose; whose eyes, like
his, from the mountain-top of vision caught the earliest light of a new day, but who have only seen it
from Pisgah, and died without entering the Promised Land. But he was permitted to see the complete triumph of his principles, and the political
institutions and policy of his country recast in con-
formity to those ideas to which he had devoted his
life. He lived to see the definite extinction of slavery and all its claims, the release of every function
in the government from its control. He heard the
roar of hostile guns settling the great debate in
which he had borne so early and so prominent a
part, with voices from which there is no appeal.
He lived to hear, also, the salvos of victory, and to
see the land covered over with the glory of freedom
as with a garment.

One other security safely locks up his fame.
" At what a price," says Landor, " would many a
man purchase the silence of futurity." Surely they
who need that silence most are those who have
once had their faces set heavenward, and then have

faltered and fallen out by the way. The energy and exaltation of soul, the uncalculating enthusiasm of humanity, which characterize revolutions, are followed by the lowering of tone, the political infidelity, the eclipse of faith, which succeed them all as the night the day. The English revolution which dethroned the Stuarts was followed by the Restoration; the French revolution, by Bonapartism and a new régime of the Bourbons; Cromwell and Hampden, by a more ignoble Charles and the successors of Strafford and Laud; Mirabeau, by Talleyrand; the overthrow of prerogative by the longing for thrones and the government of favorites.

So we, also, after the gigantic struggle to overthrow the oppression of centuries, live in a time of reaction. Wealth has usurped leadership; plutocracy, and not ideas, rules the hour; and the dry bones of the old tyranny crushed thirty years ago begin to live. The appeal to be true to the ideas of 1860 falls upon deaf ears. We would rather sacrifice to the Moloch of money; we rise no higher in our contentions than some wrangle about the tariff, or the puerility and rascality of determining how little of intrinsic value we can palm off upon the world for a dollar.

It was Mr. Hale's high fortune to escape these dangers. We have to thank God that there were no recantations and no apostacies in his later days ; that he was never overtaken by the lassitude of the moral reformer, or "the scepticism that treads upon the heels of revolutions;" nor yielded to the apostacy that clouds the fame and the memory of some who had done valiant service for the right.

And when the great struggle which had opened and closed in his lifetime was finished,—when the scene upon which he had moved was closed, how truly could he say that he had not only fought the good fight, but had kept the faith.

It is altogether fitting, therefore, that the statue of such a man, so long conspicuous in the public service, holding the highest commission the state had to bestow for nearly twenty years, and ever upholding her honor and increasing her fame before the world, should be erected here, to stand, as we trust, for centuries to come, in the grounds of its capitol. We thus pay homage to his memory in the state of his birth and his abode; in no provincial spirit, however, but as citizens of a larger country, in whose service he exerted all the powers of his heart and brain.

This monumental bronze, its pedestal inscribed with some of the great outlines of his life story, impressively conveys to the younger generations, living in the light and stirring with the sublime thoughts of a liberty kindled to a higher glow by his torch, the assurance that from his lips the accents of freedom always found unfettered utterance, that we have numbered his labors and entered into his spirit, and that more than they can pay of gratitude and veneration is due to him for the achievements and lessons of his high, and pure, and strenuous public life.

Aye more, we proclaim by this act to-day that he deserves to stand in the Valhalla of the National Capitol with the sages and worthies whose effigies adorn its rotunda, because he was the hero of the noblest of our revolutions,—that peaceful revolution of ideas in which the seed was sown of the harvest which the soldier's sword came afterwards to reap;—which overturned a giant wrong, emancipated the master no less than the slave, and gave to America that place in the political order to which she was destined by Providence; a revolution unlike those that have re-organized societies elsewhere, in that in ours there were no crimes and no excesses, no Anarchy, no Terror, no Military Despotism, no profanations and no blasphemies, no massacres and no proscriptions, to leave their ineffaceable stains upon the face of human progress.

I am quite aware that there is an appointed space prescribed by usage and good taste, by the courtesy of the press and the patience of an audience, within which what is said here should be circumscribed. That limit was long since passed, and I have lingered unduly over the great man and great actions I have sought to commemorate. With all who knew him in life, I long to-day

". . . For the touch of a vanished hand,
And the sound of a voice that is still."—

and, recalling all that he was to friends and country, "my heart, penetrated with the remembrance of the man, grows liquid as I speak, and I could pour it out like water."

And then, remembering the Protean forms in which the foes of liberty are ever appearing, and the dangers that beset the republic for which he lived and wrought, the vain sorrow and the selfish

aspiration are alike forgotten, and thinking sadly
of some crisis of Freedom in future years, and he
not here to lead on her legions in the bewildering
fight, I bid hail and farewell to this noble son of
New Hampshire, one of the chiefest jewels in her
crown of glory.

> "Ah! if in coming times
> Some giant evil arise,
> And Honor falter and pale,
> His were a name to conjure with!
> God send his like again!"

When Col. Hall had nearly concluded his oration,
he was seized with faintness, and was unable to
finish. His attack was not serious, however, and
after he was able to leave the platform the exercises
were continued.

THE CHAIRMAN:—It often happens that contemporaries and posterity are so tardy in the appreciation of true greatness, that, when the work of building a memorial is done, much, if not all, that was
personal to the honored dead, has perished from the
memories of men, or exists only as a half-forgotten
tradition. I count it the supreme felicity of this occasion, that our senior senator, in his admiration of
the character of his distinguished predecessor, reinforced by family affection, has made possible the
dedication of this statue while so many illustrious
co-laborers with Mr. Hale are among the living;
and that we have to-day, as the guests of the state,
so good a representation of the survivors of the
great anti-slavery conflict.

If memory serves me aright, forty-three years ago one of the northern districts of Pennsylvania —sometimes called the Wilmot Proviso district— elected a young man to congress, who took his seat, the next year, the youngest member of that body. July 4, 1861, he was elected speaker. Of the manner in which he bore himself in that high office, during those troublesome times, we are not ignorant.

It gives me pleasure to introduce, at this time, the young man of 1850, and the speaker of the national house of representatives in the 37th congress, Hon. Galusha A. Grow, of Pennsylvania.

HON. GALUSHA A. GROW'S ADDRESS.

MR. CHAIRMAN AND FELLOW-CITIZENS:—At midnight closing the twenty-sixth day of May, 1854, the boom of cannon in front of the nation's Capitol, echoes along the hills that skirt the Potomac. It is the jubilation of the champion of American slavery on the final vote in congress repealing the Missouri Compromise, the signature to the act by a subservient president being already assured. For the first time a restriction on the extension of the institutions of human bondage on the American continent is blotted from the statute book. With the contemplated repeal of one other restriction— that prohibiting the foreign slave trade—and the final triumph of the devotees of slavery in the legislation of the country would have been complete.

Ten years scarcely pass away, and these same Potomac hills re-echo the boom of cannon welcoming the return of the battle-scarred veterans from the victorious fields of a Union saved and a country free. The irrepressible conflict of a hundred years is ended forever.

It seems to be a part of the plans of Divine Providence that every marked advance in civilization must begin in mighty convulsions. The moral law was first proclaimed in the thunders of Sinai, and the earthly mission of the Saviour of mankind closed amidst the rending of mountains and the throes of the earthquake. The Goddess of Liberty herself was born in the shock of battle, and amid its carnage has carved out some of her grandest victories, while over its crimson fields the race marches on to higher and nobler destinies. As the lightnings of heaven rend and destroy only to purify and reinvigorate, so Freedom's cannon furrows the fields of decaying empires, and seeds them anew with human gore; from which springs a more vigorous race, to cherish the hopes and guard the rights of mankind.

In the world's decisive battles, in the onward progress of the race to a higher and better civilization, great battalions have always marched in the rear of great ideas. The armies that saved the American Union marched under the inspiration, the same as if it had been inscribed upon their banners, of that sentiment of New Hampshire's greatest son, though adopted and crowned with lasting honors by Massachusetts, " Liberty and Union, now and forever, one and inseparable."

At a time when Slavery in the plenitude of its power, dominated every branch of the government, dictated its legislation, and made and unmade pres-

idents, and, by social and business ostracism, coupled
not unfrequently with mob violence, was attempting
to stifle free speech and trammel the freedom of the
press, like John the Baptist crying in the wilderness John P. Hale stood solitary and alone in the
senate of the United States, protesting against such
domination, and, prophet-like, predicting that a better day would surely come, if its dawn was not already near at hand. But, unlike the prophets of
old, he was not without honor in his own country
and in the times in which he lived. He led the forlorn hope of a revived love of liberty, which in the
swift-coming future was to scale the ragged battlements of human bondage and bid the oppressed go
free. Thenceforth the inalienable rights of the
Declaration of Independence are to be the heritage
of every child born on American soil.

His private worth, his public acts, and his great
services to his country, as a faithful tribune of the
people in the forum of public opinion, have been
portrayed so faithfully and well by the speakers who
have preceded me, that no other words of praise or
eulogy are needed. The real hero is found not
alone in the night watch and forlorn hope of the
battlefield, but in the martyrdom of a perverse, op-
pressive public opinion, and the execution of unjust
and tyrannical laws.

Men who breathe their spirit into the institutions
of their country or stamp their characters upon the
pillars of the age can never die. Statues and monuments are erected to their memory. It is well.
For they stand through the ages, visible objects in-
citing the living to emulate the virtues and the pat-

riotic devotion of the dead. But the actors in the early or later scenes of that mighty national drama which closed at Appomattox, whether in council or on the field, need no monuments of stone or tablets of brass to perpetuate their memory. They live in the affections of the present, and will live in the gratitude of the future. Their tombs are the hearts of the great and the good; their monuments, the granite hills of a nation rejoicing in freedom.

THE CHAIRMAN:—We have the feeling, and in a few instances it has been expressed, that Massachusetts has received from New Hampshire large additions to its business and professional resources, and that we have the right to call upon our sister commonwealth whenever assistance is needed. We should not feel that this statue was properly dedicated without a word from Massachusetts. Governor Boutwell, whose life-work has been a part of the history of that state for fifty years, has kindly consented to make a brief address, and I gladly announce him as the next speaker.

HON. GEORGE S. BOUTWELL'S ADDRESS.

MR. CHAIRMAN AND LADIES AND GENTLEMEN:— If I do not err in my estimate of Mr. Hale's services, his claim to the honors that are tendered to his name and memory by his native state and by a public larger than any state, rests upon a most substantial foundation. In early manhood he was allied to a political party that was dominant in the state,—a party that for more than a generation had dictated the policy of the country. Without delay, by his talents, learning, and wisdom in affairs, he was advanced to places of honor, power, and trust, and made secure in a public confidence not limited by party lines.

When, in his thirty-eighth year, Mr. Hale took his seat in the house of representatives, there were but few, if any, whose abilities were superior, and none, probably, whose prospects in a party-political aspect were better. Before his first term in congress was ended he was forced to accept or to confront the policy of slavery-extension, to which the Democratic party was then about to commit itself. Without hesitation, and with the fervid energy of youth, he denounced the project as a crime, in which not one redeeming feature could be found. Thenceforward, and especially during the next two years, he gave himself without reserve to a contest in New Hampshire which attracted the attention and involved the fortunes of the whole country,—a contest, which, as we approach the close of a half century, is not yet ended. Disregarding these incitements to ambition, putting aside these prospects of promotion, Mr. Hale made war upon the slave-power,—not yet upon slavery itself,—in one of the strongholds of that power, as New Hampshire then was.

The generation to which Mr. Hale belonged did not comprehend that power, and to this generation all adequate statements must appear to be exaggerations. In 1839, Mr. Clay valued the slaves of the country at twelve hundred million dollars, and the auxiliary property in lands and debts whose value

8

rested upon slave labor could not have been less
than twelve hundred million more. Thus there
was concentrated in defence of the institution a sum
equal to a third or a quarter assuredly of the total
property of the country. This enormous invest-
ment was buttressed by the constitution, sustained
by a large public sentiment in which there lingered
the tradition only that slavery was a local institution. That tradition found but a feeble expression
in the press, in the bar, in the courts, in the col-
leges, in the churches, and finally in the political
parties into which the country was divided.

Fortunately for Mr. Hale the contest which he
carried on in 1845, '46, and '47 was in a state which
had no pecuniary interest in the institution of slavery-extension upon moral and political grounds,
and so dealing with it Mr. Hale achieved the first
of the long line of victories which have marked the
steps by which the foulest of tyrannies has been
destroyed, not in America only, but in Portugal,
Spain, and Brazil; and thus has humanity been
inspired with the hope that the time is not distant
when slavery shall disappear even from the savage
and semi-civilized races of men.

So much has been gained, and what has been
gained cannot be lost except in a general wreck of
human institutions; but the contest on which Mr.
Hale entered in 1845 is not ended. Indeed, a half
century is a brief period for the extirpation of
a crime and the influence of a crime that had
degraded millions of men into chattels; a crime
that had been embalmed in the constitution by the
patriot founders of the Republic; a crime that was

authorized and justified, or at least, tolerated by
the Scriptures, as was proclaimed by more than
half the teachers in the pulpits and believed by
more than half the occupants of the pews; a crime
that controlled a product that was essential to trade
at home and to commerce abroad; a crime that
thus had been raised to the dignity of a virtue in
the estimation of a vast majority of the people in
fifteen states of the Union.

It was against this formidable array of authority
and power that Mr. Hale and his associates made
war. An unequal contest in the beginning, to be
transformed into victory at the end; but the end is
not yet reached. The tone of the press, the voice
of the pulpit, the opinions of the people have been
changed, and all for justice and right. The constitution of the country has been remodeled, slavery
has disappeared, citizenship has been made national
and universal, and the equality of men in the states
has been guaranteed as the basis of the equality of
states in the Union.

To these results Mr. Hale contributed most
largely through a period of twenty years of eventful public service, and thus we justify his claim to
the honors that are tendered to his name and memory by the authorities and citizens of his native
state.

The four million of emancipated slaves have
increased to seven million citizens, a ninth part of
the population of the Republic, and of these, more
than two thirds are denied the rights of citizens in
the states where they reside. This is the remaining crime of slavery—our inheritance from that

institution—a crime that is justified in the old
slave states and tolerated and excused by influential men and bodies of men in all parts of the country.

If Mr. Hale and his associates are worthy of
monuments and statues, then it is the duty of this
generation to consummate the work which was by
them so well begun.

THE CHAIRMAN:—There is upon this platform a
distinguished citizen of the United States, who
made his first visit to New Hampshire half a century ago. He did not at that time receive the
welcome due to his manhood at the .hands of our
people generally. To-day he comes as the guest
of the state, which now makes full and glad atone-
ment for its earlier shortcomings. Mr. Douglass,
may we hear from you?

FREDERICK DOUGLASS'S ADDRESS.

MR. CHAIRMAN:—I have made no preparation
to address this audience, and had hoped that the
managers of this occasion would allow me to sit
here and only give color to the occasion. (Laughter.) I hardly ought to be here to-day on account
of my health. I am very feeble, and am suffering
from an attack which would excuse me almost for
my absence from this place; but I desired to be
here, and I may say that I never in all my life
desired more fervently to make a speech than on
this occasion, and never felt myself less able to do
so than now.

I want, however, to say that, in 1845, it was my pleasure and my privilege to look upon the manly form of John P. Hale, and thereafter to meet him often, and to hear his melodious voice and listen to the thrilling sentiments he was accustomed to utter in connection with the great cause of liberty. I travelled with him some in central New York, in company with him who was afterwards Chief-Justice Chase, and heard them both speak. I saw them in public and saw them in private, and one thing, which has not been mentioned in the elaborate, eloquent, and able discourse that we have heard, struck me in regard to John P. Hale. It was this: Wherever he stopped, and there were any little children around, little girls and boys, somehow or other they were irresistibly attracted to John P. Hale. (Applause.) They would lean on his knees, play about him; and I thought that was a good sign, a very striking evidence of the greatness of the man. It reminded me of the saying of the Saviour, " Suffer little children to come unto me, for of such is the kingdom of Heaven." And if you ever see a man in your travels anywhere in this world from whom children shrink, there is something wrong about that man. (Laughter.) I was going to say that if you see a man from whom the ladies shrink, there is something wrong about him. (Laughter.)

I wanted to be here because I am one of the vast multitude of emancipated ones whom John P. Hale devoted his heart and his transcendent abilities to liberate. I wanted to be here to represent those millions; to show you that one, at least, of those millions appreciates the greatness, the grandeur, and the devotion and the courage of John P. Hale. (Applause.)

We, in this day, can hardly understand the measure of the greatness of that man's courage, the greatness of the sacrifice he made, the greatness of his faith in the ultimate triumph of great principles. Why, he was preceded in Washington by John Quincy Adams, a man venerable for his learning in the laws, skilled in legislation, an acknowledged statesman; and yet against him came a torrent of abuse and persecution that well nigh drove him from the house of representatives. Happily for him, though not remarkable for his eloquence in his younger days, he became the " old man eloquent," and could defend himself. John Marshall, who brought in the resolution for his expulsion, remarked that Mr. Adams took longer to defend himself than it took God Almighty to make the world, for he spoke two weeks. Finally he overcame the opposition and was allowed to stand his ground; and when he came home to old Massachusetts, our poet was enabled to say to him,—

> Not from the bloody field,
> Borne on his battered shield,
> By foe o'ercome;
> But from a sterner fight
> In the defence of right,
> Clothed in a conqueror's might,
> We hail him home.
>
> Where slavery's minions cower
> Before their servile power,
> He bore their ban ;

And, like an aged oak
That braved the lightning's stroke,
When thunders round it broke,
Stood up a man.

Now, I say, we have no scales in which to weigh
the courage and the manliness of John P. Hale;
we have no means of measuring it—we of the
present generation, I mean,—but if you go back to
the time when the honest farmers of the state of
New Hampshire thought themselves justified in
yoking up ninety oxen to drag away a negro
school-house, you will see that John P. Hale had
something to meet in the state of New Hampshire
as well as in the state of South Carolina. (Applause.)

I remember the time that I came here, fifty years
ago. I was a slave, even here in New Hampshire.
Indeed, in all parts of the country I was a slave.
The country was a slave hunting-ground, all over
it. A slave could be started at Ticonderoga, and
chased down to Bunker Hill, and he might ascend
that granite shaft, with its capstone in the clouds,
and plead in the name of the blood that was spat-
tered at its base to be allowed liberty, and even
there he could be hunted, chained, and dragged
back to slavery. Not only the South, but the
North, was in a state to make it dangerous for any
man to take the side of the slave. There was no
valley so deep, no mountain so high, no glen so
secluded, no spot so sacred to liberty, in any part
of this broad land, whereon I could place my foot
and say, with safety, I am now secure from the
slave hunters.

In that day, too, the American eagle refused to give me shelter, and there was no room under the outspread wings of the eagle for the head of Frederick Douglass; but, besides, the American eagle laid bad eggs at that time. (Laughter.) It was hardly safe for us to open our mouths in the interest of liberty in those days; and the thing that pleases me to-day is the vast and wonderful change that has taken place. Yes, this audience is full compensation, full compensation for the slender audience that met me in the old town hall, with its side benches—I can see it now, but it is gone. This was not such a city then as it is now.

A VOICE.—What about suffrage down South?

MR. DOUGLASS.—I was going to say something about that. As I heard Governor Boutwell say on the floor of congress, when he was going on with a volley of eloquence, as he could then, some one interrupted him, and said, "How about this?" and he replied, Well, "I am coming to that." (Laughter.) I am coming to that.

I have often said that the want of congress now, or want of the senate, is another John P. Hale. (Applause.) We have a representative who has inherited his principles, and has the nerve to stand up on the floor of the senate and utter his convictions in regard to a free ballot and an honest count, and that is your senator, Hon. William E. Chandler. (Applause.) He is no coward. But, great as he is, he will admit that John P. Hale was a little taller man. (Laughter.)

Mr. Hale entered the senate under circumstances that would have taxed the courage of a Napoleon

—aye, more than that, for Napoleon did not have the moral courage to begin with John P. Hale. It was something for a man to come from New Hampshire and stand in the presence of Henry Clay, of John C. Calhoun, of Lewis Cass, and of Daniel Webster, their bright eyes opening upon him, and resenting his interposition—I say, it was something to stand up there in such presence and be a man, as was John P. Hale. (Applause.)

Mr. Clay tried to down him in his very suave and eloquent manner. It so happened that, during the compromise measures, Mr. Hale in several instances followed Mr. Clay, who made many speeches on that compromise measure. When Mr. Clay spoke, the senate chambers were usually full. Mr. Clay came in one morning, and after being followed by Mr. Hale, said, "It will be noticed by the senators that on almost every occasion when it is my privilege to address the senate of the United States, I am followed by the senator from New Hampshire. If that is to be taken as a desire on his part to measure arms with me in oratory, I concede the palm." Mr. Hale, sitting in his seat, said, "That accounts for the calumny." Mr. Clay sang out, "What calumny, sir?" in his imperious way. Mr. Hale says, "I answer no questions put to me in that tone." He was able to meet any occasion. His aptness of reply was wonderful, and his illustrations were striking.

I did not intend to speak even this long. I never make long speeches. This occasion requires a short speech, and I never made a short speech with which I was satisfied, and I never made a long one with which anybody else was satisfied. (Laughter.) This good man whom you have taken away [Col. Hall] has stolen much of my thunder that I thought I would use if I spoke at all. He has gone before me and has taken the bread of life out of my mouth.

I can only say to you, my friends, that I am greatly impressed with the vast and wonderful change that has taken place in the condition of my people. It seems to me that I am living in a new world; that I am seeing more than John saw in his apocalyptic vision, a new heaven and a new earth! What a transition from the past to the present! For we have heard of nations being born in a day; but this nation has certainly been turned upside down in a very short time.

Now in regard to the condition of things at the South, I am much exercised just now. I do not know what it is coming to. At this time there is a tide of lawlessness and violence sweeping over the South that is almost disheartening, and until we infuse a little more backbone into the Republican party, and that party will bring to the front the question of right, the question of justice, the question of the constitution, we shall see this tide of violence sweep on. How wonderful it is that these men, who a few years ago were on the battle field with arms in their hands and bullets in their pockets, and with broad blades and bloody hands seeking to dismember this country, that they can stand up now on the floor of the senate of the United States and tell the North, tell the world, that they mean to violate the constitution so far as

preventing the negro voting. They dare to tell us
so. Oh, if they should speak this in the presence
of that man there, he would skin them alive
(laughter and cries of " Good ") or drive them to
their homes. And it is coming, it is coming. I
think our convention at Minneapolis—I hope no
Democrat will take offence—our Republican convention there was a little more determined on this
question than heretofore. But I have to say in
regard to the Republican party that it is a great
mistake for that party to dwarf and belittle the
moral side of their character by presenting to us
on all occasions only the one theme, tariff, tariff,
tariff. These things we ought to have done, and
not left the other undone. I think that the nation
has a soul, or ought to have a soul, and I can say
to it, "What of it ? What if you gain the whole
world for your market and lose your own soul ?"
(Applause.)   The soul of a nation is its honor, and
you bound yourselves when you gave the negro
his liberty, when you gave him the right to vote,
you pledged yourselves that you would see to it
that that right would be protected. (Applause.)
What a humiliating spectacle do we present, if it
can be said that we can defend the liberty of the
American citizen in Chili, that you can defend
him in any foreign country, but you cannot defend
his liberty at home. I do not believe that to be
the case, but I believe that that is the truth to press
home upon the American people and upon the law-
makers of our time.

My friends, I have spoken longer than I intended. I did not expect to speak at all; and,

really, it is only because my style of going along in this matter is a little different from the written style which I should have' adopted if I had prepared myself, that it ought to be tolerated. After we have had so much fine and learned eloquence, so much transcendental eloquence, I thought that you could bear a few desultory remarks such as I have been trying to make. (Tremendous applause.)

THE CHAIRMAN:—Not only did Mr. Hale attach to himself all reasonable anti-slavery workers, but scholars and all men striving for the upbuilding of character in their fellows.

Among the younger of the clergy of his day, perhaps no one knew him better than Rev. Dr. Woodbury, formerly pastor of the Unitarian church in Concord, and now of Providence, R.I., whom I ask to speak of Mr. Hale as he knew him.

ADDRESS OF REV. AUGUSTUS WOODBURY, D. D.

It is an especial gratification to me that I am able to participate in the exercises of this day. My friendly relations with the generous donor of the statue, my cordial interest in all that pertains to the history of New Hampshire, and my personal admiration of the character and public service of Mr. Hale, all combine to make the occasion one of satisfaction and delight. The eloquent oration and addresses to which we have listened, in their words of appropriate and appreciative eulogy, have left but little for me to say, which can add to the dig-

nity of the theme or the method of its treatment.
It is only a simple contribution that I can make
to the united and general voice of well-merited
praise. Yet we have come together here to-day
not to praise but to commemorate, and the commemoration finds its best and highest function in
stimulating ourselves to noble living, as we turn our
thoughts to him who has won for himself a place
among the noble dead. To myself as to you, fellow-citizens, the name of John P. Hale has been
for half a century the synonym of private and public virtue, patriotic courage, unswerving devotion
to the principles of religious and political freedom,
and an unfaltering advocacy of the dearest rights
of man. Stark was the brave soldier, Webster the consummate orator, Hale the champion
of liberty for all. It is well that they should be
grouped here, their forms and features preserved in
enduring bronze, to teach the generations to come,
that fidelity of service to the Republic, in whatever
field it may be displayed, will ever be held in high,
affectionate, and permanent esteem. A sincere
feeling of gratitude for the labors of those who
have helped to shape " the fortune of the Republic "
mingles with the desire to do what we can in the
work of perpetuating the story of their deeds. But
it is ever to be remembered that it is not what we
may do or say that honors their memory   Rather
would we be assured that the opportunity which
is given to us of recalling their services, imparts an
honor to ourselves.

The word which I have to speak must necessarily
be one of reminiscence.   It was in my boyhood,

while a student at Exeter, that I first saw and heard John P. Hale. He was then in the flush of his ambition and hope. Deeply interested as I was, even at that early day, in the questions which were then agitating the public mind, I was one of the assembly that crowded the Town hall at Exeter to hear the discussion in which Mr. Hale was to take part. Of course I cannot remember the exact words which were spoken. I can only recall the impression which was made upon my youthful mind. Particularly was I struck by the sturdy independence, the outspoken boldness, which were characteristic of the orator, whose magnetic presence, good-humored wit, and resonant eloquence aroused the audience to an admiring enthusiasm. The aggressiveness of the slave power was still far from the point of actual resistance to the government, but the mutterings of the coming storm in the movement for the annexation of Texas had begun to be heard, and it was quite evident that Mr. Hale was not to be terrified or even alarmed by any threatening cloud that might appear upon the political horizon. How he met the tempest when it came, and how he bore himself in the strife of elements, is a matter of history, and has been well set forth in the addresses which have already been spoken. For myself, it is sufficient to say that the interest with which I listened to his fervid oratory grew into admiration, when, in after years, I watched his public career, rejoiced in his successes, and had the honor, for a brief period, of his personal acquaintance.

I speak of this incident to-day because it has

reference to a matter of great importance which any one who addresses a public assembly should bear in mind. Among his auditors there will certainly be a greater or less number of young hearers, who will catch the tone and spirit of the address, and who will be affected by them to a considerable degree. It is often the case, that an apparently casual word will determine the current of a young man's thought, and possibly turn the direction of his life. It may arouse his ambition to achieve a generous, brave, and honorable manhood, or it may lead him to sordid, mercenary, and unworthy courses. The young are very quick to receive impressions, and in the fresh soil of an immature mind the good seed germinates quickly, or noxious weeds find a ready opportunity for growth. As Mr. Lincoln, in one of his addresses, said, "these early impressions last longer than any others." The young men of the country set forward to true, patriotic, and unselfish living by the words of their public teachers, would, as Mr. Emerson said they should, "bind each other to loyalty" at the altar, "where genius would kindle its fires and bring forgotten truth to the eyes of men." But it is the bearing and spirit of the speaker himself that produces the effect—the unconscious influence of the character of the orator, that works out the result. A brave and manly sincerity will touch the heart of the listener, and stir the mind to noble thought. A false and insincere spirit will be sure to manifest itself. The young are quick to detect the inner soul of the man, and to those eager eyes there can be no concealment. "The style is the man," it is

sometimes said. But the style reaches farther than
the construction of finely rounded periods. In its
best expression, it is the true and noble utterance
of true and noble thought. Lincoln's Gettysburg
address, brief as it is, outweighs the stately oration
of Everett, and carries away the honors of the occasion by the sheer force of its complete sincerity.
This, as it seems to me, was characteristic of the
utterance of Hale. Although a hypercriticism
might detect some unimportant faults of rhetoric,
the most patient investigation could find nothing
to detract from the courage and truthfulness, that
gave vividness and force to his ardent and impassioned oratory.

Later on, in my early manhood, I heard Mr. Hale
on an entirely different occasion. It is well known
among his friends that he once essayed, for a sea-
son at least, the task of a lecturer in the desk of
the popular lyceum, which at one time occupied a
considerable space in the public regard. Like all
other men who are accustomed to the freedom of
extemporaneous speech, Mr. Hale's manner was
more subdued, when confined to a manuscript upon
the lecture platform, than when he spoke in the
spontaneous oratory of the public rostrum. The
subject which he chose may not have been so attractive as one more closely related to the questions
of popular debate. It was the "Last Gladiatorial
Combat in Rome," which he undertook to depict.
Nevertheless, a theme apparently so remote as that
became, in his hands, the opportune appeal to the
noblest moral instincts of his hearers. He told, in
graphic style, and in clear, incisive language, the

story of the Christian monk, Telemachus, who in
the year 404 made a special and sacred mission to
Rome, and at the supreme moment of a gladiatorial
fight threw himself into the midst of the strife and
sacrificed his life in a vain attempt to separate the
combatants and put an end to the bloody and inhu-
man spectacle. He paid the penalty of his temer-
ity. But even the hard hearts of the brutal Roman
populace were touched by the unexpected scene.
The Emperor Honorius, induced by the report of
the transaction, abolished the gladiatorial games,
and the carnage came to an end. Never again were
the sands of the arena stained by the blood of those
brave men who were brought from their distant
homes and " butchered to make a Roman holiday."
The self-sacrifice of the Christian disciple had conquered even a Roman's greed for blood.

The story having been told, the application, as
Mr. Hale made it, was obvious. In solemn, dignified, and impressive accents, he closed his address
in words like these, as they recur to me through
the remembrance of nearly forty years: " Is there
not an institution in our own land as deeply and
thoroughly seated in the social and political life of
the nation as that bloody spectacle in the social and
political life of imperial Rome? May not the time
come, when, even though it be but by a single
man's devotion to conscience and God, the spirit of
self-sacrifice, bravely moving to an offering of personal happiness and life, shall be as fully effectual
in putting an end to this barbaric power of slavery?
Surely, among American citizens such an act of
an equally supreme heroism cannot be impossible."

9

Doubtless he did not imagine, as no one among us was able at the time to foresee, that, not one, but hundreds of thousands, of American citizens, would lay their lives upon the altar of their nation's freedom, and, by the sacrifice, which had its climax in the death of the martyred president, put an end forever to the curse that had so long blighted the land that was worth loving "beyond compare."

Thus it came to pass, the impressions of my boyhood's days deepened into the conclusions of my manhood's years. In the sober light of history, too, which clearly reveals both the virtues and the weaknesses of human nature, I have seen no reason to change the opinion or lower the estimate of the character of the man in honoring whom the state of New Hampshire honors herself. John P. Hale still stands, and will always stand, as the embodiment of manly courage, of sincere, unselfish patriotism, of incorruptible statesmanship. Liberal, devout, and reverential in his religion, broad and generous in thought, as he was independent in politics, he "came full circle" in his well-rounded manhood, and thus his life career is to us and to all an inspiration, as well as a study. With him, blandishments and threats were equally ineffectual to turn him from the course which his convictions of duty impelled him to pursue. He stood upon his own feet, spoke his own words, did with all his might what his conscience bade him, and left the legacy of his independent and faithful life to his children and his children's children, to his fellow-citizens of state and nation, as an enduring memorial of his virtue. If these voiceless lips could speak, the

word would surely be: "Be brave; be bold in virtue's cause, be true, be faithful to conscience, the
deepest convictions of duty and the highest ideals
of life. Be loyal to your noblest self, your fellow-
men, your country, God, and the truth, which he is
always revealing!" What better word can there
be than that?

The granite may crumble and the bronze may
waste beneath the corroding touch of time. But
right is right, and truth is truth as long as sun
and moon endure, and he who serves them well with
self-forgetting devotion partakes of their own eternal.

The Chairman:—We have among our own
citizens. one who as an editor many years ago was
described as a " Free Soiler with abolition proclivi-
ties." Such a man must have been a close observer
of Mr. Hale's course. It gives me pleasure to introduce the Hon. Amos Hadley.

HON. AMOS HADLEY'S ADDRESS.

Mr. Chairman and Fellow-Citizens:—That
statue, mute, but eloquent in its silence, appeals to
memory and summons historic recollection. It
bids the mind recur to years nearly half-way along
the present century's course,—the years of '45 and
'46,—years of eventful significance in the political
history of our state and nation. For then it was
that, in our state, liberty, as the natural right of
universal humanity, first effectively asserted its
claim as a practical cardinal principle in political

creed and action. Then it was that the security of
a party long dominant in New Hampshire was first
seriously troubled, and its ascendancy threatened,
nay, temporarily overthrown, by the dark-looming
question of slavery. Then it was that the voice of
one of the ablest leaders of that party was heard
calling halt to it, and with the prophetic sagacity
of high philanthropic statesmanship, appealing to
it to take new bearings, and henceforth to march to
the music of union and liberty, and not of union
and slavery. That voice was the voice of John P.
Hale.

To use the pun of those days of turbid political
atmosphere, a protracted " Hale-storm " arose. It
came up from the South. It was generated of
Texas Annexation, a measure primarily designed to
sustain and perpetuate the inconsistency and sin of
human slavery in our boasted republic of the free.
A Democratic member of the lower house of congress, John P. Hale, had already shown manly, but
risky, independence in opposing the twenty-first
rule,—the infamous " Atherton gag " upon anti-
slavery petitions; but he had been renominated
with three associates upon a general ticket. Soon
the New Hampshire legislature, in its quadrennial
winter session of 1844–5, instructed the congressional delegation to support the annexation of
Texas. But circumstances had evolved a moral
hero, ready to surrender " office, place, and power,
rather than bow down and worship slavery." Such
evolution could not but work commotion. Within
ten days, John P. Hale, from his seat in congress,
boldly met the legislative instruction with a letter,

in which he flatly refused compliance, and denounced the aims and purposes of the annexation
measure, and the reasons urged therefor, as "eminently calculated to provoke the scorn of earth,
and the judgment of Heaven." That letter was a
thunderbolt, close herald of a storm—a storm of
"hailstones and coals of fire!"

There was a fearful rattling among the dry bones
of party conservatism. There was a waking up
with hornet wrath not unmixed with fear. There
was hurry-scurry among the Democratic leaders,
who said one to another, "Away with him—the pes-
tilent fellow with his twaddle of freedom!" The
state convention was reassembled, a month before
the March election of 1845, the refractory candidate was dropped, and one was substituted in
whose party subservience there was "no guile."
But while the spirit of angry revenge was thus
aroused in the Democratic party, conscience was
also awakened therein to the important issue, and
the resolute, though discarded, candidate had those
who stood by him and his righteous cause. A
cleavage showed itself in the party's hitherto com-
pact solidity. At the ensuing election, while the
other congressional candidates were chosen, the
substitute for Mr. Hale was not. Three other trials
were made in course of the year,—the last in
March, 1846,—but with no choice of the fourth
member; Mr. Hale's place in congress remained
unfilled.

The storm had been on, fiercely pelting all the
while. Hale's canvasses had covered the state from
the Cochecho to the Connecticut, and from Coös to

Strawberry Bank. His arguments and appeals, heard clear, strong, and convincing above the angry, clamorous din of overbearing, denunciatory opposition, had sunk deep into many hearts, infusing them with courage to break the ties of party, for conscience, country, truth, and liberty. Deeper and deeper had grown the cleavage in the rock of Granite Democracy, till the "Independent Democrats" had become a considerable party. Accordingly, at the March election of 1846, the Anti-Democratic parties, though retaining two organizations and supporting two state tickets, had together won, potentially, a sweeping anti-slavery triumph. Here, indeed, was something new under the sun.

It was now the first Wednesday of June, 1846— the day for organizing anew the state government. The effects of the great political storm were strikingly visible. No governor, no quorum of council or senate had been chosen by popular vote; but a house of representatives had been; and that, by wise coalition, was anti-slavery by a safe majority. And that house, too, contained among its members one John P. Hale of Dover. He there to lead the anti-slavery majority? He there with an unexpired and a full term in the United States senate at the disposal of that legislature? Were indeed "the stars in their courses fighting against Sisera?" So it would certainly seem, whether "Sisera" was John P. Hale's former party, or slavery itself.

On the bright morning of that third day of June, 1846, intense interest centered in the New Hampshire house of representatives. And here pursuing briefly a train of personal reminiscence, I will relate what I saw and heard. Standing in the crowded south gallery of the old capitol, I looked down upon that full house, comprising able men of both parties; for practically there were but two. The oath has been administered by Governor Steele, the outgoing executive, the clerk of the last house has called to order, and Thomas E. Sawyer of Dover has been chosen chairman. Now the balloting for speaker is on. The definite test of party strength is making; there is the corresponding stress of interest. The votes are gathered, sorted and counted, and the chairman announces, amidst the breathless attention of house and galleries, this result:

"Whole number of votes cast, 260; necessary to a choice, 131; Henry B. Rust has 1 ; George G. Fogg has 2; Samuel Swasey has 118; John P. Hale has 139;—and John P. Hale having a majority of the votes cast, is elected speaker."

Glad applause greets the announcement. Mr. Hale arises and passes with prompt and dignified step to the speaker's chair. No curule chair,—it seemed to me then, and it seems to me now—could ever be more becomingly filled. The new speaker was in the vigorous maturity of forty years, of strong and symmetric physical build, with a face glowing with ruddy health, bright with brilliance of intellect and genialness of heart,—a face, handsome, good-natured, jovial even, but with a will in it. A man of cool self-possession, easy dignity, and admirable poise, the speaker stood in his place, and pronounced his address of acceptance in the clear, mellow tones of that voice which had been heard enunciating with such effect, for more than a year, throughout the state, the gospel of liberty. In the course of that address, independence of opinion was urged with a most effective appropriateness, in these words:

" Coming together from the different parts of the state—representing her various interests, and, a fact neither to be denied nor kept out of sight, exponents of widely different political sentiments—entire unanimity of opinion is not to be expected, perhaps not to be desired. But if we must differ, we can respect honest differences of opinion, according to each other the same integrity of purpose which we claim for ourselves."

Never shall I forget with what rich melody of tone, impressive emphasis, and depth of conviction, the speaker uttered these, among his closing words:—

" For myself, gentlemen, in the discharge of the duties of this chair, and in every other position in which the voice of the people or the providence of God may call me to act, I shall read for myself,— and I suggest the same for your consideration,— that immortal sentiment, which the wisdom of our fathers placed as the corner stone of our constitution, 'that all men are created equally free and independent,' as the most emphatic declaration of the will of the people of New Hampshire."

The speaker had closed amid appreciative applause, when one at my side, not liking the present turn of politics, uttered to another of kindred sentiments, the sneering criticism, " Abolition ! " To which came the reply, in a similar tone, " Yes, he means the nigger." Inadvertently significant were those sneers. Yes, Hale did " mean the negro," as a fellow-man divinely entitled to all the rights of humanity, and he would mean the negro all along in the coming years; the free North, too, would get to " mean the negro," more and more; ay, and the time was coming when the voice of the God of Nations and of Justice would be heard amid the bloody terrors of slavery-engendered war,—and heard to be obeyed,—I mean the negro. "Let the oppressed go free."

But this train of reminiscence must here be left. That it has been pursued thus far, or even at all, finds a reason in the more than ordinary historic significance of its main fact. That occupancy of the speaker's chair by John P. Hale, representing, as it did, early successful resistance to the behests of slavery, was, as seen in the light of subsequent history, an important one in the series of events that culminated in slavery destroyed and the Union saved.

Did time and the scope of this effort permit, another scene might be depicted—that enacted six days later in the same legislature, when Speaker Hale, rejected by his former party from the lower house of congress, was elected to the senate of the United States for six years from the 4th of March, 1847. Oh, what revenge of fortune was this! What condign poetic justice! Verily the mills of the gods took on unusual speed while grinding with their usual fineness! Six years, then four, then six again,—sixteen years in the senate of the United States—such was John P. Hale's great opportunity; that he sacredly improved it in faithful, fearless service for country, liberty, and humanity, is his clear, safe title to enduring fame.

It is the proud honor of New Hampshire to have been the first in much of historic well-doing; but never was she more nobly first than when she elected John P. Hale as the first anti-slavery senator of the United States. As such he stood alone in his place for two years, holding his own, all panoplied as he was, in reason, wit, and good nature to attack or to defend. But there came by and by, from fair Ohio, to stand by his side, Salmon P. Chase, another stalwart son of New Hampshire, and ere long appeared Charles Sumner, the pride of Massachusetts, to reinforce the two. And there they wrought together in their good work, and there they fought together the good fight—Hale, Chase, and Sumner—an immortal three!

Thus, then, the beautiful and impressive memorial in bronze, in the unveiled presence of which we now stand, has full and glorious reason to be; for in the recent expressive words of Frederick Douglass,—honor ever be to the name of that great and noble freedman, freeman, and American citizen,— " No statue of patriot, statesman, or philanthropist of our times will convey to aftercoming generations · a lesson of moral heroism more sublime."

The Chairman:—I cannot bring myself to the point of formally introducing to a New Hampshire audience the next and last speaker. I can only say that, in looking over my list, I thought that Dr. Quint would be a good man to close the speak-

ing, and that he would manage an audience sur-
feited with good addresses better than any man
with whom I am acquainted: The Rev. Dr. Quint,
of Dover.

REV. DR. ALONZO H. QUINT'S ADDRESS.

MR. CHAIRMAN AND CITIZENS OF NEW HAMP-
SHIRE: I hope I shall not long detain you from
that doxology which is promised, but I have the
floor, and you must trust to my generosity. I
count it an honor to be invited to participate in the
exercises of this occasion, when New Hampshire,
through the thousands of citizens here assembled,
recognizes the greatness of one of its greatest sons
—great not merely because of his remarkable powers, but because the application of those powers
had its heroic and moral aspect, in which conscience and right seemed instinctive. If I had
ever had a doubt whether I did right in voting in
yonder legislative halls for the distinguished senator now upon this platform, to represent this state
in that high office,—of which I never had a doubt,
—that doubt would have ended in seeing how the
senator has intuitively interpreted the sentiments
and qualified the desires of the people of New
Hampshire by placing this noble statue in these
grounds. His act is an act for which the people
of this state will be eminently grateful. The members of the legislature, in passing up this walk,
may see the face of one who always stood for conscience and for right—a man who was willing to
be set aside and stand alone, exposed to calumny

and abuse, rather than surrender his convictions.
Legislators can then properly enter yonder doors,
and pass uncovered, as I always did, before the
torn and scarred and bullet-riddled flags, and before the portraits of noble sons of this state, who
gave their lives upon the battle-field for the flag
and liberty.

That young boy who has to-day unveiled this
statue has performed a notable act. He will remember it during his life. He has promise, but he
will have to contend with the fact, in attaining
public success, that he has a father's and mother's
father's memory with which to compete.

In early life, that is, in my boyhood, I knew
something of the man to whom we pay honor to-
day. There was in him the peculiar genial qualities which drew young life to him. He attracted
us. My father, from the same political party, went
with John P. Hale in his separation from former
associates. I remember hearing men discuss the
little convention of old "liberty men," which met
to consider whether to sustain him in his movement. Would that Moses A. and Jonathan Cart-
land, Oliver Wyatt, and others like them, had survived to be present on this occasion! I remember
a special incident. I was often in the printing-
office in Dover, where I learned to set type, and
where Mr. Hale had a warm friend in the editor
and proprietor of the political organ. The famous
letter came, denouncing the proposed annexation of
Texas. It was in type, and in the evening before
the issue of the paper I saw " in proof" the editor's
hearty commendation of the letter. You may fancy

my surprise in finding next morning, when the
paper was issued, that the commendation had been
cancelled, and that there had been substituted, if I
remember correctly, a colorless statement that com-
ment was deferred. It was learned that two distinguished politicians had driven to Dover in the
night and persuaded the reluctant editor to strike
out the commendatory paragraph. Mr. Hale felt
the defection of his staunch friend.

My distinguished relative, Col. Daniel Hall, has
told you with exquisite analysis and richness of
thought the history of those struggles so far as
Mr. Hale was the principal actor. He stood practically alone. It seemed the end of his public
career. But I believe that no allusion has been
made to what I hesitatingly will refer to. I trust
it will not be considered a violation of delicacy if
I allude to the fact that many a man gets his
noblest inspirations in the home circle, and that
this man found, in his great sacrifice, the warmest
support where he felt its value, and the strengthening of a purpose to give up everything but honor
—public office, party associates, future fame.

I must say something for New Hampshire to-
day, for New Hampshire is a grand old state.
Not the least of its glory is in that it sent this first
anti-slavery senator to the senate-house. It was
two years before another state did likewise; and it
was four years, let it be remembered, before Massachusetts sent Sumner to reinforce the great pioneer. Massachusetts is a great state, and we welcome its people every summer to our great mountains. In all soberness, I certainly cannot forget

certain relic-banners hanging listlessly in the state-
house at Boston, nor the heroic dead who carried
those flags, with whom it was my glorious privilege to be a comrade in long years of bivouac and
battle. But New Hampshire, my native state, gave
the first anti-slavery senator. New Hampshire
has usually been foremost in history. Men hear of
Lexington and Concord, but it was in New Hampshire, four months earlier, that the first armed conflict with the crown took place, when New Hampshire men captured the royal fort "William and
Mary" in broad daylight, against the fire of mus-
kets and cannon, and with cheers pulled down
the royal flag. It was a story which Mr. Hale
used to love to tell, how New Hampshire equipped
John Stark's independent command which conquered at Bennington, and thus secured the French
alliance which gave us final independence. It was
fitting that New Hampshire should lead in the contest for human liberty in the senate of the United
States. When the War of the Rebellion ended,
the close of his twenty years' contest, it was signalized by the entrance of our troops into Richmond.
Two loyal Southern women, who had long been
under guard, saw the bayonets and the flag of the
first entering regiment, and, with streaming eyes,
kneeled down upon the pavement and thanked
God for the sight. That first regiment was the
Thirteenth New Hampshire. It was the suitable
conclusion to the beginning of New Hampshire's
great senatorship; and it was right that John P.
Hale, who remembered his solitary entrance into
the Capitol, should live to see the victory.

John Parker Hale was worthy of New Hampshire, and New Hampshire was worthy of John Parker Hale. This statue is to stand here in the heat of summer and the cold of winter, just as he stood in the storms of the great contest. When next Memorial Day comes round, let the comrades of the Grand Army of the Republic strew flowers at the foot of this statue, as being the memorial of one equally deserving with every man who fell in the fight or who lived to come home from the conflict.

The exercises, after four hours, were formally brought to a close by the chairman, but the audience pressed around the platform and called for more singing, and Mr. Hutchinson, with Mrs. Abbie Hutchinson Patton,* who was present with her husband, sang various old songs of freedom, Mr. Douglass assisting in the service.

The song " The Old Granite State " was asked for and rendered in the words here given, from a draft dated Bradford, N. H., September 13, 1845, in the handwriting of Hon. Mason W. Tappan, as follows:

---

* Mrs. Patton on the tenth day of September at Amesbury, Mass., again sung at the funeral of Mr. Whittier, and she died in New York city November 24, 1892, and was buried on the 29th, at Milford, N. H. John W. Hutchinson is the only survivor of the famous quartette of anti-slavery singers. If this memorial volume were not already too large the compiler would feel impelled to publish a glowing tribute to the Hutchinson family, and especially to the sweet woman singer, written by Mr. Frank B. Carpenter and published in the New York Home Journal of December 7, 1892. A brief sketch of the Hutchinson family is also published by Mayor P. B. Cogswell in the Granite Monthly for December, 1892.

WELCOME TO HON. JOHN P. HALE.

TUNE—Old Granite State, as sung by the Hutchinsons.

From each mountain top and valley,
And from every street and alley,
Let the friends of freedom rally,
 In the Old Granite State—
To sustain the friend of freedom,
To sustain the friend of freedom,
 In his conflict for the right.

Come and let us swell the chorus
While victory hovers o'er us—
Tyrants all shall quail before us,
 In the Old Granite State.
It shall ne'er be said by any,
It shall ne'er be said by any,
 That New Hampshire's sons are slaves!

John Parker Hale of Dover,
John Parker Hale of Dover,
 In the Old Granite State,
On the right of Petition,
On the right of Petition,
Like a true-hearted freeman,
 Gave his vote against the "Gag!"

And when Calhoun would annex us
To slave-holding, slave-cursed *Texas*,
That forever they might vex us,
 And perpetuate their crime,
HALE opposed the deadly union,
HALE opposed the deadly union,
And refused the foul commission,—
 LET HIS NAME WITH HONOR SHINE!

And now when others falter,
"Burn strange fire" on Freedom's Altar,
Tamely creep, or meanly falter,
 In the Old Granite State;

Still on Justice firmly planted,
Still on Justice firmly planted,
He will face the Storm undaunted
In the Old Granite State.

May success crown each endeavor,
May success crown each endeavor,
Of Freedom's faithful friend,
And sustain him we will ever,
And sustain him we will ever,
Till oppression's days shall end.

Brave champion of Freedom,
Brave champion of Freedom,
In the Old Granite State,
We give you now a WELCOME,
We give you now a WELCOME,
To our homes among the hills!

Bradford, N. H., September 13, 1845.

Mr. John W. Hutchinson next narrated reminiscences of Mr. Hale, and spoke of his own personal relations with him. During the exercises he had sung his own tribute, as follows :

O son of New Hampshire, thy fame cannot fade.
In the hearts of our people thine image inlaid.
This statue in grandeur now points to the sky,
A lesson is teaching to each passer by :
A lesson to battle with life day by day,
And courage to conquer its foes by the way.

We must stand like our granite, and moving be strong;
Let our glory live ever in story and song.

In the hearts of our nation, as imbedded in gold,
Our Rogers and Hale, and hundreds untold
Of brave hearts who stood for justice and right,
And in every reform its battle we'll fight.
New Hampshire stands foremost and mighty in fame;
She has left a fair record and glorious name.

10

Gone are slavery's days; the oppressed ones are free,
Forever to rest under liberty's tree.
The brave men who stood forth in martial array
Are falling; like leaves they are passing away.

But they stood like our granite, and in battle were strong;
Let their glory live ever in story and song.

He whose statue to-day in honor we raise
Bared his breast to the tempest in Freedom's dark days,
And while through the world truth and justice prevail
Shall be loved and be honored the memory of Hale.

Then be true to our banner and liberty strong,
That our glory live ever in story and song.

Mr. Hutchinson also sang the verses composed
for the occasion by that veteran freesoiler, Mr.
George W. Putnam, of 130 Brookline street, Lynn,
Mass., as follows :

Here from our mountain homes we come,
    Heart answering heart, hand grasping hand,
To honor one who stood for Right
    When darkness covered all the land.

The tyrant's power with iron will
    Had hunted Freedom to her death ;
And crouching low o'er patriot graves
    Their children spoke with bated breath.

Around the Nation's Capitol
    The bondmen clanked their heavy chains ;
And " Free Speech " died when Lovejoy's blood
    Crimsoned fair Alton's distant plains.

Long years of darkness came and went,
    The weak still trampled by the strong,
Until the cry went forth that we
    Had insult borne, and shame, too long !

And then that " man John—sent from God,"
　Strong in the truth, and free and brave,
Summoned—as with a trumpet call—
　Our buried manhood from its grave.

Calmly he stood, awhile the storm
　Gathered along his darkling path,
Denunciation's thunder tones,
　And hissing waves of human wrath.

And while above, around, below,
　The tempests raged and skies grew black,
He faced the foe, and proudly bade
　The waves of tyranny roll back!

The true of heart, the strong of soul,
　With purpose grand around him came,
And soon our valleys rang with songs,
　The mountain peaks were all aflame.

Through the broad land his thrilling call
　Waked the old spirit of our sires,
And kindled high in million hearts
　The flame from Freedom's altar fires!

In the proud nation's council hall,
　Thundering beneath its lofty dome,
He met the swelling tide of crime,
　Like granite of his mountain home.

Well we recall his burning words
　For Freedom, when, with banners high,
And beating drums, and bugle peal,
　The Hampshire troops marched southward by!

Marched southward—telling all the world
　To place on Freedom's brow her crown;
With cannon's boom, and flashing steel,
　The mountain men were coming down!

And when Great Freedom's work was done,
　And red with blood were land and sea,

The wide earth heard the crash of chains,
   And shouts of ransomed millions, free.

But of the brave who came not back,
   Remember that their lives were given
To save a nation's priceless life,
   The noblest cause of Earth and Heaven !

And so to-day, with speech and song,
   And cannon's voice, and chime of bells,
We come with joy to strew afresh
   His grave with Freedom's immortelles !

APPENDIX.

APPENDIX.

LETTERS, INTERVIEWS, AND COMMENTS.

[From JOHN G. WHITTIER.]

HAMPTON FALLS, N. H., July 28, 1892.

To His Excellency Governor Tuttle :

It is a matter of very great regret to me that I find my-self unable to be present at the unveiling of the statue of the great New Hampshire senator, who so richly deserves the honor. No man knows better than myself how bravely and wisely he bore himself in the revolt and conflict which placed his state permanently on the side of freedom. He broke the chains of party, and set free the best and worthi-est of the Jeffersonian Democracy to speak and vote as their better instincts and consciences inclined them. His victory made all the after successes possible which culmin-ated in the abolition of human slavery and the establish-ment of the Union on an unmovable basis.

As one of the few now living who had the privilege of acting with him in that memorable struggle, I am glad to bear my testimony to the ability, eloquence, and devotion to principle of the man whose place in the Pantheon of his state has the permanence of her granite mountains.

I am truly and respectfully thy friend,

JOHN G. WHITTIER.*

---

* Mr. Whittier died at Hampton Falls, September 7, 1892, and was buried on the 10th at Amesbury, Mass. In a brief but impressive account of his funeral, by Mrs. Caroline H. Dall, to be found in the

[From FREDERICK DOUGLASS.]

CEDAR HILL, ANACOSTIA, D. C., June 29, 1892.

Hon. W. E. Chandler:

MY DEAR SIR:—I would gladly obey your call to Concord on the 3d of August. The occasion stirs my heart and memory. No statue of patriot, statesman, or philanthropist of our times will convey to after-coming generations a lesson of moral heroism more sublime than that proposed to be unveiled of John P. Hale, on the third of August. I remember well the man and his works, and it may be that I can be present and bear my testimony on the occasion of the unveiling, but I am not now in a condition to positively promise.

Very truly yours,

FREDERICK DOUGLASS.

[From NATHANIEL S. BERRY.]

BRISTOL, N. H., July 30, 1892.

Gov. Hiram A. Tuttle:

MY DEAR SIR:—As it is very uncertain whether I shall be able to meet you in Concord on the 3d of August, as invited, allow me to say a word to you in regard to my friendship and esteem for John P. Hale. From 1818 to

---

New England Magazine for January, 1893, it is stated that John and Abby Hutchinson (with Mr. Patton) attended the quiet Quaker service, and tenderly sung the chant, " Close his eyes, his work is done. Lay him low."

On Mr. Whittier's 80th birthday, December 17, 1887, he received a picture with this inscription, " John P. Hale Chandler sends birthday greeting to Mr. Whittier, from whom the boy, like his grandfather, shall learn to love nature, to revere humanity, to pity the downtrodden, and to trust the Eternal Goodness." Mr. Whittier, in acknowledgment, wrote on the margin of one of the printed cards which he sent out to the numerous friends who had congratulated him, these words: "I had no visitor more acceptable on the 17th than the grandson of my old friend, John P. Hale. I thank his father for sending him. I am truly thy friend, John G. Whittier."

1840 I voted with the Democratic party. In 1840 I was elected a delegate and attended the national convention held in Baltimore, and there learned, from the demands made by a leading member from Tennessee and the doings of the convention, that the extension and strengthening of the institution of slavery was the first principle acted upon by the party leaders, and not, as I had always hoped and believed, the desire to devise and carry out measures by which our nation should be freed from that great crime. I then said that I could not any longer vote to aid the Democratic party. When Mr. Hale, as a Democratic member of congress, voted against the annexation of Texas, giving his reasons therefor, I thought he was right, and when in obedience to the demands of Southern leaders, he was denounced, and his nomination for a second election as representative, which had been made, was revoked by the party leaders of this state, I did all I could to sustain him and his action. Soon after, I consented to have my name used as a candidate for governor by the Liberty or Free Soil party, with no thought of ever being elected to the office, but I did receive votes enough to prevent an election by the people, and during the following months I was waited upon by Harry Hibbard and other leading men in the Democratic party, who assured me that with the fourteen Liberty or Free-Soil members elected to the state legislature every Democratic member would vote for me as United States senator, rather than have Mr. Hale elected, and they urged me time and again before the legislature assembled to accept. I replied that I would not consent, but would do all I could for Mr. Hale's return to congress. No person in this state did more to forward the success and triumph of the Republican party than Mr. Hale, and I am very glad that his statue is to be placed in the state house yard. If I am permitted to be present for a little time during the unveiling, it will be very gratifying to me.

I am very truly yours,

N. S. BERRY.

[From A. P. Putnam.]

Concord, Mass., Aug. 5, 1892.

My Dear Sir:—From the circumstance that I have recently had some correspondence with you about certain genealogical matters in which we were alike interested, I dare say it was yourself who kindly sent to me a copy of yesterday's *New Hampshire Republican*, published in your city, and containing a full report of the proceedings at the unveiling of the memorial statue of John P. Hale, at Concord. I am particularly glad at receiving such an account of an occasion which must have been very impressive, as it was certainly one, also, that reflects great credit upon all who had to do with it. Senator Chandler's gift to the state is one for which thousands on thousands in other sections of the Union besides his own will thank him, and Colonel Hall's address is a noble and most important contribution to the history of the anti-slavery struggle. All the speakers rose to the hour, and one reads their eloquent words with a fresh and increased appreciation of the exalted worth of the man they so fitly honored.

The old Granite State has had an abundant share of illustrious names, as we all know, but I do not recall one of them that seems to me more deserving of lasting remembrance and praise than that of John Parker Hale. It required a vast deal of moral courage to withstand and fight, single-handed as it were, the pro-slavery oligarchy and party, there in New Hampshire, in 1845. To all human seeming, it meant political ostracism and ruin. Few would have ventured the contest, even for dear Liberty's sake, so proud and tyrannous and fierce was the power which was then in rule. But the man from Dover was not only a true lover of Freedom and of his race, but he was also one who knew no fear, and was perfectly willing and ready to sacrifice himself for a just and holy cause. It thrills me, even now, to recall the lofty and courageous spirit with which he threw down the gauntlet, and went before the people with his magnificent appeal.

For I was no indifferent or remote observer of what was then and there going on. In 1844 and 1845, I was a student at Pembroke, N. H. Party spirit then ran very high, and the Polk Democracy was as arbitrary as it was all powerful. The boys at the academy entered into the controversies and excitements of the time with earnest zeal, sharing in due proportion the names and sentiments of the various organizations that divided the people. It was a notable epoch when "Jack Hale" began his fight, and I well remember how a good number of the students quickly sided with him, and how stoutly they contended, in their own way, for the principles he represented, and for himself as the leader of the new, independent movement. Colonel Hall, in his exceedingly interesting and admirable address, gives an account of the famous encounter, at the old North church in Concord, between Mr. Hale and Franklin Pierce. It was but a few miles away, and some of us students went to see and hear. It was, indeed, a memorable scene. Not alone a very large number of the citizens of Concord, but hundreds of farmers from surrounding towns and from more distant places, crowded to listen to Freedom's rising orator and defender. In later years it was my good fortune to hear him speak on many occasions, but I never heard him when he appeared to better advantage, or seemed to me abler and grander, than in that "battle of the giants." After the two hours' speech by Mr. Hale, there was a loud and persistent call for Mr. Pierce by the old Democracy, and presently the local chief of his party came forward and mounted the rostrum. His address occupied about as much time as that of his predecessor. It was able, pointed, and aggressive, having a tone of severity quite in contrast with the excellent spirit of the other. Pierce was pale, excited, and passionate, more or less frequently having to stop to cool his tongue with water, though it had no perceptible effect to cool his rage. I sat quite near the stage, so that I saw and heard the whole, and I could but think that the very clever Concord lawyer's anger was a little intensified

in consequence of the fact that Mr. Hale, at the conclusion of his own speech, had quickly gathered up his papers,
folded them under his arm, stepped down from the platform, and taken a seat in one of the front pews, where,
with a calm and beaming face, and in a most imperturbable
and manly spirit, he listened attentively to his antagonist's
speech to the very end. Of course, Pierce's concluding
words, like those of Hale, were followed by uproarious
applause. Then it was that cries arose for the latter once
more, to give answer to the attack which had been made
upon him. It was a brief reply, for the hour was getting
late, and the ground had been well covered before. Yet it
was a most pertinent and effective word. I never knew the
man to be more eloquent. Voice, look, manner, thought,
language, and all, as he stood there on the seat of the pew
he occupied and fronted the vast assemblage, went right
home to the minds and hearts of his hearers in such wise
that it was evident as he closed that he had captured the
audience. The enthusiasm was far greater for him than for
Pierce, or his cause or party. A huge swarm of people followed him as he emerged from the meeting-house and proceeded to the village, full of admiration for the man and
for what he had said and done.

How little any of us who were there realized, at the time,
that both of these sons of New Hampshire were at no distant day to be candidates for the presidency, and that one
of them was actually to be elected to the high office! It
was far easier to so divine the future as to see the advancing and growing hosts of Liberty, with John P. Hale as one
of its bravest and most gallant champions in all the long
and tremendous warfare. That he was. He never be-
trayed the sacred interests of justice and right. His service to humanity, his service to his country, was heroic and
faithful and incalculable, and it is meet that his statue
should rise at last at the very capital of the state that gave
him birth.

I did not intend to write so much. Taking it for granted

that you sent me the *Republican* that has come to hand, let
me thank you heartily for it. I remain

Very truly yours,

A. P. PUTNAM.

HON. GEO. A. RAMSDELL.

[From LARKIN D. MASON.]

SOUTH TAMWORTH, N. H., Aug. 5, 1892.

DEAR MR. CHANDLER:—I had a splendid position last
Wednesday to hear every word and consider every suggestion. Notwithstanding the many long and able speeches, I
thought possibly there were some things left unsaid, and as
a gleaner I followed the reapers and picked up a few heads
which they missed, and have tied them up in a bundle and
send them for your consideration.

It was one of my best days on earth. I am nearly
through with this life and hope to meet you and all the
Hale family, and all the faithful soldiers in the late great
moral struggle, and I would not object to have Frederick
Douglass come in to give color to the occasion.

Very truly,

LARKIN D. MASON.

MR. MASON'S "GLEANINGS."

From whatever standpoint we look back upon our country's history, we find progress. This progress the great
Brooklyn divine calls evolution. I think we are all ready
to admit that society does not naturally drift heavenward,
as a tree grows up in nature, but it is always more or less
in conflict with everything that advances it to a higher
plane of life.

Such a conflict always requires personal sacrifice in order
to ensure victory. These great conflicts and victories have
grown out of individual agonizing, out of the personal conflicts of heroic souls with the powers of ignorance and

wrong, of noble men who have stepped out of the ruts of organizations and exposed themselves to calumny and censure for the sake of the good they might do to society and the benefit they might confer upon their race. And it is a fact familiar to us all, that whenever the people were ready to advance, some man with special qualifications for the emergency has appeared upon the stage.

Probably no man but Washington could have taken so feeble an army, so poorly equipped and supported, and have gained our independence. No man but Lincoln could have issued the Emancipation Proclamation at the time he did, and have been sustained in it; and perhaps no other officer in the Union army could have subdued the Rebellion without any concession or compromise, but General Grant.

I think it equally certain that there was no other man except John P. Hale who could have gone into the United States senate as early as 1846 and advocated the cause of universal liberty; standing among slaveholders and possibly duelists, and there, without faltering, presenting the evils of slavery and the dangerous encroachments of the whole system of slavery, and afterward invited by the most radical slaveholders to go to their homes and spend the Christmas holidays with them.

Mr. Hale never made an unkind expression toward his opponents, but always extended that courtesy which won their respect. Mr. Hale, from his early manhood till his death, never met an opponent and left him the victor. He treated the subject under discussion with such seriousness that he seldom failed to draw tears from his audience, and yet, if occasion called, he could improvise an anecdote that would place his opponent in an unenviable position. He could never be hired, coaxed, or driven to advocate that which he thought was wrong, or to hold his peace when error was present.

It was my privilege, as early as 1845, to take my team and carry him from one appointment to another among the hills of Carroll county. He went forth bearing precious seed. He lived to return again rejoicing, bringing his sheaves with him.

When Mr. Hale entered the political contest, slavery had such a controlling influence in this nation over parties, presses, and pulpits, that it required nerve to enter the contest against it. When he had finished his work not a slave rattled his fetters or clanked his chains.

He richly deserved the epitaph he desired to be read by the wife of his bosom and the children of his love, " This man sacrificed place and honor rather than bow down and worship slavery."

To apply a sentiment original with President Lincoln, " We sincerely regret we cannot penetrate his resting place and bear to him the evidences of our heartfelt gratitude." I rejoice in this tribute. of respect to the memory of the noble hero, and I heartily thank the distinguished son of New Hampshire for this appropriate act, and I thank the great God for putting it into his heart to do it.

———

[From CHESTER B. JORDAN.]

LANCASTER, N. H., Aug. 5, 1892.

I knew much of Mr. Hale, and greatly admired his intrepid spirit, his fearlessness in the cause of right, his loyalty to his convictions and to his country and her best interests, and his love for humanity everywhere. But I want the record where my little boys, when they become men, can know something of the first and staunchest New Hampshire defender of the rights and liberty of man.

CHESTER B. JORDAN.

———

[From CALEB A. WALL.]

WORCESTER, MASS., Aug. 2, 1892.

To the Editor of the Daily Monitor, Concord, N. H.:

Exceedingly regretting I cannot attend in person the exercises to-morrow, in tribute to the memory of John P.

Hale, I could not resist the temptation to express by letter something of my gratification that such a tribute is to be paid to one so worthy the admiration of the friends of Freedom all over the country. I am one of those enthusiastic admirers of the pioneers in the anti-slavery conflict, who have watched their course from the beginning with great interest, and none of them deserve more credit for boldness and efficiency in speech and action than the distinguished senator from New Hampshire, in and out of congress. It was my good fortune to hear the great speech he made in our city (then town) hall, Oct. 13, 1846, soon after his election as senator, over an opposition of unexampled note, and the report of that speech is the first one I ever made in my fifty years' experience as a newspaper man. How the echoes of that speech still ring in my ears! It was something after the style of his reply to the attacks and denunciations of Franklin Pierce, Isaac Hill, and other champions of the slave power of that time.

In looking over the files of newspapers for 1845, I find an item, probably contributed by myself, containing the following extract from a speech then made by Mr. Hale in answer to his antagonists and former friends, who had excommunicated him from their support because of his opposition to pro-slavery measures:

"In conclusion, I may be permitted to say that the measure of my ambition will be full, if, when my earthly career shall be ended and my bones are laid beneath the soil of New Hampshire, and when my wife and children shall repair to my grave to drop the tear of affection to my memory, they may read on my tombstone, ' *He who lies beneath surrendered office, place, and power rather than bow down and worship slavery.*'"

These were indeed fitting words with which to close that memorable controversy, which, it is said, lasted all night; the triumph of Hale before the people, over the myrmidons of the slave oligarchy in the persons of Pierce, Hill, and others.

CALEB A. WALL.

[From the Worcester *Spy* of July 31, 1892.]

Mr. Wall then referred to the matter of the dedication next Wednesday, in Concord, N. H., of the monument to that eloquent pioneer champion of human rights, John P. Hale, the first Free Soil senator in congress, and Free Soil candidate for president in 1852. A well deserved tribute was paid to Mr. Hale, for his fidelity, boldness, and effective advocacy of the cause of freedom during his sixteen years in the senate, and as a platform speaker. A sketch of Mr. Hale's powerful speech in the City hall in Worcester, October 13, 1846, after his first election as United States senator, over the pro-slavery Democracy of the Granite State, led by Franklin Pierce, was read, to show the quality of Mr. Hale as a speaker.

Mr. Wall closed his eulogy of Mr. Hale by reading lines of poetic tribute to him by a son of the Granite state, in which were the following beautiful stanzas, expressive of the modest wish of the deceased illustrious champion of human rights:

> "When kind affection e'er shall place
>   An humble shaft above my grave,
> These simple words are all I ask—
>   'He sought to help the helpless slave.'
>
> "He lived to see the good work done,
>   The land redeemed from slavery's thrall;
> No more the scourge of whips and chains,
>   But freedom reigning over all."

[From JOHN D. LYMAN.]

The unveiling of the statue of the brilliant, brainy, and whole-souled John P. Hale reminds me of my first vote for member of congress. I have never since seen so much interest, or excitement so intense, about the election of a member of the national house of representatives. Hale and Pierce were the two most gallant and prominent Demo-

11

cratic leaders at this time in the state. Hale had served one term in congress, and, according to usage, had been re-nominated. After this nomination he had addressed his celebrated letter to his constituents in opposition to the annexation of Texas without some provision against slavery. A convention, managed by Pierce and other leading Democrats, had been called, at which Hale's nomination had been repudiated and John Woodbury nominated in his place. New Hampshire had not then obeyed the law of congress requiring the states to be districted for congressmen, and they were voted for on a general ticket. In my town, Milton, at the preceding presidential election in November, the Polk electors had received forty-five votes, the Clay electors, ninety-four, and the Free Soil candidate, twenty-seven. Hale's letter and his repudiation inspired the Whig leaders with hope and enthusiasm, rejoiced the Free Soilers, led away a part of the Democrats, and enraged the others. These last named denounced Hale in language more vigorous than polite as a renegade and traitor. All were earnest. My political views were largely centered in love of protection, the "American System" as advocated by Clay, Webster, and other famous statesmen of that and earlier days, and in my hatred of human slavery.

I did not consider Hale sound on the question of protection, and disliked his opposition to the West Point Military academy, his support of James K. Polk, pledged to the pro-slavery schemes of the South, and his opposition to the law of congress requiring the election of members of congress by districts. But on the other hand, I far more disliked the idea of his being defeated for doing right in refusing to further bow down to the domineering and wicked slave power.

When our leading Whigs found me electioneering for Hale, their appeals for me to stick to the Whigs were the most earnest and intense political entreaties I have ever received. It seemed that they could not give me up. So provoked were they that for several years they defeated me whenever my friends nominated me for any office. I need not say that my active work for Hale disgusted the regular Democrats, for they hated him with a newer and hotter hatred than they did their old antagonists, the Whigs.

But Milton did well that day, for Woodbury received only thirty-one votes, while Hale received seventy-three, outrunning in this strong Whig town, all other congressional candidates.

Going home to vote in 1853, I was greatly surprised at being elected representative, for the town had never elected so young a man, and I had not heard my name mentioned in connection with the office. All shades and grades of the opposition in the house that year, I think, numbered about seventy-nine, with eleven Democratic and one opposition senator. The repeal of the Missouri Compromise aroused the indignation of the free states before the election of 1854. To the remarkable legislature of that year I was elected, running, I think, some forty votes ahead of our state ticket. This session of 1854 was to the Democrats what Gettysburg was to the rebels. Pierce was president. The able Charles G. Atherton, known as "Gag" Atherton, had died, and Moses Norris's term would expire the next March, thus leaving the charming mannered and yielding. president between the upper and nether millstones of the forces of liberty and slavery. The opposition in this legislature consisted of Whigs, Free Soilers, and Independent Democrats, who united upon Mason W. Tappan for speaker, and we then and now believe that we would have elected him but for from one to three traitors in our ranks, who enabled Frank R. Chase to be elected without a vote to spare.

A disappointed Democrat from Newington voted scattering. The election of two senators was the great absorbing object of the Democrats, and to defeat these elections, and keep the senatorial seats vacant till the next year, when the opposition felt sure they could fill them with liberty-loving men, was the great object of the opposition. So intense a strain for so many days I have never since felt. The long-time dominant Democracy, backed by the power of a national Democratic administration and the slave power, with a New Hampshire president, exerted its utmost power of persuasion and other arts in vain. It was one continuous strain. Generally a caucus every night, with a statement of every member's whereabouts. One of our men went home one night, and bidding his dying wife a last good-bye hastened back to vote. Who can look back upon that session and not feel proud of New Hampshire! George W. Nesmith was our manager-in-chief, Daniel Clark our eloquent exhorter, and Mason W. Tappan and others our earnest field marshals. Honored and lamented leaders! Thus by earnest labor were our senatorial seats saved to be filled at the next session by John P. Hale and James Bell. Thirty-eight years have passed since that eventful session, but in all these years no lover of slavery or sympathizer with rebellion has sat in the national senate as a representative of New Hampshire.

Since the advent of our Saviour has there ever been any other thirty-eight years so crowded and crowned with events so momentous and progressive?

J. D. LYMAN.

NEWSPAPER INTERVIEWS.

[From The *Monitor*, July 30, 1892.]

Hon. Sylvester Dana, of this city, was intimately acquainted with the late John P. Hale. He was associated with him politically, and was very close to him in social relations. The invitation upon which the late Mr. Hale visited Concord, and made his famous speech in the Old North church on election day, June 5, 1845, was written by Judge Dana. It was signed by six prominent citizens, who had previously acted with Mr. Hale politically. Large hand-bills were posted in Concord and vicinity, giving notice of the meeting, ending with the prophetic stanza, afterwards so well fulfilled,

"Truth, crushed to earth, shall rise again,
The eternal years of God are hers."

The judge remembers distinctly to have seen Mr. Hale as he entered the church edifice. He was escorted by the late James Peverly, a resident of this city, then a prominent trader here and a very estimable gentleman.

The house was crowded, the legislature having adjourned to allow members to attend. The Whigs had previously held a convention in the building, and the platform erected for the purposes of it still remained. It was from this platform that Hale made his memorable speech. He was not introduced to the audience, but immediately upon his arrival came forward and began his remarks. The newspapers and documents to which he made reference were wrapped in a large red silk handkerchief. He spoke with great earnestness and force, and was greeted with frequent applause. His peroration was especially cheered. He occupied more than two hours, and was listened to throughout with intense attention.

As Judge Dana remembers Mr. Hale on that day, he was a rotund, well-proportioned man, weighing more than two hundred pounds, symmetrically and strongly built; handsome and prepossessing in appearance. He had a smooth-shaved face, and a powerful and persuasive voice. His gestures were graceful and frequent, and he seemed to be thoroughly absorbed in the great issue that he so ably discussed. His subject was the vindication of his vote against the annexation of Texas as a slave state to the Union. Hale took strong ground against such annexation. It was plain from the beginning to the end that Mr. Hale had perfect command of himself, and perfect command of his subject.

When he had concluded his speech, he came down from

the platform and took a seat in a pew immediately in front. Then the late Franklin Pierce, afterward president, ascended the platform and answered Mr. Hale, speaking something over an hour. Pierce, as is well known, was a polished orator, and represented his side of the case as well as any man could do it. He urged all available arguments in justification of the annexation, and criticised Mr. Hale's course severely. When he had concluded, Hale stood upon the seat where he had been sitting, and facing the audience, replied. He spoke perhaps five minutes, his remarks being, as Judge Dana says, the most eloquent that he ever heard fall from human lips. His closing sentence, as Judge Dana remembers it, was as follows: "When filial affection shall erect an humble monument to show where rest my mortal remains, I wish upon it no other epitaph than this: Here lies one who surrendered office, place, and power, rather than bow down and worship slavery."

He had the sympathy of a sincere following, and those who heard him then were not surprised that he should become chief of the great anti-slavery leaders.

Although the meeting was largely attended, there were many people in Concord who were busy on election day, and were unable to hear the great orators, Hale and Pierce, and Mr. Peverly and others thought it desirable that Mr. Hale should visit Concord again when people could have a better opportunity to listen to him. It was arranged that he should be present on the afternoon of the next Thanksgiving day in November. He came then, and delivered an address in the old court house (town hall), which was packed to overflowing. It was a very able speech that he made, and is remembered by many of our citizens.

Hardly had this second meeting closed when Carlos G. Hawthorne, of Hopkinton, sought the statesman, and acquainted him with the fact that arrangements had been made for a meeting in Hopkinton, to be addressed by him that evening. The air was chilly, and Mr. Hale was wet with perspiration from his efforts in the town hall here, but he consented to accompany Mr. Hawthorne, which he did in a'chaise, and addressed a large and intelligent audience in the old Academy hall in Hopkinton village.

The interest in Concord was such that Judge Dana and others chartered a four-horse stage-coach, and attended the meeting there.

His remarks at Hopkinton, Judge Dana says, were in some respects even more impressive than those made at Concord, his speech there dealing more especially with the moral aspects of the great question of human slavery.

[From The *Monitor*, August 2, 1892.]

Hon. Henry P. Rolfe, of this city, now beyond three-score-and-ten, is blessed with a remarkable memory. For many years he was prominent in the practice of his profession, and in the politics of New Hampshire. Associated personally, as he was, with many of the central figures during important epochs in the history of our state, his reminiscences are very valuable. In conversation to-day, he spoke very feelingly on the subject that just now is being revived so pleasantly and profitably, that of the work and worth of the late John P. Hale, whom the splendid statue to be unveiled in the state house park next week is to commemorate. Having paid a tribute to Senator Chandler for his generous appreciation of Mr. Hale, Mr. Rolfe's talk was caught stenographically, and with his permission made available, as follows:

In the latter part of the summer of 1842, during my vacation while fitting for college at New Hampton, I attended court one week at Laconia, then Meredith Bridge. His Honor Judge Tebbetts presided. Hon. Henry Y. Simpson and Hon. Thomas Cogswell were side judges. I had never been in a court room before, and everything that transpired was to me novel. I saw there, for the first time, John Parker Hale, then in the practice of the law in Dover. He was thirty-six years of age, had been United States

district-attorney seven years, having been appointed by
General Jackson in 1834, and afterward removed by President Tyler in 1841. He was the finest appearing man I
ever beheld, about five feet, eleven inches tall, neatly
dressed, of perfect form, hair black and straight, face somewhat florid, and a countenance beaming all over with emotion and expression, and his manners were elegant.

I heard him try several cases before the jury. When the
court was not in session, I kept as near him as I could, to
hear all he said. When he addressed the court his language was refined, and his arguments to the jury could
hardly be resisted. Everything he said, everything he did,
seemed to me to carry an irresistible charm with it. I
heard him say out of court that Judge Tebbetts was the
most perfect exemplar of a trial judge that he had ever seen
upon the bench. He said to him during a trial, where the
judge ruled against him, " Your honor holds the law differently from what I understand it, but I bow with perfect
respect to your honor's decision," at the same time bowing
with a graceful dignity and urbanity which must have delighted the court. It certainly delighted me. He tried a
case before the jury wherein a brother of General Tuttle, of
Meredith, was a party, and there were two witnesses in the
case by the name of Chattel. They testified against his
client's interests, and in his argument he spoke of them in
a most sarcastic way as " these living Chattels."

William C. Clarke was then practising at Meredith
Bridge. He was afterward attorney-general of the state
for several years, possessing as fine a personal appearance
as one would wish to look upon, but Mr. Hale eclipsed him
entirely. The next spring after this Mr. Hale was elected
a member of congress, and in 1844, Polk was elected president, and President Tyler was moving every available force
to annex Texas; and, to the surprise of many, Mr. Hale
opposed the annexation. He served two years as a member
of congress, and when nominated for a second term wrote
his constituents that if they wanted a representative to vote

for the annexation of Texas they must choose another man. Another man was nominated, and Mr. Hale joined issue with the Democracy. He was defeated. Then followed the great contest in New Hampshire which made Hale immortal. The history of that contest is known everywhere, and John P. Hale is known as the gallant political pioneer who first assaulted the bulwarks of American slavery. He went before the people of New Hampshire in the campaign of 1845, and in that of 1846, and won in the last. He was elected a member of the legislature from Dover, speaker of the house, and United States senator for six years from March 4, 1847.

In June, 1845, during the session of the legislature, in the Old North church, came off the contest between him and Gen. Franklin Pierce, the most renowned of any in the country, except that in 1858 between Stephen A. Douglas and Abraham Lincoln.

In the year 1872, being then in Dover on business as United States district-attorney, I was, by Mr. Joshua Varney, in his tailor's shop, introduced to Mr. Hale as one who formerly occupied the office I then held. He was at leisure and so was I, for the afternoon. I referred to the time and the circumstances when I first saw him at Meredith Bridge. He at once became very communicative, told me of his ministry in Spain, his entrance into the United States senate, and other incidents; but the interesting and thrilling part of his conversation was in regard to his meeting in Concord in the Old North church. He had been invited by some one,—Judge Dana, I think,—to come to Concord, and make a speech to vindicate himself. I will tell the story as he told it, as near as I can remember it.

"I had been invited to go to Concord during the session of the legislature and make a speech to the citizens there. I was little acquainted with the people in that vicinity. I knew of George G. Fogg, James Peverly, Jefferson Noyes, Sylvester Dana, and a few others. I accepted the invitation, and when I reached Concord I was met upon the

arrival of the stage coach by Mr. Peverly, Mr. Fogg, and
two or three others. They waited upon me to the house
north of the American House, and put me in a room on the
back side of the house that looked out on a stage stable and
stage yard, and left me, telling me when the time for the
meeting should arrive they would call for me. When the
time for dinner arrived, I was called and went down to dinner, no one speaking to me or seeming to know me. No
one called upon me till the time for the meeting. Then
Mr. Fogg, Mr. Peverly, and Mr. Jefferson Noyes called for
me. When I came out on the street it was still as Sunday,
not a person to be seen except the three men that were
with me, not a carriage anywhere in sight. We walked
along in silence; the gentlemen with me said nothing, and
I said little to them. I was gloomy and despondent, but
kept my thoughts to myself. As we turned around the
corner of the old Fiske store, and I looked up and saw the
crowd at the doors of the old church surging to get in, the
people above and below hanging out of the windows, first a
great weight of responsibility oppressed me, and in a
moment more an inspiration came upon me, as mysterious as
the emotions of the new birth. I walked into the densely
crowded house as calm and collected and self-assured as it
was possible for a man to be. I felt that the only thing I
then wanted—an opportunity—had come, and I soon gathered that great crowd into my arms, and swayed it about as
the gentle winds do the fields of ripening grain. That
inspiration never for a moment left me. It followed me
over the state, during the ensuing campaign, into the senate
of the United States, remained with me there, and subsided only when the proclamation of President Lincoln
declared that in this land the sun should rise upon no bondman and set upon no slave; and now when I turn my eyes
heavenward, I can in imagination see hanging out from the
battlements of Heaven the broken shackles of four millions
of slaves, which for nearly twenty years I did all in my
power to rend.

" When I entered the senate I supposed every man's hand would be against me, but I very soon found a friend in Thomas H. Benton. I was one day speaking in the senate on a subject I was not so familiar with as I ought to have been, when one of the pages handed me a note. I looked at it and found it was from Mr. Benton, containing just the important information I needed, and ever after this when I was speaking he would watch me, and if he thought I needed any facts he would come behind me and post me up, or send the information on a slip of paper which a page would place on the desk before me ; and what is most singular, I never knew him to make a mistake, and I relied upon him as confidently as though I were reading it out of a book."

In 1851, Mr. Hale and Richard H. Dana, Jr., were counsel for the men who were tried for the rescue of Shadrach, a fugitive slave in Boston. He was taken from the United States marshal and his posse, carried to a place of safety, and finally transported on the underground railroad to Canada. Mr. Hale and Mr. Dana made an able and tenacious defence, and no convictions were obtained. Several years after, during the war, Mr. Dana was in one of the rural towns near Boston, when a gentleman accosted him with much cordiality, saying, " How do you do, Mr. Dana ? " Mr. Dana returned the salutation with much civility, and said to him, " Sir, you have the advantage of me. I think I have met you somewhere before ; your face is somewhat familiar, but I cannot 'recall your name." " It is not strange," the gentleman replied, " for I do not think that I have met you since you and Mr. Hale defended the rescuers of Shadrach, the fugitive slave. My name is Mr. Blank. I was a member of the jury who tried them." " Indeed," said Mr. Dana, " I am delighted to see you." " I think," said the gentleman, " I never saw two gentlemen more anxious than you and Mr. Hale were about the safety of your clients." " Certainly we were," replied Mr. Dana. " But," said the gentleman, " I did not feel the least

anxiety in the world. I saw from the beginning that there
was no danger of your clients' conviction." "Why not?"
said Mr. Dana. "Because," said the gentleman, "I was the
man who took Shadrach at the door of the court house, put
him into a cab, and took him to a place of safety at Mr.
Blank's in old Concord, and I concluded from the beginning
of the trial that there was no danger of those other fellows
being convicted while I was on the jury."

This story was told to me by Hon. Albert R. Hatch, of
Portsmouth, and in 1886 I told the story to Judge Gray at
Boston, and he confirmed the truth of it, for he said he had
repeatedly heard Mr. Dana himself tell the story·substan-
tially as I have told it.

___

As Mr. Parker Pillsbury, of this city, one of the very
foremost of the anti-slavery leaders, stopped a moment to
look deferentially at the Hale statue as it was being put in
position, his mind must have filled with memories of that
important epoch in our national history in which he himself was so intensely interested and took so active a part.
He sacrificed almost everything to the cause of freedom,
and among the able lecturers who canvassed the country
there was no more vigorous thinker, more forcible writer,
or more devout devotee to the interests of humanity.

Mr. Pillsbury is comparatively little known to the rising
generation, but he was one of the foremost characters in
the great American crisis wherein Mr. Hale figured so con-
spicuously. Mr. Pillsbury admired him, and respected him,
and loved him, and as he stood there gazing upon the granite and the bronze that are to perpetuate his honor, he
seemed absorbed in deep and tender thoughts.

This remarkable man was found soon afterward in his
scholarly, well-conned library, at his home on School street,
this city. Over his head, as the modest minister, editor,
lecturer, and statesman sat there, hung an excellent portrait
of Wendell Phillips. On one side was a copy of the famous

engraving entitled "Waiting for the Hour," representing the affecting scene of slaves gathered together, one of their number holding a watch, anxiously waiting for the minute to come when by the emancipation proclamation of President Lincoln they were to be free.

Not far from it hung a printed advertising poster, characteristic of the days when human beings were subjects of barter and sale and every-day traffic. It reads as follows :

RAFFLE.

Mr. Joseph Jennings respectfully informs his friends and the public that at the request of many acquaintances he has been induced to purchase from Mr. Osborne, of Missouri, the celebrated dark bay horse, " Star," aged 5 years, square trotter and warranted sound ; with a new light trotting buggy and harness ; also the dark, stout mulatto girl "Sarah," aged about 20 years, general house servant, valued at $900, and guaranteed, and will be raffled for at 4 o'clock p. m., Feb. 1st, at the selection hotel of the subscribers.

The above is as represented, and those persons who may wish to engage in the usual practice of raffling, will, I assure them, be perfectly satisfied with their destiny in this offer.

The whole is valued at just what it is worth ; $1,500 ; 1500 chances at one dollar each.

The raffle will be conducted by gentlemen selected by interested persons. Five days will be allowed to complete the raffle. Both of the above described can be seen at my store, No. 78 Common street (New Orleans), second door from Camp, at from 9 o'clock a. m. to 2 p. m.

First throw to take the first choice ; last throw remaining prize ; and the fortunate winners will pay $20 each for the refreshments furnished on the occasion.

P. S. No chances recognized unless paid for previous to the commencement.

JOSEPH JENNINGS.

Mr. Pillsbury said :

" I came into the movement in 1840, just at the time when the country was agitated with Texas. When the annexation of Texas came before congress, Mr. Hale was the only Democrat who voted against it. I was in the whirl, and Nathaniel P. Rogers, editor of the *Herald of*

Freedom, had been before that time, and there was a dissatisfaction between him and some of the society, and he dropped the paper, so I had to pick it up out of the mud and dust, and carry it on. I remember very well Mr. Hale's course and position. I was editing the paper at the time, and lecturing a great deal besides, and he was rather our text, and I kept him before the people all I possibly could.

"Of course there was a fragment of the Whig party in New Hampshire, and they saw their opportunity, and were pretty friendly to us, and so we had the support of New Hampshire, which had been almost unanimously Democratic. We three, Stephen S. Foster, the editor, Nathaniel P. Rogers, and myself, were all of us Non-Resistants from principle, and the other two, Rogers and Foster, officers of the Non-Resistant society. We were all of us non-voters from principle, and we said, and we had reason to say, that the reign of Democracy was nearing its end in the state. I have no hesitation in saying that we three, non-voters though we were, undoubtedly had much more to do with the changing of the politics than any other three persons in it. In four years we had shaken the state pretty clean of that kind of Democracy, and John P. Hale was sent to the senate and kept there eighteen years, whereas, he was only in the house as a Democrat when they cast him out.

"At that time I wrote him a letter. He was then in Washington. I told him that his course would be approved by the people of New Hampshire, and that I had been over the state so far, and understood so well the feeling, that I felt warranted in saying to him that he would be sustained, and I hoped he would not falter. It happened that just then the Hutchinson family, who were famous singers, were in Washington giving concerts, and he invited them to dinner, and read them this letter as part of the entertainment. They were greatly pleased with it, 'For,' said they, 'we, too, are in the state and among the people of New Hampshire, and we know as well as he.' That, perhaps, is the best incident I can think of, for I was editing and lecturing both, and running wherever there was a chance to have anything done. In that letter you got pretty much my whole temper and spirit. I wanted to give him a full view of it, and he deemed it of sufficient consequence in inviting them there to dinner to read it as a part of the dessert, and they were very much pleased with it.

"I was not here when he made his speech. I began in 1840 on my mission of anti-slavery, and I never left off until the last slave was free. I do not remember ever to have had a conversation with Mr. Hale in my life. My wife once had a little correspondence with him on account of the Woman's Anti-Slavery society.

"I have n't any recollections of Mr. Hale that would be worthy your noticing, only that whenever I had an opportunity of hearing him, I improved it. I heard him in Massachusetts in two or three places, but never here. He stumped the country a great deal with very good success. The slaveholders could never get angry with him. They got angry with Charles Sumner, and tried to kill him, but Hale always kept them good-natured. He was a good deal like Tom B. Reed. Hale had that same vein of humor, rather cold, but always keen and effective. But I had personal acquaintance with hardly any of the public men and grandees. I had two years and a half in England, or at least in Europe. I did accidentally once meet the queen, and called on the lord chancellor of Ireland, and had a fine interview with him."

It was a very pleasant call that the writer had upon Mr. Pillsbury at his home, and the pleasure was heightened not a little when Mrs. Pillsbury, a very estimable lady, who has done much for charity, came forward with kindly greeting and to express her interest in the unveiling of the statue of Mr. Hale. She said :

"An anti-slavery society was formed by a few of the women of Concord in the year 1838. It was called the Woman's Anti-Slavery society. It was a very unpopular

society. Only those who had rare moral courage felt as
though they could belong to it. We used to have our meet-
ings around at the houses of the different women. Occasionally we would have an anti-slavery fair or sale on a very
small scale, to raise money to help send slaves to Canada,
and help carry on the anti-slavery paper, the *Herald of
Freedom*. We used to have colored people in the house,
sometimes three days at a time, until we could get them
away in the night to another place further toward Canada.

"There were not many members of our society, for few
dared to belong to it. The only members now living in
Concord are Mrs. Amos Wood, Mrs. Nathaniel White, and
myself. Some of the other members were Mrs. N. P.
Rogers, Mrs. Mary Ann French, Mrs. John D. Norton,
Mrs. Joseph G. Wyatt, Mrs. Esther Currier, Mrs. Enoch
Perkins, Mrs. Elbridge Chase, and Mrs. Mary Ann Allison.

"The society was in existence from 1838 to 1844. It
was about the time the society was formed that we were
talking of the annexation of Texas to the Union, and Mr.
Hale lost his seat in the house. As I was secretary of the
society, they thought I ought to write a letter to Mr. Hale
telling him how much we indorsed his course; and I addressed him in this way. I said: The women of Concord's
anti-slavery society wish me to write you, thus and so.
He replied in an autograph letter. He said he was gratified to receive the letter, very much gratified, but first of
all he wished to say how much more gratifying it was to
receive a letter of that import from women than from ladies,
for, he said, 'In my experience thus far with the world, I
have found that there is this difference,—God made women;
dancing-masters and milliners made ladies.'

"When this letter came to me I opened and read it, and
laid it in the record book of the society. I tied it between
the pages and left it. Some one took my place as secretary,
and book and all were lost. In after years when he called
to see us in Concord, he would almost always make allusion
to that letter, for he said it was the only one he ever

received wherein the writers wrote as women. He said it took women in those days to work for the slaves. As I wrote him in that letter I said something like this,—"We are all in sympathy with you in this work that you have done, and were we allowed to vote, how zealously we should all vote that you should retain your place."

FUNERAL CEREMONIES.

[From a contemporaneous publication.]

The death of Hon. John P. Hale, the distinguished and eloquent champion of liberty, took place Wednesday evening, November 19, 1873, after more than three years of serious illness and suffering. The record of his life is full of honor and heroism, and his noble services in behalf of the oppressed will never be forgotten, but will illumine the pages of American history with glorious lustre.

The city of Dover made appropriate and sincere observation of the sad funeral occasion, Saturday, November 22. Business was generally suspended, and large numbers of people from surrounding places, and many from various sections of New England, were present. An almost Sabbath stillness reigned in the stricken city. Bunting draped in mourning was displayed at half mast, and at various places, and the bells tolled their solemn requiem as the ceremonies were in progress.

At 1.30 p. m. family prayers were held at the late residence of the deceased on Pleasant street, and the remains were then taken to the Unitarian church on Locust street, Rev. Thomas W. Brown, pastor. The church was filled with sorrowing people, long before the services began, including many distinguished persons from this and other states. The pulpit was draped in black and bore a floral tribute. At the foot of the casket was a cross of white roses with trailing smilax; at the head, a very large crown of the same surmounted by a floral cross, and encircling the

12

plate a beautiful wreath. The plate was inscribed, " John Parker Hale, aged 67 years."

The services were deeply impressive, and were conducted by Rev. Thomas W. Brown, pastor, assisted by Rev. John Parkman, of Boston, in former years pastor of the church and a personal friend of the deceased. The opening service was a chant by the choir, followed by selections from the Scriptures.

Rev. Mr. Brown then delivered the funeral address, referring in an appropriate manner to the greatness of soul, the thrilling eloquence, the championship of the rights of the oppressed, the deep religious character of the deceased statesman, and closing with the words :

> " And now he rests; his greatness and his sweetness
>   No more shall seem at strife ;
> And death has moulded into calm completeness
>   The statue of his life."

Rev. John Parkman then gave some touching reminiscences of his acquaintance with the deceased, thirty years ago, showing the lofty character and nobility of soul of Mr. Hale, and referred to his firm religious faith.

The closing services were prayer by the pastor and a hymn sung by the choir. The remains were then taken in solemn procession to Pine Hill cemetery, which spot the deceased loved to visit and view the beautiful scenery it affords.

The committal service was there performed by Rev. Thomas R. Lambert, D. D., of Charlestown, Mass., of St. John's (Episcopal) church, a brother-in-law of the deceased.

The pall bearers were Hon. E. A. Straw (governor), Hon. Walker Harriman, Judge Daniel Clark, Gen. Gilman Marston, Hon. George G. Fogg, Hon. Mason W. Tappan, Hon. E. H. Rollins, Hon. James Pike, Hon. Charles H. Horton (mayor), Hon. John H. White, Hon. Oliver Wyatt, and Benjamin Barnes, Esq.

MEMORIAL SERVICES.

At the Unitarian church, Sunday morning, November 23, memorial services were held in honor of the late Hon. John P. Hale. The attendance was very large, including friends from all denominations.

The usual services were given, the selections by the pastor and choir being appropriate and with especial reference to the occasion.

[FROM A SERMON BY REV. THOMAS W. BROWN.]

*   *   *   *   *   *   *   *   *   *

"Faithful unto Death."—*Revelation* 2: 10. I think that they who are accustomed to judge our friend's life (and perhaps of the motives of that life) by its successes instead of its sacrifices, are at fault in so doing. The successes came, indeed, as the divine Providence that guides the world, and its destiny sometimes permits such triumphs to follow upon human endeavor and righteous service. But the successes came, not without long waiting, and many, many dark days and deeds of sacrifice. Said one, who was not in political affinity with our departed friend, and whose testimony is therefore of the more value, "When Mr. Hale took his seat in the senate, he was almost alone, and had to combat, single-handed, against the political giants of those days. Sometimes he was met with labored arguments, and again by bitter reproaches. Sometimes those who were his peers would affect to ignore him, and again they would mercilessly denounce him, as advancing doctrines dangerous to the Republic. But he was not to be silenced, or intimidated, in the discharge of what he believed to be his duty. So high were his aims, and so conciliatory his manners, that before the close of his senatorial term he had beaten down the barriers of opposition and fairly conquered. *   * He was thus not only the standard-bearer, but the pioneer of the North, in the senate."

And all this is true. But who of us shall tell, who of us

can even conceive, the immense cost at which all this well-earned triumph was achieved? The alienations of old friends; the unjust 'suspicion of motives; the bitter sarcasms heaped upon his conscientiously avowed principles and purposes; the loneliness of a position which left him, for a time, in a kind of banishment, and under party proscription; the fierce fightings with temptations to yield, where to yield was treason to the right; and the long, long catalogue of self-denials and self-sacrifices and resistances to the sophistry of self-seeking, in order to be the great and noble soul he was; and, if it be true, as doubtless it is, that one who now stands foremost in that national chamber in which our departed friend won laurels which shall never fade,—but which reverent hands shall ever twine freshly about his venerated memory,—if it be true, I say, that such an one exclaimed, " Ah, Mr. Hale has said wiser, and done better, things than we all," is it not because he who is thus so justly eulogized *won* his robes of glory and honor through much patiently endured mental tribulation?

If, now, we analyze this greatness of his, this *genuine* heroism which compelled, in spite of themselves, the admiration, even of his political adversaries, we shall find it, I think, to be very largely of a moral character. Even of intellectual power, indeed, it is easy enough to see that he was a remarkable possessor; and if the question were one of daring merely, of the bare courage to *say* bold and startling things in his place in congress, few could equal him. But there was something beside and better than these, something as far above and beyond these as heaven is above and beyond the earth on which we dwell; and this was his moral fearlessness. Indeed, it would almost seem as if he scarcely knew the meaning of the word fear. He must have known his danger. His friends at least knew of it, and had many fears for him. How could they help it? How could he help it? Yet he never took so much as the slightest precaution against such danger. Others went armed, about the streets of the capital and into its perilous

suburbs; and some of *these*, even, were attacked and assaulted. But he, without a single weapon, without a single
apparent feeling of the need of one, went everywhere and
anywhere, alone and unguarded. We read to-day with
a smile the threats which were fulminated against his life
and safety. But they were no idle threats then; and still,
walking in his integrity, panoplied by his *mens sibi conscia
recti*, he was without fear as he was without reproach.
Sullen looks, harsh threats, bitter invectives glanced off
from his armor of proof, and left him as undismayed as he
was unharmed by them.

And this was the courage, not simply of the martial hero
but of the Christian hero; not the mere daring of reckless-
ness or passion, but of lofty principle. He knew himself to
be right; and thus to be on the side of Him who has
pledged His Almighty power to the defense of the right.
He knew, too, that the life or safety of man—of *any* man—
was of less consequence to the world and the truth than
fidelity to duty and consecration to principle; and *this* is
why he was fearless; this is why, like a great apostle of
the olden time, whose life he must often have studied, and
whose fearless devotion to duty he so frequently emulated,
he did not count his life, even, dear unto him, if so that
he might win the right and the true.

* * * * * * * * * *

But what was the occasion, what the inspiration, of our
friend's courage? It was this: To set at defiance all the
promptings of interest, and dare all the dangers of enmity,
in behalf of the oppressed, the down-trodden, and the
despised; to stoop to lift up a mere chattel, that he might
transmute it into a man! And then, as if this were not
enough,—as if his great heart were large enough, as it was,
—to take in the needs of a people more numerous than the
enslaved, he reaches out his hand in deprecation, and lifts
up his strong voice in rebuke of that barbarous, that brutal
custom,—since abolished through his instrumentality—of
plying the cruel lash upon the bare backs of the seamen in

our national ships. Could courage be sublimer than this, friends ? And yet, this was the courage which dwelt in the heart, this the temper that glorified the life, and will immortalize the memory, of him whom to-day we miss from among men. And is it not the pure instinct of justice, as well as of admiration, which prompts us to exclaim,

> " Thanks, for the good man's beautiful example,
>   Who in the vilest saw
>   Some sacred crypt, or altar of a temple
>   Still vocal with God's law."

How conspicuous an element, too, in our friend's greatness, how largely contributive to the rich completeness of his character, was his wondrous self-control! There was power in him, as we all know, fit to crush and wither at will; and there must have been times, when to use that power, and perhaps to abuse it, must have been one of the strongest of temptations. But did any one ever know him to do this? No man, I think, was likely to have had stronger feelings than he, or more fierce uprisings of that nature in us, that leads to passionate, or at least to petulant, outbreak into sharp speech. No man, too, could have been more outraged in his better nature, not only at the sight of the wrongs which were countenanced, but at the wrong-doings that were excused and approved by law or long established custom. And then there were the personal taunts to which he was at times subjected, and the sarcastic allusions to professed principles, and the domineering spirit of opposition to his views, and the thousand things beside, which were calculated to aggravate and annoy any man. But while these things must have sometimes provoked him to indignation, and indignant protest, and dignified self-assertion, yet I recall not a single instance in which he actually lost temper, or fell into passionate recrimination over them. Instead of this, his apparently imperturbable good humor, his conquering pleasantry, his witty retort, his manly dignity, and equipoise of temper were only made the more conspicuous by such instances and experiences. Of course I do not claim that he was perfect. No man that lives is that. But I do mean to say, that whatever may have been the inward struggle, and the undetected strife within his breast, he appears always to have been the victor. Nay, he often even disarmed opposition, and turned strife into silence, and passion into peace and friendliness, by the very contagion of his own inexhaustible good humor. And if it be true, as the Scripture alleges, that "he that is slow to anger is better than the mighty, and he that ruleth his spirit than he that taketh a city," then he whom we to-day mourn was even mightier than many who wear the laurels of chivalrous conquest, gained upon some battle-field of worldly strife.

But, co-existing with this dignity and equableness of temper of which I have just spoken, enriching and glorifying it, as well as all beside in his character—was his Christian faith; his trust, pure and unshaken, in the great God, who guides and governs all things. I am not aware, indeed, that he had much to say about this Christian faith. Least of all, is he likely to have been one who would ever boast about it, or parade it before the gaze of others. That was not like him at all. But that he was filled and fired with it, I cannot see how any man who knew him can well doubt. In fact, his entire life is the sufficient evidence of this. What was that life, indeed, except a giving forth of itself for the good of others; a deep and long devotion and fidelity to the advocacy and advancement of causes and interests, which, at the outset at least, seemed calculated to meet only with failure? And *could he have lived* such a life, could he have endured such wearying opposition and self-denial in the way of duty-bearing, except as he was sustained and nourished by a devout faith in God and the right?

He lived, it is true—and in this respect he was far more favored than are the majority of the great workers for humanity—he lived to see all, and more than all he had anticipated and hoped for, splendidly achieved. But in the helping to bring it all to pass, what discouragement and deferred hope ; what slow progress and persistent encounter of opposition ; what liability to misapprehension on the part of others, and half distrust of one's self, perchance! What a perpetual challenge to one's patience, too, and what a seemingly unending demand for effort and struggle! Yet he proved equal to it all.   Not because he had faith in himself simply—which every good man ought to have ; not because he trusted in others merely, or in the final triumph of abstract principle ; but because he trusted in God, and leaned upon the arm which is Almighty.   He himself might perish in the contest.   All others might.   But the right, and the true, and the good, must survive and succeed, though the heavens themselves fell.   "Time and myself" is said to have been the motto of one of the old Spanish kings, "time and myself against the world."   "God and myself" seems to have been the motto of our departed friend, "God and myself against a whole universe of evil and wrong."   And this faith of his conquered ; as all such faith in the Highest eventually must, by whomsoever cherished.

But he is dead, alas! this noble defender of the right, this champion of freedom, philanthropy, and human rights! *Dead!* did I say?   Nay, he has but just begun, in the highest sense, to live.   Lives like his,—noble and Christian careers of usefulness and godly service, do not end at the gate-way of the grave.   They cannot.   There, on the contrary, they commence to put on immortality ; not alone the immortality of heaven, but that of earth.   Dying, such men yet live.   Passing on and up, they do but become the more imperishable possessors of the earth, which they have enriched by their noble service.   Their influence, their memories, the inextinguishable grace of a something in them, which death only transfigures into a more enduring substance, these all survive.   Like the fragrance of flowers, which goes out into the air even when the flowers themselves are crushed, or when they droop and die at the touch of some sudden blight—so the aroma of a good life sends out an incense of spiritual fragrance into the atmosphere of men's lives, which abides, and enriches, and influences long after the career of the departed has become little else but a memory.

It is related of one of the early chieftains of a Scottish clan, that as he fell one day mortally wounded upon the field of battle, bleeding and gasping, his followers seemed ready to give way. All was lost, they thought, if he were to perish. But just then the glance of the expiring hero fell upon their wavering ranks, and, dying though he was, the spirit of a hundred heroes still burned in his heart. Raising himself heavily and most painfully upon his elbow, and looking undauntedly and gloriously out upon his wavering band through the gathering mists of death, he exclaimed, "My children! My children! I am not dead; I am only looking on, to see that you do your duty."

So with the honored friend and leader who has just gone before us, and upon whose placid, peaceful countenance—typical of the undying peace into which he has entered—we looked for the last time yesterday. "Only looking on" upon us is he, "to see that we do *our* duty," as *he* so grandly did his. Looking on upon us, out of his grand and completed life of duty, and from his exalted seat in heaven; looking on, too, to shame our shortcoming and wavering, and to stimulate our faith and steadfastness. And as we remember, that

> "Round his grave are quietude and beauty;
> And the sweet Heaven above,
> The fitting symbols of a life of duty,
> Transfigured into love!"

let us remember, too, that this quietude, and beauty, and sweetness of peace, are to be our inspiration as well as our comfort, our quickening in the way of duty as well as our confirmation in the trust of that life everlasting, upon which he himself has so triumphantly entered.

[From a Sermon by Rev. George B. Spaulding.]

The following extracts are from a discourse commemorative of the character and career of Hon. John Parker Hale, delivered in the First Parish church, Dover, N. H., on Thanksgiving day, November 27, 1873, by the Rev. George B. Spaulding:

Let us, as best we may, bring back before us the character and career of our illustrious townsman,—the brilliant lawyer, the fearless, indomitable public leader, the untarnished senator, the true brother and champion of his entire race, John Parker Hale.

The first glimpse which I catch of him is full of pathos, and is most significant. In his early boyhood he lost his father, a parent tenderly loved and revered. It is said, by neighbors who sympathized with the boy in his early sorrows, that for a long time he was wont to go forth at early morning hour, or in the solemn evening twilight, and kneel down by the father's grave to pray. The figure of that kneeling boy, in that rude graveyard, is the most fixed and prominent recollection which some have of him whom we honor to-day.

If I know anything of New England character and of the power of New England training, I know that both have from the first been so distinctly religious that most of our great men have had their natures permeated with great religious sentiments and principles. I think of John Adams, taught in his infancy to repeat the prayer which he never after forgot to utter to the close of his magnificent career, "Now I lay me down to sleep;" I think of Webster, who, according to his own words, was taught to lisp at his mother's feet and on his father's knee, texts from the Scripture; I think of this young boy, easing his breaking heart in prayers to God over his father's grave; and I see how it was that one and all of them in all after life, despite all their mistakes, despite, it may be, the absence of an open and professed piety, manifested the presence and power in them of a profoundly religious nature. In this I find the key to their characters. In this I see an explanation of that deep moral earnestness, that solemnity and grandeur, which came out in all their great speech and action.

* * * * .* * * * * *

Mr. Hale was preëminently an advocate. His real place was before a jury. He understood law,—but its great principles rather than its technicalities. And these first he had mastered, not by close, severe study, but by a kind of intuitive insight, coupled with a quick, retentive memory, which treasured up for his ready use decisions and arguments to which he had once listened, or of which he had once cursorily read. As he stood up before the jury, not drilled to his task by painstaking care, but inspired by the occasion, by the very faces which confronted him, with his large, generous form, his free, open gestures, all lighted with a soul that was earnest with conviction, with words singularly facile, but terse and full of force, holding his flashing lance straight and steadily to the one point in the case, and driving it home with his splendid bursts of feeling, he was well-nigh irresistible. He was full of imagination, but his imagery never blunted the edge of his blade, nor impeded the vigor of his blow. His speech was like an eastern scimitar, bright and dazzling, and yet keen in edge, cutting to the marrow.

Let me give you an instance : It was during one of those famous trials growing out of the rescue of the slave Shadrach at Boston. Mr. Hale had read from the reports numerous decisions to the effect that slavery is against the laws of God, the law of nature, and the laws of England and Massachusetts. He also read from the laws of Virginia and other southern states to show that a person of Shadrach's color (not a negro) is even there presumed to be free, and cannot be proved a slave except by evidence of descent from an African slave-mother, and that possession and holding of a slave did not afford a presumption of slavery. He then said, "Now, gentlemen, it appears that there is no slavery by the law of England, by the law of Massachusetts, by the law of nature ; and these old judges say,—mind, your excellency, I do not say this; it would be treason ; so unequivocal a recognition of the higher law would be treason in me,—but these old judges say that it is against the law of God ! Against all these laws, against all this evidence, against all these presumptions, comes one John Debree from Norfolk, Va., and says that he owns him ! This is all the evidence. The mere breath of the slave-catcher's mouth turns a man into another man's chattel ! Suppose John Debree had said that he owned the moon, or the stars, or had an exclusive right to the sunshine, would you find it so by your verdict? But, gentlemen, the stars shall fade and fall from heaven ; the moon shall grow old and decay ; and heavens themselves shall pass away as a scroll,—but the soul of the despised and hunted Shadrach shall live on with the life of God himself! I wonder if John DeBree will say that he owns him then ! "

It is said that neither court nor marshals could check the long and tumultuous applause which followed. Here is finest wit and genuine humor, and vivid, bold imagination, and most felicitous language ; but under all, like an organ's peal, we hear the solemn movement of a profoundly earnest soul.

I think that, as we follow the man on in his great career, and note those passages which have been and always will be treasured up as specimens of masterly power and eloquence, we shall find that they, one and all, were spoken when his moral nature was most deeply stirred, when his soul quivered with a sense of God and his eternal and immutable truths.

*   *   *   *   *   *   *   *   *   *

At the closing session of the twenty-eighth congress, a resolution was introduced, under the stimulus of President Tyler's message, for the annexation of Texas as a slave state. It was not a measure of the Democratic party ; it was, rather, a personal scheme of the president's. It was

denounced by prominent Democratic congressmen; and I
think that the testimony of the party in this state was, for
a time at least, straight against it. Mr. Hale put himself
on record, by speech, resolution, and ballot, as opposed to
the measure. He was not long in discovering that his position was not approved at home; and, further on, he came
to see that his continued opposition to the annexation
would prove his political death-warrant. He was at this
time the nominee of his party for re-election; but he knew
that his votes and action on this measure would result in
his being finally repudiated by his political friends. Still,
he wavered not. Rather, he went forward and forestalled
his doom by writing a letter, addressed to his constituents, in
which he declared that the reasons given by the advocates
of the annexation scheme "were eminently worthy to provoke the scorn of earth and the judgment of Heaven."
In the convention of his party, which immediately followed,
Mr. Hale's name was struck from the ticket by a unanimous
vote. Mr. Hale then began to make those appeals to the
people, in which the powers of his peculiar and versatile eloquence had full play. He spoke before crowded audiences
in great halls, or to the few who gathered in school-houses,
or in the open air, to listen to his impassioned vindications.
The meeting in the Old North church, at Concord, will
never be forgotten. Mr. Hale went there an object of bitter hatred to his old friends, not accepted by the other
great party,—alone. In that speech in the church, in the
presence of an excited, crowded audience, his voice attuned
to the promptings of his deepest convictions, rang out those
ever memorable words,—"I expected to be called ambitious, to have my name cast out as evil, to be traduced and
misrepresented. I have not been disappointed, but if
things have come to this condition, that conscience and a
sacred regard for truth and duty are to be publicly held up
to ridicule and scouted at without rebuke, as has just been
done here, it matters little whether we are annexed to
Texas, or Texas is annexed to us. I may be permitted to

say that the measure of my ambition will be full, if, when my earthly career shall be finished, and my bones are laid beneath the soil of New Hampshire, and my wife and children shall repair to my grave to drop the tear of affection to my memory, they may read on my tombstone, 'He who lies beneath surrendered office and place and power, rather than bow down and worship slavery.'" I think that the bitterest political opponent who to-day survives Mr. Hale must admire his lofty, intrepid spirit, as thus manifested; concede his perfect honesty, and confess that, now, as he sleeps beneath New Hampshire soil, after nearly thirty years of fearless and persistent opposition to a great wrong, he may fairly claim the proud epitaph which he once craved.

* * * * * * * * * *

James Otis and Patrick Henry were the evangels of our American liberty. Theirs were the voices which were heard ringing in the wilderness. They did a work as mighty as that of Washington and Adams, whose genius·it was to organize the forces which these others had called into life; to put them into serried columns on the field of battle, and construct them into the union of states and the constitution of a great nation. Mr. Hale was the Patrick Henry of our Revolutionary age. His clarion voice, wherever heard,—in the congressional hall, or from the platform,—electrified the people, and challenged them, for twenty long years, to a deeper and deeper indignation against the great wrong of the nation. His speeches in the senate chamber were meant for other ears than grave and reverend senators. They were not carefully prepared orations. They were not for the elucidation of some perplexing subject of finance. They were brief, witty, scathing replies, or magnificent bursts of feeling and righteous wrath, or jocose allusions and illustrations, under the fun and laughter of which the keen blade glittered, or solemn, prophetic warning and appeal,—all these, from first to last, bearing upon the one great evil, and all addressed to that vast, to him ever visible, audience, which, in all the cities and villages and in every hamlet of the North and West, were listening,—some in rage and some in fervid sympathy—but all listening with profound interest to the words which leaped from his lips.

And how skilfully Heaven fitted its chosen instrument for this great, perilous work. It was wonderful. Other congressmen spoke in opposition to slavery, and then became silent through fear. Others only evoked an answering wrath, which took from their arguments half their power. But here was one who stood, through the battle of twenty years, the most conspicuous knight of them all, striking with the heavy and lightning stroke of a Cœur de Lion, but with such good heartiness, such imperturbable temper, such rollicking fun, in the wild medley of the great fight, that his enemies fell back to pay homage to his magnanimity, his courage, his genuine feeling, his irresistible, large fellowship and good nature.

I remember when, in 1858, I was acting as a reporter in a southern commercial convention in Savannah, where Yancey and Rhett and Barnwell and DeBow, and other fiery sons of the South, poured out in red-hot invective and abuse their hatred of northern men,—I remember of hearing them speak of " Jack Hale," as they and you loved to call him, as a "prince of good fellows." In an after-sojourn of a year in the South, mingling with the great southern leaders, just on the eve of those great events which broke upon us, when men's minds were infuriated with hatred of the North, I do not recall that I ever heard from any of these men any word which indicated a bitter feeling against Mr. Hale.

Now, such a man, one who could hold his place and yet all the time be true to it, faithful and yet courteous, speaking the severest truth with such an inimitable grace of soul that his foes must needs join in admiration of it,—such a man, my friends, is not born in centuries. It was our happiest fortune that Heaven sent him into our age and into the awful crisis of our affairs. One less courageous than he

would have failed us. One less amiable and good-hearted
would have been useless.

*   *   *   *   *   *   *   *   *   *

With his private life, with the charms of his personal
character, you are all familiar. His sweetest and most
attractive trait was his love of nature. He loved the great
hill-tops where he could see village and hamlet, plain and
forest, and the horizon stretching away into its infinitude.
He loved the ocean, and would sit for hours entranced by its
ever-varying sights and sounds. He loved especially the
hillside where he now lies, and from it he was wont many
and many times to gaze in mute rapture upon the sun sink-
ing into the western heavens. He loved his old ways and
old places. He was full of the simplicities of nature,—childlike, sportive, notional, hearty, always natural. And for it
all you loved him with a rare fondness and pride. No party
prejudice kept your hearts from him. When he came back
from his foreign mission, his old political opponents vied
with his strong party friends to bid him warmest welcome.
In his sickness and sad infirmities, your pities and prayers
mingled. And when at last God had called him, and you
went forth to bear him to his loved and longed-for resting-
place, without thought of party differences, you, with tears
and tenderness, laid him with his mother earth.

He must have been a rare man to have thus won your
hearts,—rare in the qualities of his social nature and the
sweetness of his character, as well as in his splendid intellectual capacities, his keen, broad mind, his intuitive insight,
his fervid imagination, and eloquent speech. Already we
yearn to honor him with the full meed of his honor, but
that cannot be. The smoke and dust of a tremendous conflict still cover the field. We, and he who moved so grandly
in it, are not to be seen in due clearness and proportion, but
the day is coming when the mist shall have cleared away,
and all will stand forth in the revealing light of history in
their true place and stature. When that day comes, among
the greatest who wrought with equal skill and force to lift

man into higher dignity and knit the race into closer brotherhood, and who taught succeeding generations the solemn,
inspiring lesson of loyalty to God and right, will be seen, in
all the loftiness of his full stature, him whom to-day we
honor—John Parker Hale.

NEWSPAPER EXTRACTS.

[From The *Journal*, Augusta, Me., August 3, 1892.]

To-morrow the statue of John P. Hale, which has been
erected in the Capitol park, Concord, N. H., by the munifi-
cence of his son-in-law, Hon. W. E. Chandler of the United
States senate, will be publicly presented to the people of
New Hampshire and dedicated with appropriate exercises.
The honor to be thus paid to the memory of this incorruptible statesman is well deserved, for in the contest over
slavery which ended with the freedom of the slave, he was a
brave and fearless leader. As all readers of American history know, the Free Soil movement, which led to the Rebellion and the proclamation of emancipation of President
Lincoln, began in the American congress over the passage of
the resolutions providing for the annexation of Texas, without recourse to the treaty-making power, the vote on which
was had in the house of representatives on the 25th of
January, 1845. The Democratic party, which had just
elected James K. Polk president, made the support of these
resolutions the test of party fealty. Of the ninety-eight
negative votes but twenty-eight were cast by those classed
as Democrats, all of whom were from the free states. One
of these twenty-eight was John P. Hale, of New Hampshire, then serving his first term in the house.

He was in his thirty-ninth year, and had only recently
been nominated by the Democrats of his district for re-
election. For his disobedience to the orders of the slave
power, the party leaders in New Hampshire determined to
discipline him, but they never made a more fatal party

13

blunder.   He was denounced as. a traitor to his party, a
new convention was called and another candidate nominated, the result of' the election being that there was no
choice, and for the next two years the district was unrepresented in congress.   The next year, 1846, Hale was elected
to the New Hampshire legislature by his Dover friends, was
elected speaker, and then United States senator for the full
term of six years, as an anti-slavery man, and in December,
1847, he entered the United States senate, the first distinctively anti-slavery member of that body.   He thus became
the recognized leader of the Free Soilers throughout the
country.   He would doubtless have been their standard-
bearer in the presidential campaign of 1848, had not the
party decided to take advantage of the Barnburner thirst
for revenge on Lewis Cass, and so placed Van Buren at the
head of its ticket, but in 1852 the Free Soilers turned to
him as their natural leader.   He was one of the bravest and
most fearless champions of the cause of human rights, and
his courage, ability, and thorough steadfastness in support
of freedom and national unity were of the highest value,
both before and during the Civil War.   In the light of history, John P. Hale, the anti-slavery Republican, stands far
higher in the roll of New Hampshire statesmen than
Franklin Pierce, the pro-slavery Democratic president.

[From the Camden (Me.) *Herald*, August 12, 1892.]

The unveiling last week of the beautiful statue of John
P. Hale, presented to the city of Concord, N. H., by Hon.
William E. Chandler, his son-in-law, was an occasion of
interest, not only to New Hampshire but to the country.
The eloquent eulogies delivered did but simple justice to
one who bore so brave and manly a part in the great anti-
slavery struggle from 1845 to 1865.   John P. Hale was a
magnificent man, physically, mentally, and morally.   He
was formerly a Democrat, and a friend and political asso-

ciate of Franklin Pierce, but on the slavery question they divided, Pierce taking the pro-slavery and Hale the anti-slavery side of the question. It was like the sundering of family ties, for they had been friends and associates since their college days at Old Bowdoin.

The work which John P. Hale did as a senator from New Hampshire can hardly be adequately appreciated. His bravery, combined with his eloquence and humorous style, made him a formidable adversary for the champions of slavery to meet. In many respects he was superior to Charles Sumner as a debater and controversialist. The work that he did will stand in history more enduring than the bronze statue erected to his blessed memory.

Many of our older people well remember hearing John P. Hale speak here on the political issues of the country in the great Lincoln campaign of 1860. The meeting was one of the largest ever held in Camden, the people coming not only from all parts of the county, but from Bangor with "wide-awake" uniforms and banners. It was held in the Buchanan grove at the foot of Mount Battle on Mountain street. We shall never forget the stirring eloquence of the speech he made on that occasion. His humor was magnificent. We remember distinctly one happy hit of the speech. There was a great complaint at that time against the ministers for preaching politics. Mr. Hale said this preaching against sin had always been unpopular with sinners. He remembered that Paul preached on one occasion at Ephesus, where many of the merchants and manufacturers were engaged in the making and selling of silver images of the Goddess Diana. One of these rich and influential gentlemen was walking up to the church with Paul where he was going to preach. He said to Paul that the people of Ephesus had heard a great deal about that eloquent sermon which he preached at Athens, and he thought they would like very much to hear him repeat that sermon; but Paul, knowing the peculiar sins of Ephesus, pitched right into the silver image business, and Paul received no call to preach any more at Ephesus! The humor of the illustration was irresistible.

We remember very distinctly the simplicity and delightfulness of the man while he was a guest at our home. We invited to dine with him at our table two of the veteran Abolitionists who had voted for Hale as the Free Soil candidate for president in 1852, George W. Cobb and Nathaniel Hosmer. The meeting of these men was one we shall never forget. We remember how they talked of the obloquy of carrying the banner of Free Soil in the dark days of persecution, and the prospect and outlook for the future.

If ever man was worthy of a statue it was John P. Hale of New Hampshire.

———

[From The *Press*, Portland, Me., August 1, 1892.]

John P. Hale was one of the earliest in the field of the group of great anti-slavery statesmen. When the war with Mexico opened the eyes of the North, both of the great parties contributed men who thenceforth became famous anti-slavery champions, Seward, Wade, Fessenden, Giddings, and Stevens came from the Whig party; and John P. Hale, Hamlin, Wilmot, and Chase from the Democratic party. Hale's path as an anti-slavery leader in New Hampshire was not strewn with roses. Franklin Pierce tried twice to discipline him for opposing the annexation of Texas; but he beat Pierce twice before the people, defied the Democratic party, and was elected to the United States senate as a Free Soiler. But Pierce triumphed in the election of '52, when he was elected president, receiving 1,601,274 votes to 1,386,580 for Scott (Whig), and 155,825 for Hale, who ran as the Free Soil candidate. But Pierce's triumph was only for a time; and in the light of history John P. Hale, the anti-slavery Republican, stands far higher in the roll of New Hampshire statesmen than Franklin Pierce, the pro-slavery Democratic president.

[From The *Journal*, Augusta, Me., August 5, 1892.]

The ceremonies at Concord, Wednesday, in connection with the dedication of a monument to the memory of John P. Hale, were a fitting and impressive tribute to one of the grandest figures in New England history, a man who could not be driven or cajoled from his convictions of duty, and who took his stand for free soil, free speech, and free men at a time when the championship of those principles cost something.

[From The *Advertiser*, Boston, Mass., August 6, 1892.]

Senator Chandler of New Hampshire never did a better deed than when he promoted the placing of a statue at the capital of his state, to that brave and effective champion of freedom, his predecessor in the senate—John Parker Hale of Dover. Senator Hale deserved the honor more than Webster, whose statue was first set up there; and not less than John Stark, the hero of Bunker Hill and of Bennington; for he had the courage that Webster needed, and that Stark showed so often in battle. Obstinate courage is the ordinary virtue of New Hampshire,—so common that its presence is hardly noted; but the absence of it excites remark and opprobrium at once. The warfare carried on by Hale against the arrogant slave masters of Carolina and Virginia was longer, and at first seemed more hopeless, than the fight of Stark, Weare, and Langdon against King George; but the final result was similar.

The "Granite State," as her sons like to call New Hampshire, was united against England, and furnished Washington with his most efficient soldiers; she also stood by Washington in peace as in war; and when she saw Jackson, with equal bravery, if with more passion, defending his country, she stood by him also. This had the ill effect to throw the state upon the wrong side in the early years of the anti-slavery conflict; for Jackson, though he had put down the revolt of Calhoun in 1832, was a slaveholder, and an advocate for annexing Texas. Hale, like his college-mates, Hawthorne, F. Pierce, and J. Cilley, was a Jackson Democrat,—had even been appointed to office, when a young lawyer, by President Jackson; but when the scheme of annexing Texas, merely to aid slavery against freedom, was pressed upon him, he refused to follow the party flag any longer.

I well remember the excitement aroused by his bold course. Pierce, afterwards president, was then the Demo-cratic leader in the state—a handsome, genial, plausible gentleman, son of a Revolutionary officer, and without any great personal ambition. Hale, also, was a popular lawyer, humorous and plain in manners, but of an earnestness till then unsuspected. His own section—the counties of Rock-ingham and Strafford, which had been almost the whole state in the Revolution—stood by Hale, and the Demo-cratic strength was broken there, never to return in full vigor. The little town of Hampton Falls, from which Whittier dates his admirable letter in praise of Hale, threw more Democratic votes for Hale, as an independent candi-date for congress, than for Pierce's man, John Woodbury. Two years later, Hale took his seat in the senate, the first avowed anti-slavery senator for twenty-five years. He was chosen in 1846.

Calhoun of Carolina was then a senator, as he had been for more than twenty years,—so were Benton of Missouri, Clay of Kentucky, and Webster of Massachusetts. Hale was a new man, though he had served a term in the house, but he was not long in coming to the front. In March, 1848, he introduced a bill in the senate applying Jefferson's ordinance forbidding slavery in Oregon, which was soon to come in as a state. In his remarks supporting it, he said: " I am willing to place myself upon the great principle of human right, to stand where the word of God and my own conscience concur in placing me, and then bid defiance to

all consequences." Calhoun maintained that congress had
no power to prevent a slaveholder from emigrating to any
territory, and there holding his slaves, and that even the
people of the territory had no right to say no.

A few days later Calhoun declared the same opinion,
adding: "If the historian who shall record the destruction
of our Union should be disposed to look to its remote and
recondite causes, he will trace them to a proposition which
is the most false and most dangerous of all political errors,—
that all men are born free and equal. As understood, there
is not a word of truth in it." In the following month
(April, 1848), Hale having introduced a resolution based on
a law of Maryland making the District of Columbia respon-
sible for property destroyed by a pro-slavery mob, Calhoun
said, "I am amazed that even the senator from New Hampshire should have so little regard for the constitution of the
country as to introduce such a bill as this." It was such
utterances as this, no doubt, that led Lowell, in the "Big-
low Papers," to make Calhoun say:

> We stan' on the Constitushun, by thunder!
> It's a fac' uv wich there's bushels uv proofs:
> Fer haow c'd we trample on 't so, I wonder,
> Ef 't warnt thet 't is ollers under aour hoofs?

In the same debate, Senator Foote of Mississippi distinguished himself, even among slave-masters, by charging that
Hale was "as guilty as if he had committed highway rob-
bery;" adding, "I invite him to visit Mississippi, and will
tell him beforehand that he could not go ten miles into the
interior,.before he would grace one of the tallest trees of
the forest, with a rope round his neck; and that, if necessary, I should myself assist in the operation." Such were
the fair humanities of old slave-masters. Little did Hale
care for such threats.

Hale was twice nominated for the presidency—in 1848,
when he declined in favor of Van Buren, and in 1852,

when another New Hampshire man was elected,—Franklin Pierce, who had vainly tried to put Hale down, in 1845, on the Texas issue. This time Pierce had the people with him, and was triumphantly chosen over his old commander, Scott, as well as over Hale. It was a barren triumph.

*   *   *   *   *   *   *   *   *   *

Hale was then recalled to the senate, ... and from 1855 onward, New Hampshire led the opposition to slavery, as she had formerly led the Jackson Democracy. To Hale and his following this change was chiefly due, and it came in spite of the fact that Webster, Cass, Pierce, and the other eminent "Sons of New Hampshire" were all on the other side. The stone which the builders rejected became the head of the corner, as so often happens; and Hale was that stone. Now he stands in permanence at the corner of the state house yard—a sign to all the world that men love a brave man.

F. B. SANBORN.

Concord, August 5.

────

[From The *Spy*, Worcester, Mass., August 3, 1892.]

To-day the citizens of New Hampshire are doing a creditable thing in honoring the memory of their most distinguished and patriotic statesman of the last generation, by the dedication of a monument at the state capital in Concord to John P. Hale. . . . . The political revolution accomplished by Mr. Hale, and those who stood by him in his refusal to bow down to the Baal of slavery at the bidding of Franklin Pierce, Isaac Hill, and others forty-six years ago, is the most memorable in the history of that state or of any other state. It was a first great step toward the accomplishment of the subsequent grand national political revolution, by which Abraham Lincoln was elected and slavery abolished in the country. Hale's triumph over Pierce in 1846 was but the forerunner of the triumph of Lincoln over Douglas and Breckenridge in 1860, and of freedom over slavery as a necessary result. The platform on which Mr. Hale was nominated for president in 1852 had for one of its planks the resolution that "slavery is a sin against God and a crime against man, and we will use our utmost efforts to abolish it;" and another, that "we go for free soil, free speech, and free men, and will fight ever for these principles until victory shall reward our efforts." These views were more radical than those put into the platforms of 1856 and 1860, but the nation had to come up to them before the war was over. In honoring John P. Hale his state honors the platform of principles on which he stood, to which, thank God, the nation has at last come.

[From the Haverhill (Mass.) *Bulletin*, August 2, 1892]

Many men have been born and reared in New Hampshire, men who have helped shape the destiny of the nation. Among these, few, if any, occupied a grander or more influential position than the late John Parker Hale. He was born in 1810, and grew up a Democrat after the strictest measure of the party of his state.

In 1834, while residing in Dover, he was appointed United States district attorney by President Jackson, which office he held until removed by President Tyler in 1841. In 1843 he was elected member of congress, and in 1844 Polk was elected president, and President Tyler was moving every available force to annex Texas, and to the surprise of many, Mr. Hale opposed the scheme. Two years later he was defeated, and a man friendly to annexation was elected. Then followed the great contest in New Hampshire which made Hale immortal; he was from that time onward the recognized political anti-slavery leader in the Old Granite state. He went before the people of the state in the 1845–46 campaign, and won. He was elected a member of the legislature, speaker of the house, and United States senator for six years from March 4, 1847.

The campaign of 1845 and 1846 completely revolutionized New Hampshire. Hale's brave words for freedom awoke the echoes among the hills and through the valleys of the old commonwealth, arousing the hardy yeomanry everywhere to a sense of their duty to humanity. Men who had been life-long Democrats threw off the yoke of bondage and rallied under the new standard raised by the "Renegade Jack Hale," as he was called in derision by the old "hunkers," of the Democratic party. On one of these occasions, soon after this memorable campaign began, Mr. Hale, by invitation, made an address in the North church at Concord. It proved the event of his life. He entered the church a stranger to almost everybody present in the vast audience. He was there to vindicate his action in leaving his old associates and organizing a new party. He was, as he afterwards said himself, gloomy and desponding. But the inspiration came and he held the listeners in breathless silence to the end. That inspiration, said Mr. Hale, lasted him during the entire campaign and never left him, and subsided only when the proclamation of President Lincoln declared that in this land the sun should rise upon no bondsman and set upon no slaves. And this enabled him to say afterwards, "Now when I turn my eyes heavenward, I can, in imagination, see hanging out from the battlements of Heaven the broken shackles of four millions of slaves, which for twenty years I did all in my power to rend."

John P. Hale was a great man, and his life left an impress upon New Hampshire which will never fade out. When he left the Democratic party of his native state, that party was bound hand and foot to the slave power of the South, and the grand old state seemed to be doomed to wear the shackles and chain forever. But his voice broke the spell, and such men as the late William Hoyt of Danville and others heard and spurned longer to remain in the ranks of a party pledged to sustain slavery; they joined the new movement, and New Hampshire soon took its stand on the side of freedom and humanity.

And now, while John P. Hale needs no monument to perpetuate his memory or his worth, it is well to give this splendid statue, now ready, a place in the State House park at the capital of the state. The unveiling of this fine work of art is to take place on Wednesday with imposing and appropriate ceremonies.

> "Once to every man and nation
> Comes the moment to decide,
> In the strife of truth with falsehood,
> For the good or evil side."

That time came to John P. Hale when he refused to do the bidding of the slave power. Noble was the stand he took; grandly did he sustain himself, and win the name he sent down to posterity.

[From the Boston *Traveller*, July 29, 1892.]

The dedication of the statue of John P. Hale, which will take place at Concord, N. H., next week, will be an occasion of unusual interest. The honor which is paid his memory is well deserved. In the contest over slavery, which ended with the freedom of the slave, he was a brave and fearless leader. The Free Soil movement in the national congress, began, as it will be remembered, over the passage of the resolutions providing for the annexation of Texas without recourse to the treaty-making power, the vote on which was had in the house of representatives on the 25th of January, 1845. The Democratic party, which had just elected James K. Polk president, made the support of these resolutions the test of party fealty. Of the ninety-eight negative votes but twenty-eight were cast by those classed as Democrats, all of whom were from the free states. One of these twenty-eight was John P. Hale of New Hampshire, then serving his first term in the house.

He was in his thirty-ninth year, and had only recently been nominated by the Democrats of his district for re-election. For his disobedience to the orders of the slave power, the party leaders in New Hampshire determined to discipline him, but they never made a more fatal party blunder. He was denounced as a traitor to his party, a new convention was called, and another candidate nominated, the result of the election being that there was no choice, and for the next two years the district was unrepresented in congress. The next year, 1846, Hale was elected to the New Hampshire legislature by his Dover friends, was elected speaker, and then United States senator for the full term of six years, as an anti-slavery man, and in December, 1847, he entered the United States senate, the first distinctively anti-slavery member of that body. He thus became the recognized leader of the Free Soilers throughout the country. He would doubtless have been their standard-bearer in the presidential campaign of 1848, had not the party decided to take advantage of the Barnburner thirst for revenge on Lewis Cass, and so placed Van Buren at the head of its ticket, but in 1852 the Free Soilers turned to him as their natural leader. He was one of the bravest and most fearless champions of the cause of human rights, and his courage, ability, and thorough steadfastness in support of freedom and national unity were of the highest value, both before and during the Civil War.

The statue is the gift to the state of Senator William E. Chandler, who will formally present it. . . . . The statue is a fitting tribute to the memory of a devoted and patriotic son of the Granite state, and it is fitting that it should have a place in Capitol park, by the side of that other great son of that state, Daniel Webster.

_____

[From The *Journal*, Boston, Mass., August 4, 1892.]

The ceremonies at Concord yesterday, in connection with the dedication of a monument to the memory of John P. Hale, were a fitting and impressive tribute to one of the grandest figures in New England history, a man who could not be driven or cajoled from his convictions of duty, and who took his stand for free soil, free speech, and free men at a time when the championship of those principles cost something.

[From the Boston *Herald*, August 4, 1892.]

The statue unveiled at Concord yesterday renders a tardy tribute to the memory of one of the great men of New Hampshire, its first abolition senator, one of the first men in congress to labor for the freedom of the slave, and a man whom the state rightly honors for his personal and political worth. Senator Chandler deserves the thanks of New England people for erecting this statue to the memory of his distinguished kinsman, and his speech on the occasion was a fair and just summary of the place which Senator Hale held in the history of the struggle over slavery and in sustaining the efforts of his countrymen to secure its abolition during the Civil War. Governor Tuttle and Colonel Hall were equally happy in their efforts, and the dedication of this statue will long be remembered as a notable event in the political history of New Hampshire.

[From the Boston *Herald*, August 5, 1892.]

The early services of John P. Hale in the cause of freedom are not likely to be overestimated. He fitted in admirably with Seward, Sumner, and Wade, and supplied an element of humor, in which they were all deficient, to the anti-slavery debates of the senate. His portly personality admirably accorded with his general good nature, and he could say very sharp things without appearing malicious or bitter in so doing. He so exasperated that queer character, Senator Foote of Mississippi, one day, that the latter told him they would hang him to the nearest tree if he came into the southern state. Hale turned this upon him with imperturbable phlegm, neither posing as a possible martyr nor showing any special resentment toward his adversary, but treating him with the ridicule he deserved.

[From the Boston *News*, July 29, 1892.]

One of New Hampshire's ablest, and certainly one of her bravest, statesmen was John P. Hale. He was in public life when it required courage to openly denounce the institution of slavery, and never shirked nor faltered in his devotion to the cause he early espoused. Both before and during the Civil War, both at home and abroad, he performed valuable service for the nation, and it is fitting that his memory should be honored. On Wednesday next a statue will be dedicated at Concord, presented by Senator William E. Chandler, and being accepted by the state will stand through the years to come to call attention, not only to John P. Hale, but to the respect in which he is held by those who follow him.

[From the Hartford (Conn.) *Courant*, August 6, 1892.]

John P. Hale's statue should have been standing in the New Hampshire capital these twenty years past; but much better late than never. He was the first of the anti-slavery senators, and he had a pretty lonesome time of it, politically, until Chase and Sumner arrived on the scene.

When the committees of the senate were made up at the opening of the session, he was left out in the cold altogether. The explanation given on the floor by one of the little great men of the day was, that Hale was "outside all healthy political organizations." A man of a different temperament in his place would have lost his head and raged, or lost his pluck and moped. Hale laughed and waited. He was as cool, as bright, and as irrepressible as a May morning. After a little the senate discovered that the "Abolitionist" from New Hampshire was a thoroughly good fellow, and that he had the invaluable faculty of being able to make it laugh. He could be serious enough on occasion, but it was as natural to him to joke as to breathe. What with his geniality and his irresistible drollery, the slaveholders of the senate presently found themselves distinguishing between the man and his opinions, and liking the one as cordially as they detested the other. In this respect his case presents a marked contrast to that of Seward. The Southerners not only hated Seward's politics, but they hated Seward himself. He lacked Hale's bonhomie and charm; he was always serious.

But the New Hampshire man's jokes and stories did n't make him any the less faithful and useful soldier of the good cause of human freedom to which he and his great comrade from New York devoted so many years of arduous service and whose triumph they lived to see. Each had his own place and work, and both deserve to be held in gratitude and honor.

[From the New York *Times*, August 4, 1892.]

It is fitting that the statue of John P. Hale, just erected by Senator Chandler, should have a place in the state house yard at Concord, the capital of the state which he represented at Washington, first as a congressman, and then as a senator. In no other New Hampshire man's life, not excepting even Daniel Webster's, may the people of the Granite state find solider ground for state pride. Mr. Hale was one of the great men of his time, and that is saying much, for his public career covered the period in which was fought out the contest which culminated in the War of the Rebellion. There doubtless were profounder men than Mr. Hale in that period—although he had a strong and well-disciplined mind—but there was no man of all his contemporaries who over-matched him in courage and resoluteness. It was by the consecration of his powers to the anti-slavery cause, and by his unswerving adherence to what he conceived to be the line of his duty, that he made himself a man of the nation before he reached his fortieth year.

The crisis of his life came when as a congressman he faced the question of the annexation of Texas. The position that he took upon this matter was regarded with disfavor by his constituents, and he heard from them. Replying to their protests, he wrote that if they did not approve of his course they would better nominate another man to be his successor. That very thing they did. They had already made Mr. Hale a candidate for reëlection, but they held a second convention, in which they repudiated him, denouncing him as a traitor to his party. Not a word of regret came from Mr. Hale for the course which had precipitated this action, but when congress adjourned he went home and announced himself as an independent candidate. He failed of election, but so did the regularly nominated candidate of his party, and Mr. Hale was well satisfied, seeing that he had defeated the Democratic party in a fair contest in which he had squarely met the issue. This outcome of the campaign was far more than he had hoped for at first. In the beginning he had regarded himself more as a propagandist than as a candidate.

It was very early in this campaign that he had that memorable meeting with Franklin Pierce in the Old North church at Concord. Mr. Hale had been invited by a few of his friends to make a speech in vindication of his course in congress. He found the church packed with an audience that was far from friendly to him. His address took the form of an out-and-out anti-slavery argument. Not a word of apology was in it; not the sign of an acknowledgment of error; not one concessionary sentence. Mr. Pierce followed with a review of Mr. Hale's address—a review full of spirited denunciation, at times almost cruel in its severity. At the close came a taunt in which Mr. Hale was reminded of his prompt repudiation by his constituents, and was warned that persistence in his course would result in his permanent retirement from public life. Mr. Hale could hardly contain himself as these last words were speaking. As Mr. Pierce finished, he leaped upon the seat of the pew where he had been sitting, faced the great audience, and burst into speech. He spoke for about five minutes, and one who heard him has lately said that in that five minutes he was moved by the "most marvellous eloquence that ever fell from human lips." In closing, Mr. Hale said:

"When filial affection shall erect a humble monument to show where rest my mortal remains, I wish upon it no other epitaph than this: 'Here lies one who surrendered office, place, and power rather than bow down and worship slavery.'"

The next year Mr. Hale was chosen a member of the legislature, and was made speaker of the house. The same year he was elected United States senator by a combination of men of different parties. He was but forty-one years old when he entered the United States senate, the only one of his kind, the sole representative in that body of the anti-slavery sentiment of the country. Referring to Mr. Hale's election as speaker of the New Hampshire house of representatives, and anticipating his election as United States senator, the poet Whittier wrote a letter in 1846, in which he said:

"He has succeeded, and his success has broken the spell which has hitherto held reluctant Democracy in the embrace of slavery. The tide of anti-slavery feeling, long held back by the dams and dikes of party, has at last broken over all barriers and is working down from your northern mountains upon the slave-cursed South, as if Niagara stretched its foam and thunder along the whole length of Mason and Dixon's line. Let the first wave of that northern flood as it dashes against the walls of the Capitol bear thither for the first time an anti-slavery senator."

No doubt this language seemed extravagant to those who read it when it was newly written, but certainly it was prophetic. The young man who had made so bold and gallant a fight in his own state was destined for a great and influential career in the senate of the United States. The story of his work at Washington is an important part of the history of the country. Fearing nobody, always ready

14

to meet an emergency, invariably earnest, intrepid, and aggressive, he justified the expectations which his election as a senator had aroused. Excepting two years, he was a member of the senate up to 1865, so that it was permitted him to see the work completed in the inauguration of which he had participated. He was fortunate enough, too, to live to know that he, who at one time had been despised and hated by thousands of persons all over the country, had at last won the respect and admiration of the great American people by his manly independence and his magnificent courage.

The lesson of Mr. Hale's life is easily read. His career is a striking instance of the high regard which the common people have for men who are fearless in the exercise of the functions of public office. The average American citizen has no place in his heart for the coward, but he esteems nothing too good to give the man who is willing to sacrifice himself rather than forego a principle.

———

[From the Brooklyn (N. Y.) *Eagle*, August 4, 1892.]

A bronze statue of John P. Hale, presented to the state of New Hampshire by his son-in-law, Senator William E. Chandler, was yesterday unveiled at Concord. Hale was a Democrat when the state produced, as it does now, some of the stoutest Democrats anywhere to be found. At the time of the annexation of Texas and the war with Mexico, he left his party and was afterward classed as an Abolitionist, though he was more practical than the Extremists, who insisted on immediate emancipation or non-communion with the Union. The Abolitionists builded a good deal better than they knew, although somewhat differently, as is apt to happen with the best of men. Their agitation kept alive the anti-slavery sentiment until its realization fell into the hands of those who applied to it the political forces which the Abolitionists rejected, and the institution was finally destroyed, incidentally to the defense and salvation of the

Union which they denounced. Hale was an able, accomplished, eloquent man, who was appreciated and liked by many who differed most widely with him in opinion. As some of the bitterest of the Abolitionists, contrary to their expectations, lived to see freedom universal, so now, in the better days of a restored brotherhood of free states, the Southerner from the remotest boundary of the Gulf, traveling among the White hills of New Hampshire, will rejoice, as he looks at the figure of John P. Hale, that there is not a slave in the length and breadth of the land.

[From the Utica (N. Y.) *Herald*, August 5, 1892.]

The statue of John P. Hale, presented to New Hampshire by Senator William E. Chandler, was unveiled in the state house yard at Concord, Wednesday, with appropriate ceremonies and in the presence of a distinguished company. It is a fitting tribute to the memory of the first distinctly anti-slavery advocate who ever entered the United States senate. He took his seat in December, 1847, and stood alone as the champion of a great cause until joined by Salmon P. Chase, two years later, and by Charles Sumner in December, 1851.

[From the New York *Tribune*, August 4, 1892.]

Not only the state of New Hampshire but the whole country is under obligation to Senator William E. Chandler for the gift of the statue of John P. Hale, which was unveiled at Concord yesterday. There are no more eloquent voices in behalf of patriotism and good government than the echoes of those which, when the great cause of human rights was on trial, rang out clearly and fearlessly on the side of humanity and justice, and refused to be silenced by political proscription. They speak to us like the deeds of those who died at Gettysburg, as the heroes of Marathon spoke to imperial Athens.

[From the New York *Press*, August 5, 1892.]

The speech of Senator William E. Chandler, on the occasion of the unveiling of the statue of John P. Hale at Concord, was a strong and patriotic address, worthy of the fearless champion of human rights whom it commemorated. The New Hampshire senator uttered a great truth in a striking form when he said : " Men who breathe their spirit into the institutions of their country, or stamp their characters upon the pillars of the age, can never die." A grateful people may rear visible memorials to men of this type; but their truest memorial is the Republic they helped to make, not merely great in a material sense, but grand in a moral sense. John P. Hale was one of the most courageous of the little band that boldly defied the insolent slave power in congress; the effect of the example of those emancipators and regenerators was potent and permanent. The good they did is immortal.

———

[From the Syracuse (N. Y.) *Journal*, August 6, 1892.]

The monument erected this week to the memory of John P. Hale, in the state house yard at Concord, was the gift of his son-in-law, Senator William E. Chandler, to the state of New Hampshire. The tribute conveyed in this memorial is most richly deserved. Mr. Hale was a pioneer Abolitionist, and the first distinctively anti-slavery man to be chosen to the United States senate, where he led in the warfare against human slavery. He entered the senate in December, 1847, and stood alone in that body in defense of manhood and liberty, till Salmon P. Chase joined him in December, 1849, and Charles Sumner in December, 1851. * * * He stands unchallenged as New Hampshire's greatest orator, next to Daniel Webster, and his service in the anti-slavery cause was of the highest value.

[From the Philadelphia (Pa.) *Press*, August 4, 1892.]

The unveiling of a statue in Concord, N. H., yesterday, of John Parker Hale, will serve to recall to the memory of the American public a man who acted a prominent part in the great slavery conflict which waged so fiercely between 1840 and 1860. It is less than nineteen years ago since Mr. Hale died; but so rapidly is history made in these days that the majority of men in active life now will be compelled to ask why he deserves the honor of a statue erected to his memory in the capitol yard of his native state. Even this distinction might have been denied him had not the admiration of Senator Chandler led him to perform this duty to a man who reflected such honor upon New Hampshire.

The present generation can scarcely realize the heat and bitterness of the conflict with slavery, or the kind of men needed to withstand its encroachments. Southern statesmen well understood the spirit of the North in those days, and its eagerness to develop the resources of this section and take advantage of the marvellous opportunities for growing rich. The South ruled the country with an iron hand. Its threats of dissolving the Union were generally effective in forcing congressmen from the North to do its will; for few constituencies were brave and far-sighted enough to support an intrepid senator or representative who ventured to cross swords with a Southern fire-eater. History proves that the title of "doughface" was well earned by too many Northern congressmen.

But John Parker Hale was one of the few exceptions. He shrank neither before the crack of the slave-owner's whip nor the anger of his constituents. He dared to oppose the annexation of Texas, because he believed it was sought in order to strengthen and perpetuate slavery; and he had the principle to tell his people that they must choose another man to represent them if they wished him to support that measure. It was a small thing to him that his district withdrew his renomination to congress, and that he was defeated as an independent candidate on that issue. Like a sagacious statesman, he could look beyond the next election and leave his vindication to the future. It came in a few years, when the change which was gradually spreading over the North on the subject of slavery resulted in his election to the United States senate, where, with a brief interval, he remained until 1865, when the conflict was ended, freedom had triumphed, and the slave was a free man.

The rugged features of Mr. Hale's political principles made him a marked character in the forum of debate. No man who sat in congress from the North was more feared by the defenders of slavery. He could not be cajoled or intimidated. Fear for his own interests never influenced him. He believed slavery to be a wrong; and he stood, like one of the granite hills of his native state, immovable before the assaults of its friends in the North as well as in the South. The specious arguments of those who upheld the "peculiar institution" will grow moldy and musty with dust; but the declaration of John P. Hale for "free speech, free men, and free soil" will never cease to re-echo through the corridors of time.

It is well to recall such a life as Mr. Hale's, and by paying distinguished honor to his memory prove to young men that devotion to principle is certain to receive its just recognition. The men who defended human bondage have few to do them honor now, and the record of most of them is forgotten. But the memory of John P. Hale will grow brighter the further the nation recedes from the events in which he acted so conspicuous a part. The dedication of a statue in his honor comes at an appropriate time, for in the same week it occurs 100,000 ex-slaves and their descendants are permitted to prove their manhood by exercising the inestimable privilege of the suffrage in Alabama.

[From the Portland *Oregonian*.]

John Parker Hale Chandler, a boy of seven, unveiled a statue of his grandfather, John P. Hale, on the public square of Concord, New Hampshire, last Wednesday, presented to the city by his father, Senator Chandler. John P. Hale should not have waited so long for a memorial, nor should his city and state have waited for filial solicitude to provide it. He was the worthiest son of his state and his name is associated in a peculiar way with a vital crisis in national history.

John P. Hale was something more than the first Abolitionist in the United States senate, where he fought the battle for freedom for two years before he was joined by Chase and for four years before Sumner came. He was the first Abolitionist in public life after John Quincy Adams; the first of a long line of conscientious Democrats, from 1844 to 1861, to sacrifice public office and break party ties for the sake of the cause of human freedom. He did not enter the senate till 1847. Three years before, he fought the gag law for anti-slavery petitions in the house of representatives, as Adams had fought it for eight years in the senate. Adams died in 1846, and for the last two years he had a constant and courageous ally in the representative from New Hampshire, in the contest whose brunt he had so long borne alone. Indeed, circumstances made Hale's opposition more dramatic and effective than Adams's. The event which finally determined his break with the Democratic party attracted popular attention more sharply and gave the cause of abolition more conspicuous and solid standing than all the brave and patient work of the Massachusetts representative.

This event occurred in 1845. The New Hampshire legislature had instructed representatives of the state in congress to support the annexation of Texas. Hale was then in congress and a candidate for reëlection. His instant response to the resolution was a letter refusing to obey the

instructions and condemning annexation. At a state Democratic convention, six weeks later, his name was stricken
from the ticket and another substituted. He was made an
Independent candidate, and the election that spring was the
opening skirmish in the long contest over the slavery ques-,
tion. There was failure to elect, and the contest was
renewed, at special elections, four times between March,
1845, and March, 1846. During all this year Hale canvassed the state vigorously, with Franklin Pierce for his
chief opponent, taking what was then very advanced ground
on the slavery question. It was in a joint debate with
Pierce in this canvass that he made the memorable retort to
the taunt that his constituents had repudiated him : " When
filial affection shall erect an humble monument to show where
rest my mortal remains, I wish upon it no other epitaph than
this : 'Here lies one who surrendered office, place, and
power rather than bow down and worship slavery.'" It is
not stated whether Senator Chandler placed this insciption
upon the pedestal of the statue he presented to the city of
Concord. It is permanently preserved in the history of the
country. It was really this contest that made Hale senator. The three-cornered contest of Whigs, Independents,
and Democrats prevented the election of a Democratic governor in March, 1846. The Whigs and Independents had a
majority in the legislature and fused, making Hale speaker
and electing a Whig governor. A little later the same
legislature elected Hale senator. He remained in the senate,
with an intermission of two years, from 1853 to 1855, till
1865, and lived until 1873, his active public life covering
the whole anti-slavery conflict, from its weak beginnings to
its triumphant conclusion.

For nearly ten years from the death of Adams, Hale was
regarded as the leader of the anti-slavery party in the
country. It nominated him for president in 1847, though
he refused and supported Van Buren, the Barnburner candidate of the following year. He was a Free Soil candidate in
1852 and got nearly 160,000 votes. He went to the senate

once more as a Free Soiler, but the Republican party was born and Fremont carried the state in 1856. Hale's last election in 1858 was as a Republican, and he was one of the pillars of the party in congress all through the war.

Hale's title to eminence in the anti-slavery conflict was that of a pioneer. Less cultured than Sumner, less powerful than Chase, he was a clear thinker, a hard fighter, and a most courageous follower of his moral convictions. He did his work when work was most needed, and when one man counted for more than a hundred later. None of the greater men who served the cause of freedom afterward merits tenderer and more honorable remembrance than this man, who fought its battles alone in a hostile senate as John Quincy Adams fought them in a hostile house of representatives. They were the two pioneers of freedom.

———

[From The *Post Intelligencer*, Seattle, Wash., August 13, 1892.]

On the 3d inst. a fine statue of John P. Hale, presented to the state of New Hampshire by United States Senator Chandler, was unveiled at Concord. The growing generation need to be told the story of John P. Hale's career, for it is worth the telling in these sordid days when statesmanship too often stands for political sycophancy and petty selfishness. John P. Hale early in life achieved brilliant success as a lawyer; he was a handsome man, possessed of great natural gifts of wit and humor; he was genial and popular, and was the favorite orator of the Democratic party of his day; he was the associate and friend of Franklin Pierce, who became president in 1852. Mr. Hale was elected representative to congress, and was the idol of his party in New Hampshire until he was called upon in 1845 to support the forcible annexation of Texas and an unjust war with Mexico, in order to extend the dominion of human chattel slavery and to bring more slave states into the Union. Then Mr. Hale rebelled, and wrote his famous Texas letter, for which he was expelled from his party.

Mr. Hale bluntly told his constituents that they must choose another man to represent them if they wished him to support the annexation of Texas. His district took him at his word and withdrew his nomination to congress, and he was defeated as an independent candidate on that issue.

The vast moral courage of Mr. Hale's act can hardly be appreciated at this distance of nearly a half a century from its date. The Whig party of the North at that day contained some able men vigorously opposed to the annexation of Texas, but there were very few in the Democratic party, for Martin Van Buren had just been beaten for the Democratic nomination in the national convention of 1844, solely on the ground that he had once expressed himself in very moderate language as opposed to the annexation of Texas, and Henry Clay, who had expressed a similar opinion, had just been defeated for election for the presidency, in the splendid maturity of his fame and popularity, by obscure James K. Polk. The presidential election had turned on the question of the annexation of Texas, and the Democratic victory over Clay had been won on this issue.

When Mr. Hale rebelled against this test of party fealty he knew he was parting with a splendid popularity; he knew that by this act he became a political outcast; there was no home for him within either of the great parties, for the defeat of 1844 had silenced nearly all its great anti-slavery voices. After 1844 Webster's voice lost all its old anti-slavery ring, so that by 1850 we find him bidding for the presidency by helping Henry Clay carry the compromise measures, including the fugitive slave law of that year. In 1845, when Hale revolted, there was no home for him in either of the great political camps, and he knew it; he knew that this act would lose him the friendship of Pierce and all the party leaders in New Hampshire, and yet he did not hesitate; he turned his back on fame and friendships; he accepted obloquy and insult and courageously bided his time. It was not much for a fanatic to do, but Hale was not of the fanatic breed; his training as a lawyer, his early convivial habits, his genial temper and social talents, his political training as a Democratic politician, had made him anything but a man of sombre, fanatical type. His act was due to the natural benevolence and kindness of his nature; he abhorred slavery, and he would not load his conscience with any responsibility for the acquisition of a single foot of slave territory. He had never been an Abolitionist; he had always been willing to give to the old slave states all that the constitution had secured to them, and trusted, like Clay, to time and the decent opinions of mankind to lead up to gradual emancipation by the states or by the nation sanctioned by the states; but when it came to enlarging the area of the evil, Mr. Hale revolted, and always remained a rebel. When Hale revolted, among the few writers that blessed him for his moral courage was the poet Whittier, who wrote:

"God bless New Hampshire; from her granite peaks
Once more the voice of Stark and Langdon speaks."

From this time forward Mr. Hale's voice was heard protesting against the sale of slaves under Federal law in the District of Columbia; against flogging in the navy; against the enslavement or degradation of either the bodies or the souls of human beings of any race, color, or condition. Mr. Hale's day of triumph came at last. He led the forlorn hope of the Free Soil National party in 1852; he was elected three times to the United States senate, and was United States minister to Spain. He died, full of years and honors, surrounded by troops of friends who venerated him for the noble object lesson of moral courage in political life that his career had furnished.

The glory of Mr. Hale is that he was an anti-slavery man when the courage of his convictions stood for the complete sacrifice of all the earnings of a brilliant political past in the ranks of a party that had always honored him and was ready to give him further honor, but

> "He scorned their gifts of fame, and power, and gold,
> And humbly joined him to the weaker part,
> Fanatic named, and fool, yet well content
> So he could be the nearer to God's heart,
> And feel its solemn pulses sending blood
> Through all the wide-spread veins of endless good."

—

[From The *Bee*, Omaha, Neb., August 7, 1892.]

Less than forty years ago the name of John P. Hale was
on the lips of every American, for his fiery denunciation of
his party in its annexation of Texas, and subserviency to the
growing slave party by the repeal of the Missouri compromise. He was one of the greatest anti-slavery agitators in
the history of America, but his memory has almost passed
away. Last week a statue of this man was presented to
the state of New Hampshire by Senator Chandler, and the
celebration of that event will serve to awaken in the minds
of men a knowledge of one of the really courageous men of
American history.

—

[From the Manchester (N. H.) *Mirror and American.*]

John P. Hale was not a military hero. He was not a
matchless orator. He was not a great statesman. But in
the long list of the illustrious sons of New Hampshire there
is scarcely another name which shines with greater or more
enduring lustre than his. He was a strong, well-balanced
man, of sublime courage, of thorough honesty, of unwavering faith, and of unfailing sagacity. He was one of the
few who instinctively go to the front when truth needs a
champion and righteousness a defender, whose leadership is
gladly accepted because they inspire faith in their sincerity
and confidence in their capacity, and who lead so steadily
and successfully that they command the respect and admiration even of their opponents.

Mr. Hale was born in Rochester, March 31, 1806; was

educated at Bowdoin college with the class of 1827, and read law in Dover, where he began the practice of his profession in 1830. He grew to manhood under Democratic teachings, and upon reaching his majority was identified with the Democratic party, which promptly recognized his ability and responded to his desire for political preferment. In 1832 he represented Dover in the state legislature; two years afterwards he was appointed United States district attorney, and in 1843, when thirty-seven years of age, he was elected to congress. He served one term, and was renominated; but before the canvass opened he took occasion to repudiate the party doctrine upon the slavery question, and a second Democratic convention was called, which denounced him as a traitor and nominated another man in his stead. He then announced himself as an Independent candidate, and appealed to the people of his district to elect him as a Free Soil Democrat. He received more than 3,000 votes, but was defeated. The next year Dover returned him to the house of representatives at Concord, in which the Whigs and Free Soilers outnumbered the regular Democrats. A combination of these parties resulted in making him speaker, and later on electing him United States senator, while the Whig candidate for governor, Anthony Colby, was elected, there having been no choice by the people.

At the end of his first term in the senate, the Democrats controlled the legislature, and he was retired; but in 1855 he was again elected to fill an unexpired term, and served until 1865, when President Lincoln appointed him minister to Spain. In 1869 he returned, with his health much impaired, and died Nov. 18, 1873. In 1852 he was the candidate of the Free Soil party for president.

When Mr. Hale severed his connection with the Democratic party, it was at the height of its power in the state and nation, and only the eye of faith could see any prospect that its grasp would be broken, while the Free Soilers were so few and feeble that neither Democrats nor Whigs regarded them with anything but contempt. In 1841, of a total vote of 51,689 in New Hampshire, the Democrats cast 29,116, the Whigs 21,230, and the Free Soilers but 1,273, and four years later the Free Soil ticket received less than 6,000.

To all appearances, a man like John P. Hale had but to stay with the Democratic party to reach any post of honor to which he might aspire, while to leave it and defy it was to invite defeat and humiliation through life. But he neither stayed nor stopped. As soon as it became apparent that the party with which he was allied, and of which he was a leader, was to become the agent of the slave power and be used to support the South in its aggressions, as soon as he saw that Democracy was going wrong deliberately, persistently, and hopelessly, he left it, and, without counting cost or considering consequences, cast his lot with the despised Free Soilers, and from that time on, through all the struggles of the party of freedom, he was one of the bravest of its captains, one of the wisest of its counsellors, one of the stanchest and strongest of its supporters.

For more than twenty years he stood for the awakened conscience, the emancipated judgment, the love of liberty, and the loyalty to right of the people of New Hampshire and of the entire North, for his fame was as wide as the continent, and his followers were wherever freedom had a friend. At every turn the slaveholders and their northern allies found him equipped, fearless, and ready for combat. Defeat, and there was little but defeat for the anti-slavery cause for two decades, only nerved him to new endeavors, and success always inspired him to new advances. He never retreated, never parleyed, never compromised. At all times, in all places, he dared fight for the right, and he fought as stoutly when the odds were overwhelmingly against him as when the advantage was in his favor. In this, in his moral courage, was the grandeur of his character, and in this respect he had few peers among the public men of his time. A state honors itself when it does

homage to the memory of such a man as John P. Hale, and
New Hampshire may well congratulate herself that, through
the generosity of William E. Chandler, a successor in the
senate, she is given an opportunity to testify now and in all
the coming time her admiration for the character, and her
appreciation of the services, of John P. Hale, the gifted,
gallant, and unswerving champion of freedom.

———

[From the Manchester (N. H.) *Union*, August 3, 1892.]

It is fifty-three years since John P. Hale took the unexpected step which separated him from his former political
associates, turned politics in New Hampshire topsy-turvy,
and led, by a much shorter path than he could have foreseen, to the United States senate. Half a century is a long
time in the history of party politics. In that time the
actors of a given period pass from the scene. Of the leaders in New Hampshire politics who were surprised, disappointed, maddened, or encouraged by Hale's independent
course in 1845, not one remains. Those who blamed and
those who praised have alike passed away, and the issues of
that time have passed with them. Much of intensity, perhaps something of bitterness, in politics still remain, and must
remain so long as men differ and parties struggle for the
mastery; but such opposition as Hale met from the Democratic party of his day, and such misrepresentation and contumely as honorable and conscientious Democrats suffered in
their turn a few years later, are, it is hoped, buried forever
with the dead past. Hale's special greatness lies in the fact
that he stood by his convictions when, for all that he or any
one else could see, it meant the blasting of what promised to
be a brilliant future. In this respect he differed widely from
others who afterwards attained to equal prominence and
were more abundantly rewarded, but who waited before
casting their lot with the new movement until they were
sure that the party that grew from it had control of the

loaves and fishes. He was not the earliest opponent of negro slavery; but it was his fortune, through an unexpected turn in the political tide, to be the first Free Soiler in the United States senate, and as such he stood for some time alone, conspicuous, by reason of his unique position no less than by his acknowledged ability, over all others who sat in that body with him. It is fitting that the statue of so distinguished a son of New Hampshire should stand in the park that surrounds its capitol, and it is to be hoped that fair skies will smile auspiciously upon the ceremony of unveiling.

[From the Manchester (N. H.) *Press*, August 3, 1892.]

The dedication to-day at Concord, in the state house yard, of a statue to John P. Hale recalls a political history in New Hampshire that is unique and inspiring. Of the period when John P. Hale flourished it may be well said, "There were giants in those days," and among the giants John P. Hale stood among the foremost.

Senator Hale was the pioneer senator who represented that class of Democrats on whom the light, showing in its true colors the deep damnation of the system of human slavery in this country, fell with convincing power. As the first anti-slavery United States senator, battling with his former associates in the Democratic party, and leading the scattered elements of opposition to the national disgrace for many years, Hale was at once the national centre of anti-slavery sentiment and in his state the champion of an awakened public conscience.

His senatorial career, reflecting the success or failure of his combats at home, presents as much of the romantic and the inspiring as ever characterized the days of chivalry in other fields. John P. Hale was a warrior, fully armed at all points, and fighting valorously the battle for human rights. No sentiment more inspiring than that uttered in the Old North church at Concord by him when the world, the flesh, and the Hunker Democracy were uniting for his defeat, which looked inevitable, was ever uttered in New Hampshire, and it is worthily chiselled on his monument:

"I wish no other epitaph than this : Here lies one who surrendered office, place, and power rather than bow down and worship slavery."

Nor is his anti-slavery record alone to be remembered, for the efforts of Senator Hale secured the abolition of flogging in the navy and of the ration of grog.

[From the Concord (N. H.) *Monitor*, August 4, 1892.]

It was emphatically a "Free Soil, Free Speech, and Free Men" day Wednesday. The dedication of the statue of John P. Hale called together such an assemblage as will never be witnessed again in New Hampshire. Survivors of the Old Guard who rallied around John P. Hale when he wrote his famous letter to his constituents in the opening days of 1845, concerning the annexation of Texas, came from the hillsides and the valleys to do honor to his name and fame. Men in the active walks of life, whose enthusiasm was stirred in their early years by the bugle blasts for freedom blown throughout our New Hampshire hills by John P. Hale, were present in force. Young men, whose knowledge of Mr. Hale was learned from the lips of their fathers and the study of the political history of our state through one of its most eventful periods, were also present to catch the inspiration of the hour. Women, too, who extended their sympathy to the great leader in the hour of his need, and who have an instinctive love for courageous and conscientious men in the great battle of right against wrong, were present in great numbers to listen to the lengthened exercises of the occasion. All in all, it was a notable gathering, and a spontaneous tribute to the memory of one of New Hampshire's most distinguished sons.

15

[From The *News-Letter*, Exeter, N. H., August 5, 1892.]

Senator Chandler's monument to his father-in-law, the late Senator John P. Hale, was formally dedicated in the state house yard on Wednesday. The statue was modelled and cast in Munich at the foundry of F. von Miller, who first gained reputation in this country by his admirable design for the Tyler Davidson fountain of Cincinnati. His firm later cast the Webster statue which is near that of Hale on the state house grounds. Mr. Hale is represented as speaking, holding in his left hand a roll of manuscript, while the right is raised in gesticulation. The head is inclined slightly to the left, with the face nearly in front. The expression is majestic, and the dress is copied from the clothes he actually wore when in the senate.

Mr. Hale was brilliant from his boyhood. He studied law, and practiced it in Dover for many years. He was always more of a politician than legal student, however, and was soon prominent in the legislature. He was then an orthodox Democrat. In 1843 he was elected to congress, and was faithful to party interests, until it was proposed to admit Texas as a slave state, in all probability to be cut up into two or three more states, and so balance the growing strength of the free North.

His first step was to propose that only a part of Texas should be devoted to slavery. For this he was reprimanded by his legislature, and virtually ordered to advocate unqualified admission. This he refused to do. Then his party managers nominated in opposition John Woodbury, a native of Salem, but a resident of Exeter, where he had served as register of deeds. Mr. Woodbury, who lived in the Shute house on Court street, was a well intentioned but mentally narrow man. In those days, a majority, not a plurality, vote for congressman, as now, was required, and there was no choice. Mr. Woodbury gave up the contest and returned to Salem. There was a second unsuccessful trial, and it was in the congress preceding election, that Mr.

Hale, in a speech at Concord, uttered the remarkable words quoted on his monument.

His example proved contagious, and New Hampshire had henceforth a Free Soil party, mainly recruited from the Democracy. Some of the most important movements of the new departure occurred in Exeter. The old Whigs, hitherto in a hopeless minority, joined with the seceders, and as a result carried the legislature. In 1846, Mr. Hale was elected to the United States senate. In 1848 he declined a nomination to the presidency in favor of Martin Van Buren, the third party candidate. In 1852 he ran for that office, receiving nearly 156,000 votes.

For a number of years he was the only Free Soil member of congress, and was constantly in a hopeless opposition. Yet he scored many an important point, and was popular with Southern members, both from their conviction of his honesty and from his ready wit. He had the rare art of saying unpleasant things without losing his temper, or arousing that of his hearers. He was not reëlected at the close of his first term, but the Know-Nothing triumph gave him a new chance, and he filled the unexpired term of Charles G. Atherton, deceased. At the close of this he was elected for another full term, expiring in 1865. He was then sent as minister to Spain, where he remained five years. His main work was performed in congress, and his health was now breaking. He returned home, to die on the 19th of November, 1873, at the age of sixty years. He gave reputation both to his state and the nation, and was one of the most effective pioneers in the cause of freedom. No man better deserved a statue.

———

[From the Nashua (N. H.) *Telegraph*, August 3, 1892.]

No more fitting statue could adorn the grounds of the state house at Concord than that of John Parker Hale. Above all things it stands for a man. "He was a man, take him all in all.". Among the founders of the Free Soil party Mr. Hale was first to attain a high civil position. How he reached that position constitutes one of the most interesting and instructive episodes in the politics of this country. The son of a lawyer, educated at Exeter and Bowdoin, and choosing the law himself for a profession, his humor, eloquence, and ability opened the way to immediate success. At twenty-six, he was elected to the legislature; at twenty-eight, he was appointed United States district attorney of New Hampshire; at thirty-seven he was elected a representative in congress, and at forty he was chosen United States senator, which position he held, altogether, sixteen years, covering the most eventful period in this century in the history of the country.

In his early career Mr. Hale was a member of the Democratic party. It controlled absolutely the politics of the state. The path of preferment alone lay through its favor. He had tasted its sweets, and there was apparently no honor to which he could not aspire and reach. It was in this blaze of success that Mr. Hale, as a Democratic member of congress, was instructed by the legislature to vote for the annexation of Texas. John P. Hale now stood at the parting of the ways. To vote for the admission of Texas and the further extension of slavery was to secure his relations with the dominant party of his state and of the nation. To vote almost alone against annexation was to sever those relations, retire to private life, and become an object of derision and hatred among his old associates. Mr. Hale chose to give up everything rather than bow the knee to Baal. He was ostracised, both politically and socially. Long years after, when other events had crowded upon the country, President Pierce deliberately turned his back upon Senator Hale at a White House reception.

Mr. Hale became the candidate of the Independent Democrats and Free Soilers for congress, but there was no choice; the same result followed a second and even a third election.

In 1846, Mr. Hale was elected a member of the legislature from Dover. By a fusion of the Independent Democrats, Free Soilers, and Whigs, he was elected speaker, and later, at the same session, United States senator for six years. The result electrified the anti-slavery element of the entire country, and until reinforced by Sumner, Chase, Seward, and Wade, he was the most conspicuous leader of the anti-slavery party in public life. In all this John P. Hale stood for principle against the hope of reward. His intrepid stand called forth many encomiums, but the best was the poem written by the poet Whittier. The original of this poem was placed in our possession last winter. Its re-publication now seems most opportune.

[From Rochester, N. H., Mr. Hale's Birthplace. Proceedings of the City Government. Address of Mayor Charles S. Whitehouse.]

Gentlemen : On Wednesday, August 3d, at Concord, in the state house grounds, will be unveiled, and dedicated to the people of New Hampshire with appropriate ceremonies, a statue of John Parker Hale; a native of Rochester, a learned lawyer, a profound statesman, a heroic defender of human liberty, and a man of national reputation.

Born in Rochester, March 31st, 1806, within a "stone's throw" of where we are sitting, educated in the common schools of this village and at Exeter academy, and graduated at Bowdoin college in 1827, he studied law with Jeremiah H. Woodman of this town, and with Daniel M. Christie of Dover and began the profession of his life in the latter city, where he ever after lived. He was elected to the state legislature from Dover in 1832, when but 26 years old. In 1843 he was elected to congress and served one term. In 1846 again elected to the state legislature from Dover, chosen speaker of the house, and by the same legislature elected a U. S. senator for a full term of six years. Again elected for an unexpired term of four years in 1855, and for a full term of six years in 1859. Nominated as the Free Soil candidate for the presidency in 1847, but declined. Again nominated for the presidency by the Free Soil convention in 1852. At the close of his senatorial term in 1865, he was appointed minister to Spain, where he remained five years, much of the time in ill health, and died in Dover, November 19th, 1873. In the words of another distinguished son of Rochester, Hon. Jacob H. Ela, "bearing with him the blessings of millions who had been raised from the sorrow and degradation of human servitude, and of millions more, who had admired his unselfish fidelity to the cause he had espoused, and his unwavering integrity."

Such in the briefest manner possible, I have named the dates and principal events in this distinguished man's career, who shed lustre and honor on the nation, the state, and his native town. But to speak of his high rank as a lawyer, his power with a jury, his skill in handling witnesses, his "keen wit, burning indignation, and touching pathos," needs an abler tongue than mine. As a statesman loyal to his convictions of right, undaunted when standing solitary and alone in the U. S. senate, fighting the encroachments of a domineering and arrogant slave oligarchy, unmindful of the threats and persuasions of his (at that time) political associates, thrusting aside the brilliant prospects that loomed up before him, looking with the faith of a prophet to the ultimate disenthrallment of a race from human servitude, he presents to this generation a figure heroic and grand, such as no other state in the Union can show, and one which the people of his native town can do homage to with commendable pride.

On the 3d of August, his statue, the gift of his distinguished son-in-law, Senator William E. Chandler, is to be publicly unveiled and formally dedicated to the people of New Hampshire, whom he loved so well and served so faithfully.

It seems to me eminently fitting that the people of his native place through this council should take cognizance of this important event by some official action.

In council July 19, 1892, the following resolutions were unanimously adopted:

We, the representatives of the city of Rochester in council assembled, recognizing the national reputation of John Parker Hale, a native of this town, his labors in the cause of human liberty, his profound statesmanship and lofty standard of political citizenship, and appreciating the great honor conferred upon his native place, therefore

Resolved, That the mayor and city clerk, with such of the council as may join, attend the public unveiling of his statue at the state house in the city of Concord, the 3d day of August, 1892.

FERDINAND VON MILLER, JR.

Ferdinand von Miller, Jr., the artist who designed the statue of John P. Hale, was born June, 1842, and early put to practical work. His father was Stieglmayr's successor as manager of the Royal Art foundry, and had, soon after assuming charge and as the result of a fall, contracted a severe and dangerous lung trouble, and King Ludwig I asked the sick man to provide a suitable successor to himself in the management of the works as speedily as possible. Miller therefore put his two young sons, who had scarcely finished the public school, to work with the artisans. His condition having improved, he devoted more time to the theoretical education of his sons, and Ferdinand von Miller, Jr., entered the Royal Industrial institute (now the Royal Academy) at Berlin in 1856. Besides the study of the technical branches, he here received from Professor Kiss his first instructions in modelling. Returned to Munich, he entered the Royal Academy of Fine Arts as a pupil, at the same time working part of the day as modeller and founder in the Royal Art foundry. His further education in the arts was attended to by Professor von Widemann at Munich; later he studied under Professor Haenel in Dresden, in whose studio he worked.

In 1863 he was sent to Paris, and the young artist found work in the bronze foundry of Barbedienne, where he worked two years. Afterwards he studied the systems of the bronze foundries in London, Vienna, and Florence, and at last finished his art studies during a long stay at Rome. In 1866, at the breaking out of the war, Miller joined the army as a volunteer and did not return to his art until after the conclusion of peace. And when the great struggle with France called the German people to arms, he would not remain at home, and voluntarily exchanged the tools of the artist for the sword, and served during a large part of the campaign as lieutenant in the Fifth regiment of chevaux-legers. From Paris, where his regiment had participated in the siege, he returned to the workshop.

Soon after, while erecting the large fountain at Cincinnati, he had occasion to witness the enthusiasm over the great German victories then prevailing among his countrymen in America.

While on an interesting tour through the West to San Francisco, Miller stopped at the Rocky mountains to study some Indian settlements. Here he learned to know the habits and modes of life of these people, and wrote interesting descriptions of them to his home. The life-size figure of an Indian discharging his arrow may be considered the result of his observations on this occasion.

The people of Munich have learned to know Ferdinand von Miller, Jr., outside of his art work, as president of the successful seventh meet of the German Rifle league, the ceremonies on which occasion bore a decided artistic character; also as president of the Munich Artists' league, in which capacity he directed the international art exhibition. Elected to the city council, he was chosen second chairman.

Especially important among the more recent productions of Von Miller by reason of the persons represented thereby, are the statue of King Ludwig I, placed in the Walhalla, and the equestrian statue of Emperor William I, erected at Metz, which two commissions he secured in a prize contest against many prominent competitors.

Of his former productions may be mentioned figures of Shakespeare, Humboldt, and Columbus, made for St. Louis in the United States, and which are widely known. He has modelled up to the present time thirty-one colossal monuments, and is now engaged in the work of modelling the large Warrior monument for Munich, the equestrian statue above mentioned of Emperor William, for the city of Metz, a colossal statue of Emperor William for the city of Trier, and another monument for Mittenwald.

The honorary distinctions awarded to him personally are many. He has the large gold medal of Bavaria for art, the silver medal of the Munich exposition of 1873, the first medal awarded at the exhibition of art in Vienna, the gold medal of Melbourne, and the first medal awarded at Sidney.

He is an honorary member of the academy of fine arts of Munich, but has refused to accept any honorary title offered to him.

Of decorations, he has the Cross, with Star, of a Great Commander of the Spanish Order of Isabella, the Commander's Cross of the Danish Danebrog Order, the Commander's Cross of the Italian Crown Order, the Knight's Cross of the Bavarian Crown Order, the Knight's Cross of the first class of the Bavarian Michael Order, the Knight's Cross of the third class of the Prussian Crown Order, the Knight's Cross of the first class of the Swedish Vasa Order, the Knight's Cross of the first class of the Wurtemburg Fredericks Order, and the war medals of the Austria-Prussian War, 1886, and the Franco-German War of 1870–'71.

THE MUNICH ROYAL ART BRONZE FOUNDRY.

Statement of the monuments cast at the Royal Art bronze foundry at Munich in Bavaria, omitting single statues.

There have been made forty-five large monuments for North and South America, comprising eighty-four figures all told. Among these are three equestrian statues like that of General Washington in Richmond, for which rider and horse are twenty-four feet in height. They have also furnished seven large fountains, among which are those at Cincinnati, the Central park in New York, and one at Philadelphia.

For the different states of Europe there have been completed in their works 220 colossal monuments with a total of 350 figures. This includes seventeen colossal equestrian statues and twenty-three fountains, also the largest monuments of the world that have ever been cast in bronze, The "Bavaria" of Munich and the "Germania" on the "Niederwald."

At all exhibitions where their statuary foundry exhibited, it always received honorable distinction by being awarded the first medal; at London, 1851, the large gold medal, in Munich on each and every exhibition the first medal, and the same distinction in Vienna and Berlin.

The statue of Lincoln at Washington, with a negro kneeling at his feet with broken shackles, was cast at Munich; also the Daniel Webster in the state house yard at Concord.

JOHN PARKER HALE.

[Concord *Monitor*, December 16, 1887.]

This first distinctively anti-slavery United States senator was born in Rochester, N. H., March 31, 1806, and died in Dover, N. H., November 19, 1873. His father was John Parker Hale, a lawyer in Rochester. He was educated at Phillips Exeter academy, and graduated at Bowdoin college in 1827, Franklin Pierce being a college associate. He studied law with Jeremiah H. Woodman, of Rochester, and Daniel M. Christie, of Dover, and was admitted to the Strafford county bar, August 20, 1830, and commenced practice in Dover.

In March, 1832, he was elected to the state house of representatives, and took his seat June 6, and again November 22, at the extra session. Franklin Pierce, then twenty-eight years old, was speaker. On March 22, 1834, he was appointed U. S. district attorney by President Jackson; was reappointed April 5, 1838, by President Van Buren, and removed for political reasons by President Tyler, June 17, 1841. Joel Eastman was appointed to succeed him.

On March 8, 1842, he was elected representative in the Twenty-eighth congress, and took his seat December 4, 1843. He opposed the twenty-first rule, suppressing anti-slavery petitions, but supported Polk and Dallas in the presidential canvass of 1844, and was renominated on a general ticket with three associates. The N. H. legislature, December 28, 1844, passed resolutions instructing their representatives to support the annexation of Texas, and President Tyler, in his annual message of that year, advocated annexation. On January 7, 1845, Mr. Hale wrote his noted Texas letter to "The Democratic Republican electors" of New Hampshire, which may be found published in the first number, dated May 1, 1845, of the *Independent Democrat*, started at Manchester by Robert C. Wetmore.

The letter is dated at the House of Representatives, Washington. He says he cannot support the annexation of Texas, and that the reasons alleged by the administration justifying it are "eminently calculated to provoke the scorn of earth and the judgment of heaven; and I cannot consent by any agency of mine to aid in placing our beloved country in such an attitude. When our forefathers bade a last fare-well to the homes of their childhood, the graves of their fathers, and the temples of their God, and ventured upon all the desperate contingencies of wintry seas and a savage coast, that they might in strong faith and ardent hope lay deep the foundations of the temple of liberty, their faith would have become scepticism, and their hopes despair, could they have foreseen that the day would ever arrive when their degenerate sons would be found seeking to extend their boundaries and their government, not for the purpose of promoting freedom, but sustaining slavery."

The state convention of his party reassembled at Concord, February 12, 1845, and, under the lead of Franklin Pierce, struck Hale's name from the ticket for representatives in congress, and substituted that of John Woodbury. Mr. Hale was supported as an Independent candidate. On March 1, 1845, Mr. Hale and one other Democrat, R. D. Davis, of New York, voted with the Whigs against the joint resolution which passed congress admitting Texas to the Union.

On March 11, 1845, the election took place: 23,141 votes were necessary to a choice. The highest of the three Dem-ocratic candidates who were elected had 24,904 votes; the highest Whig candidate had 15,177. Woodbury had 22,314, Joseph Cilley had 4,827, and Mr. Hale had 7,788. On the second trial, September 23, 1845, Ichabod Goodwin, Whig, had 10,055, Woodbury, 17,936, and Hale, 8,355. On the third trial, November 29, Goodwin had 12,187; Woodbury, 19,916; Hale, 9,766. On the fourth trial, at the annual election, March 10, 1846, Goodwin had 16,617, Woodbury, 26,806, and Hale, 11,475.

During these repeated trials Mr. Hale thoroughly canvassed the state. At his North church meeting in Concord, June 5, 1845, General Pierce and other Democrats attended, and after Mr. Hale closed his impassioned speech with the words, " People change, public opinion changes, and parties change ; but the principles of justice, moral obligations, and the God who sits upon the throne of the universe, never change," General Pierce, being called for, replied with vehemence and bitterness. Mr. Hale rejoined as follows:

" As I expected, and as I anticipated in my former remarks, it is all ' Abolitionism and Whiggery.' I expected to be called ambitious, and to have my name cast out as evil ; to be traduced and misrepresented, and have not been disappointed. If conscience and her voice are to be publicly held up to ridicule and scouted at with impunity, as has just been done here, it matters but little whether we are annexed to Texas or Texas annexed to us. In conclusion I may be permitted to say that the measure of my ambition will be full if I may feel that when my earthly career shall be finished and my bones be laid in the grave under the soil of New Hampshire, and my wife and my children shall repair thither to drop the tear of affection to my memory, they may read on my tomb-stone that he who lies beneath surrendered office, place, and power rather than bow down and worship slavery."

The growth of anti-slavery sentiment in the state was so great and rapid that at the above election of March 10, 1846, the Whigs and Independent Democrats not only again defeated a choice of representatives in congress, but also prevented any election of governor, and elected a majority of the state legislature. The total vote was 55,194 ; necessary to a choice, 27,598 ; scattering, 368. Nathaniel S. Berry (Free Soil) had 10,379 ; Anthony Colby (Whig), 17,707 ; Jared W. Williams (Democrat), 26,740.

The result of this election in 1846 gave great courage to the friends of freedom throughout the country. In The-

Independent Democrat of March 26, 1846, is a letter from John G. Whittier, dated Andover, Mass., 3d mo., 18th, 1846, in which he says of Mr. Hale :

He has succeeded, and his success has broken the spell which has hitherto held reluctant Democracy in the embraces of slavery. The tide of anti-slavery feeling, long held back by the dams and dykes of party, has at last broken over all barriers, and is rushing down from your northern mountains upon the slave-cursed South, as if Niagara stretched its foam and thunder the whole length of Mason & Dixon's line. *Let the first wave of that northern flood, as it dashes against the walls of the Capitol, bear thither for the first time an anti-slavery senator.*

When the legislature met June 3, 1846, Mr. Hale was elected speaker, receiving 139 votes ; Samuel Swasey, 118 ; scattering, three. In his address he invoked " that immortal sentiment which the wisdom of our fathers placed as the corner stone of our constitution, that all men are created equally free and independent." On June 5, Anthony Colby was elected governor, receiving 146 votes, and Jared W. Williams, 125. On June 9, Mr. Hale was elected United States senator for the six years to commence March 3, 1847, receiving in the house 139 votes against 122 for all others, and in the senate eight against four for others. On June 12, Joseph Cilley was elected to fill the existing vacancy, created by the resignation of Levi Woodbury to become an associate justice of the United States supreme court, and Mr. Cilley took his seat as senator June 22.

From his election as United States senator in 1846, to the close of his last term in 1865, Mr. Hale was a prominent Free Soil and Republican leader. On October 20, 1847, he was nominated for president by a National Liberty convention at Buffalo, with Leicester King of Ohio for vice-president, but declined the nomination and supported Mr. Van Buren, who was nominated at the Buffalo convention of August 9, 1848, by a majority of 22, Mr. Hale receiving 180 votes.

On December 6, 1847, he took his seat in the senate, which contained 32 Democrats and 21 Whigs. An attempt being made to class him as Whig, he repelled the classification, was excused by a vote of 17 to 16 from serving on committees, and he remained the only Free Soil senator until joined by Salmon P. Chase on December 3, 1849, and by Charles Sumner on December 1, 1851. Mr. Hale commenced the agitation of the slavery question, in connection with the Mexican War, on January 6, 1848, and continued it in frequent speeches during his whole term.

Shortly after his entrance into the senate he began the work of securing the abolition of flogging and the spirit ration in the navy. On July 19, 1848, he introduced a resolution relative to punishments on shipboard, and July 21 moved an amendment to the naval appropriation bill abolishing flogging and the spirit ration; but only four senators rose with him in the affirmative. On September 28, 1850, however, he secured the adoption, on the appropriation for the naval service, of the following proviso: "That flogging in the navy, and on board vessels of commerce, be and the same is hereby abolished from and after the passage of this act." But it was not until July 14, 1862, that he accomplished the abolition of the spirit ration by a clause as follows: "From and after the first day of September, 1862, the spirit ration in the navy of the United States shall forever cease, and thereafter no distilled spirituous liquors shall be admitted on board vessels-of-war, except as medical stores, and upon the order and under the control of the medical officers of such vessels, and to be used only for medical purposes. From and after the said first day of September next there shall be allowed and paid to each person in the navy now entitled to the spirit ration five cents per day in commutation and lieu thereof, which shall be in addition to their present pay."

In 1852 Mr. Hale was nominated at Pittsburgh, Pa., by the Free Soil party for president, with George W. Julian as vice-president, and they received 157,685 votes.

His first senatorial term ended March 4, 1853, on which day Franklin Pierce was inaugurated president. The succeeding winter Mr. Hale commenced the practice of law in the city of New York. The repeal of the Missouri compromise measures, however, again overthrew the Democrats of New Hampshire. They failed to elect United States senators in the legislature of June, 1854, and in March, 1855, they completely lost the state. On June 13, 1855, James Bell, Whig, was elected United States senator for six years from March 3, 1855, and Mr. Hale was elected by 218 votes against 101 for all others for the four years of the unexpired term of Charles G. Atherton, who had succeeded him and died in office. On June 9, 1858, he was reëlected for a full term of six years, to end March 4, 1865. On March 10, 1865, he was confirmed and commissioned minister to Spain, and went immediately to that court. He was recalled April 5, 1869, and took leave July 29, 1869.

The above statement of dates and statistics connected with Mr. Hale's life was prepared for Appleton's Cyclopædia of Biography, and is here printed as likely to be interesting to many readers. A most striking fact is the constant contact of Mr. Hale's life with that of Franklin Pierce. They were together at Bowdoin college. In 1832 both were in the legislature, Hale being twenty-six years old, and Pierce twenty-eight and speaker. In 1833 Pierce entered the national house of representatives, continued there four years, was elected in 1837 to the senate, and remained until March 1, 1842. In 1834 Hale became United States district attorney, and held the office until 1841, and was elected representative in congress in 1842, entering the house shortly after Pierce left the senate. Up to 1845 they associated and agreed in politics as Jackson Democrats, and together in 1844 they stumped New Hampshire for Polk and Dallas. But when in 1845 Hale left the Democracy on the Texas issue, Pierce became his opponent, and dictated his decapitation as a candidate for reëlection to the house, at the convention of February 12, 1845. From that time their lives were antagonistic. In 1846 Hale went to the senate, and in 1852 was the Free

Soil candidate for president with a view to defeating Pierce. In 1853, as Hale left the senate, Pierce entered the White House as president, having also forced the nomination and election of Charles G. Atherton as senator in Hale's place. But in 1855, before Pierce's term as president had expired, Hale, as the successor of Atherton, who had died, again appeared in his former place in the senate to assail the administration of his old friend.

The political separation of these former associates was signalized by their famous North Church debate June 5, 1845. In this discussion Pierce bitterly complained that Hale had concealed his sentiments on Texas annexation while upon the stump in the presidential canvass of 1844, to which complaint Hale's reply was that not until after Polk had been elected was the purpose avowed of bringing Texas into the Union as a slave state. The parallel careers of these two distinguished sons of New Hampshire, both orators of graceful and fervid eloquence, who gave their lives, one to the service of slavery and the other to the advocacy of freedom, one of whom became a pro-slavery president, and the other an anti-slavery senator, are an interesting study for the young men of their native state.

W. E. C.

INDEX.

www.ingramcontent.com/pod-product-compliance
Lightning Source LLC
Chambersburg PA
CBHW030815020726
47499CB00006B/1931